W9-CMG-722

The Tobermory Manuscript

A Western Story

***Other Five Star Titles
by James C. Work:***

Ride South to Purgatory

The Tobermory Manuscript

A Western Story

JAMES C. WORK

Five Star
Unity, Maine

Five Star First Edition Western Series.
Published in 2000 in conjunction with Golden West Literary
Agency.

Cover illustration by Robert Work

Set in 11 pt. Plantin by Al Chase.

Printed in the United States on permanent paper.

Library of Congress Cataloging-in-Publication Data
Work, James C.
    The Tobermory manuscript : a western story / by James C.
Work. — First ed.
        p.   cm.
    "Five Star western" — T.p. verso.
    ISBN 0-7862-2103-8 (hc : alk. paper)
    1. Estes Park (Colo.) — Fiction.   2. Nugent, James —
Fiction.   I. Title.
PS3573.O6925 T64 2000
813´.54—dc21   00-023518

To The Reader

Professor David Lachlan McIntyre and Professor Henriette Palmer were born in my imagination. James "Rocky Mountain Jim" Nugent was real, as were Griffith Evans, Lord Dunraven, Dr. George Kingsley, William Brown, and Jenny Evans. All were living in Estes Park, Colorado, on the day in 1874 when Griff Evans shot James Nugent. Isabella Bird and Enos Mills were also real; in 1873, Isabella Bird saw and heard a portion of Nugent's manuscript, and it was Enos Mills, writing in 1904, who reported that a "mass of written matter" by Nugent had disappeared following his murder.

Likewise, certain documents cited in this novel actually exist; others are of my own creation. The locations in Colorado, England, and Scotland are as authentic as a writer's imagination will allow.

Fort Collins, Colorado
J.C.W.

The Prologue to the Puzzle

The Nineteenth of June, 1874 was a Friday. Another perfect Rocky Mountain morning lounged lazily along toward midday. Motionless air of flawless clarity and brilliance lay lightly on the Estes Park meadows; it did not bend so much as a single slender blade of the new spring grass. Down at the river, a fisherman felt the glacial water freezing his legs while the sun roasted his back. A quartet of dudes, sweating aboard their borrowed horses, rode into the pine shade and shivered with the chill. It was calm and bright and quiet. A perfect day. Perfect, that is, for the shooting.

James Nugent and William Brown came riding across the hill, heading for the Evans house. They expected to find Griff Evans puttering around outside somewhere, and maybe one of Lord Dunraven's arrogant English guests on the premises. The stocky little Welshman, however, was not outside. He was lying in bed, sleeping. Passed out, to be more accurate. Someone had been helping him get drunk that morning.

An Englishman—whom witnesses and local historians usually identify as Lord Haigh—sunning himself on the bench next to the door also appeared to be asleep. But when Nugent and Brown came over the hill, he jumped up as if he had been expecting them. "Jim's on the shoot!" he cried out. "Evans! I want you to protect me!" He hurried inside and seized a shotgun leaning against the wall, just inside the door.

Evans came stumbling from the bed; a weapon was jammed into his hands as he lurched outside, blinking into the glare of the morning, cocking both barrels of the English .10-Gauge loaded with heavy buckshot known as blue whistlers. Groggy with whisky, half-blinded by the sun, Evans aimed in the direction of the horsemen and pulled the trigger.

According to Dr. George Kingsley, who arrived a few minutes later, the shotgun blast left Nugent with "five small bullet-wounds about the head and face," one of which shattered his nose and one "which had most certainly penetrated the cerebellum."

The result was proof that a human brain can sustain serious trauma and yet continue to function. At first, James Nugent was carried to a grove of trees where he was expected to die. He did not die, however, and so a wagon was commandeered to haul him over forty-five miles of rough and winding mountain roads to a hospital in Fort Collins. There his more superficial wounds were treated, but surgeons did not disturb the lead ball in his brain.

His condition gradually improved; he was moved into a nursing residence. A full recovery, however, was not to be; on September Seventh, fifty-one days after the shooting, James Nugent died. The autopsy, according to a letter from Dr. Kingsley to his daughter in Ireland, showed that one small piece of lead and one larger one had entered the back of Nugent's skull to lodge deeply in his brain where they festered until the fluid pressure against the tissue mass cut off its blood supply. Before dying, James Nugent wrote a long letter to the editor of the Fort Collins *Standard*, containing his own narrative of the occurrence.

On the day of the shooting, one of the Dunraven group advised Evans to go to Longmont, twenty miles away, and turn himself in—James Nugent still had friends in Estes Park. Evans, still not wholly sober, headed for Longmont without finding out whether his victim was dead. Along the way, he must have sobered up enough to think things over; when he got to the municipal courthouse, he did not turn himself in, but, instead, swore out a warrant for the arrest of James Nugent on charges of assault.

Someone—one of Dunraven's English party, it is believed—provided bail and an attorney, and Griff Evans was speedily acquitted. So speedily, in fact, that neither he nor James Nugent ever testified before a judge.

In an account by Enos Mills, a local historian, "the first shot probably missed Jim and hit an old stagecoach that stood by; but Jim fell from his horse with a load of buckshot in his body as the result of the second shot." Dr. Kingsley did not mention any pellets being found in the body, but said that Jim's horse was killed with the first blast.

Kingsley's narrative differs from Enos Mills's story in several ways. In his version, Jim had come walking up to the cabin, leading his horse, and had "sheltered himself behind the wheels of the timber machine"—a pair of large wheels used to haul logs—and tried to "draw a bead" on Lord Haigh who was "seated on the doorstep." Kingsley also said that Evans always kept his scatter-gun loaded and standing beside the door, as a cure for such pests as skunks and porcupines.

The murder narrative is further complicated by the presence of William Brown. Brown told people that he and Nugent had been riding peacefully toward the house when Haigh appeared in the doorway, shouting that Jim was coming to kill him. Evans then came out with the shotgun, which he aimed and fired. Brown said the first shot missed both Nugent and himself. "Jim was so taken by surprise," ran Brown's account, "that he did not move his rifle from its position across the saddle in front of him."

Brown came up with a theory to explain the pellet in the brain, the wound that proved fatal. In his theory, some pellets from a second shotgun blast struck "a broken down old wagon that stood by the side of the road" and ricocheted from "a tire or some other iron part and caught Jim on the back of the head at the base of the brain."

William Brown vanished from the territory before the coroner's inquest, never to be seen or heard of to this day.

One Colorado newspaper editorial did not blame James Nugent's death on his head wound. The editor, instead, blamed it on Nugent's resumption of his "wild life" and drinking whisky before he was fully recuperated.

But not all newspapers were unsympathetic. In his book, THE ROCKY MOUNTAIN NATIONAL PARK, Enos Mills quoted brief editorial notices from the Boulder *News*.

> . . . [T]he Boulder *News* for November 14, [1873] says of him:
>
> " 'Rocky Mountain Jim' came down from Estes Park last Tuesday, bringing along 300 pounds of trout for a share of which he has our thanks. Jim never forgets a friend, nor enemy, either."
>
> On October 17, the same paper contains this item:
>
> " 'Rocky Mountain Jim' is talking of writing a book. Jim has, under a rough crust, no mean abilities, coupled with a heart that beats right, and if he writes a book we predict it will not be tedious and unreadable."
>
> It is known that Jim had a mass of written matter just before he was shot, but I have failed to find any of it.

As James Nugent was convalescing, he composed his own version of the incident. It is a disappointing account, mostly because he was not strong enough to go to Estes Park to talk to witnesses. He had to depend upon word of mouth and newspaper stories to learn what the investigating "grand jury" had said; he was never called to testify concerning the accusation that he was guilty of assault on Evans.

"Haigh swore he was sitting in Evans's door," wrote Nugent, "saw James Nugent and Brown coming down the road. He got up, went into the house where Evans was lying on the bed, and said: 'Evans, Rocky Mountain Jim is coming, you will not see me shot down like a dog, will you?' Evans said no, and got up and took a double-barreled shotgun, went out towards Jim with the gun in his hands. Jim raised his gun, when Evans shot him from his horse, and then shot him while down upon the ground."

Nugent failed to mention a detail that was included in one of the newspaper accounts. This version maintained that Haigh, seeing Nugent down but not wounded, said to Evans: "Give him the other barrel." Perhaps Nugent didn't hear those words; a short-range shotgun blast aimed in his direction could easily have deafened him temporarily. But who gave this version to the newspaper?

Griff Evans was a stodgy Welshman, a cordial host, an outgoing and cheerful sort of man, engaging and friendly. They say he was the best shot in Estes Park. He owned a few cabins and a string of horses and had aspirations of becoming a successful mountain innkeeper. Toward Lord Dunraven and the English gentry, he was openly deferential if not downright obsequious.

But suddenly at mid-morning of a beautiful June day, this amiable self-styled host, inexplicably drunk early in the day, fired two barrels of blue whistlers at a man he had known for several years. And he missed.

Had Evans lived up to his reputation as a marksman, the twin blast would have torn James Nugent in half. If Evans had aimed at the head, it would have blown Jim's face into small pieces. But only five pellets or fragments of pellets hit Jim. The one that proved fatal, according to the unscathed and soon missing William Brown, ricocheted off the steel rim of a wagon wheel.

Why was Evans drunk that morning? What prompted him to pull the triggers? Why did he almost miss? Why did Lord Haigh assume that Rocky Mountain Jim was coming to kill him that morning? How did Lord Dunraven and Dr. George Kingsley arrive on the scene so rapidly? Who did Brown talk to before disappearing?

That 1874 murder and the motives behind it were never subjected to criminal investigation; however, it was something more than a chance outbreak of violence between a mountain man and some foreigners. Had James Nugent written a book including facts about The English Company and their fraudulent, illegal scheme to monopolize the Estes Park valley? Who were his enemies, and what did he know about them that might drive them to murder? The answers probably lie in the "mass of written matter" that Enos Mills failed to find.

Chapter One

Being professional first and female second, I don't mind it that he's the only reasonably attractive male on the faculty of Arts and Social Sciences—married or single—who has never made a pass at me. I don't mind that he publishes his offbeat literary articles while my academic history of Rocky Mountain hotels languishes in university press purgatory. But I do most certainly mind it that Professor David Lachlan McIntyre, Ph.D., could read two chapters of my manuscript on Rocky Mountain history and have only one question. And an irrelevant question at that.

Students had me tearing my hair that week; the tin bleating of the telephone buzzer did nothing to improve my mood.

"Professor Palmer," I snapped.

A pause ensued. Then a masculine voice. "So where's Mountain Jim Nugent's lost manuscript?" It was Lachlan.

"What manuscript?" I replied. "I don't recall . . . oh, you mean the one mentioned by Enos Mills? It's not significant."

"But where is it?"

"Lachlan, no one knows. That's probably why it's called *lost*, you see."

"Do you think Enos Mills saw it, in person? How did he know about it?"

"In case you failed to notice, my manuscript concerns hotels, not the scribbling of some mountain man. Nor Enos Mills, for that matter."

"Did you by any chance run across anyone saying that Lord Dunraven may have taken it?"

"Forget Mountain Jim," I said. "My last class lets out at three P.M., unless I assassinate them all. You would not believe the sort of week I've had. Shall I come to your office and pick up my manuscript?"

"I guess you'll have to, if you want it back. Not being Domino's, I don't deliver." Same old Lachlan.

By 3:15 P.M. I was in his office with the door closed, ranting my litany of complaints about student irresponsibility, administrative ministrations, and college non-collegiality. He and I shared these little after-hours sessions more or less monthly. I cherished them as a way to let off steam. Lachlan relished them, I think, mostly as an excuse not to go home. Our chats made a pleasant alternative to what was waiting for him there. We never spoke of that. This is not my ego talking, by the way; it's just one of those facts.

On this particular afternoon, he listened with a bright sparkle in his eyes, eyes the color of polished chestnut. While I went on and on, he took a Jameson's bottle and two souvenir shot glasses from his card file drawer. He held the glasses to the light to choose the one with the fewest scratches and chips and fingerprints, then filled and handed it to me when I finally finished the peroration portion of my tirade.

"Well," I breathed, "as the comedian says, that's enough about me, let's talk about you. What do you think of my manuscript so far?" I took a sip. The whisky had a peat-flavored burn to it.

"It's good," he said.

"*Good?* That's like having my mother tell me it's nice. Come on, Lachlan. What do you really think?"

"As history, I think it's better than average. As rhetoric, it's pretty dull. Then, again, you're in the Department of History. Your colleagues not only accept congenitally drab writing, they reward it with promotions and tenure. In that context, my dear Henriette, you are a pearl among porkers."

"And you're an enormous help."

"OK, OK." He took Howarth's book from the neat stack on his desk and leaned back, opening it to a page marked with a yellow slip. The sun coming in the office window shyly stroked his sandy hair and highlighted his excellent cheek bones. As I said . . . he is not what one calls an unattractive man.

"You cite Howarth . . ."—he leaned forward and flipped open my manuscript—"on page ten . . . as saying the first hotel in the Grand Valley was a boarding house at Lulu City. But then . . ."—he flipped to another page—"you mention on page seventeen that Jim Baker should be credited for starting the first boarding house, which was near Grand Lake. Your history colleagues would be delighted to split that particular hair with you. And I've marked about six other minor discrepancies you make. Check your consistency, and try to liven up your style. A little, at least."

Lachlan removed a paper clip holding together three pages and handed them to me. Three pages of comments he had typed out for me, single-spaced, each comment corresponding to a number written in red ink on my manuscript.

"These are mostly places where you could change your style. You can find similar dull parts for yourself. Mostly you overdo the passive voice and periodic sentences. You write like you're translating from German. Didn't your little prep school let you girls read T.H. Huxley, or E.M. Forster? How about Winston Churchill's HISTORY OF THE ENGLISH SPEAKING PEOPLES? You could do worse for models, you know, even if they were all males. Or there's Mary Wollstonecraft, who's OK only if you like a balance of wit and reason."

"Thank you for the reading list, Professor," I snipped.

"I'm certain that it and your comments will be most helpful. And now you may tell me exactly why that one small sentence about Rocky Mountain Jim's manuscript caught so much of your attention." I asked the question primarily to get him off the issue of my style.

"My God, Hank! You even *speak* in periodic sentences!" He laughed. David Lachlan McIntyre's laugh is, well, masculine. I enjoy it. I don't even mind when he calls me Hank rather than Henriette.

"You're not thinking of making a search for this manuscript," I said. "Just last spring you took off to go find that desert rock that was sat upon by Willa Cather. Dean Rolman was made none too happy about that."

"Hey, I covered my classes. My teaching assistant did a great job filling in for me."

Lachlan pointed to the other books on his desk. Almost every one of my Stanley Hotel and Estes Park research sources was there.

"They all include the same story," he said, "how the Irish Lord Dunraven and his aristocratic English cronies came in the Eighteen Seventies, discovered a hunter's paradise in Estes Park, and proceeded to acquire hundreds of thousands of acres through fraudulent homestead claims. They very nearly succeeded in bringing the whole valley under their control. Mountain Jim opposed them, Mountain Jim was killed, and then Enos Mills says that Mountain Jim's manuscript went missing. And you're honestly more interested in how many Eighteen Seventy-Two hotel rooms had indoor plumbing?"

It was just as I feared it would be, as the chap said in the limerick when seated next to the flatulent duchess. The missing manuscript. What had I done, letting Lachlan read about a missing manuscript? That gleam in his eye. Shots of whisky in the office. The energized dialogue. Other men discover the fire in the belly, but D. Lachlan McIntyre just gets the gleam in the eye. On the strength of a single sentence, he was poised to launch himself into another so-called "literary archaeology" project.

Vacations, I called them. At the drop of your fedora, this man can be off searching out some obscure literary site or following Zane Grey's handmade map to the *real* Surprise Valley. I should never have given him the chapter with the mention of Nugent's manuscript in it. Missing mountain man journals, Baby Doe's love letters, anything might set Lachlan off again.

"You have read everything I know about it," I said. "Enos Mills wrote that there had a been a manuscript and that it was missing when they went to Nugent's cabin in Muggins's Gulch after he died. That's it."

"Who are *they,* and what was in it?" Lachlan asked.

"How should I be expected to know? That *is* the problem with missing manuscripts, you know. They *are* missing."

"How would you like to help me look for it?"

"Certainly," I said, trying to make my voice drip with sugary disdain. "After all, I look as much like Indiana Jones as *you* do."

"No, I'm serious."

"Come on, Lachlan. How many lost manuscripts still exist out there, do you think?"

"That's like asking the rangers at Carlsbad how many undiscovered rooms there are in the caverns," he said.

"Consider," I said. "Major authors of the last fifty years have had access to typing machines, tape recorders, carbon paper, photo duplication, even word processing. The problem isn't that some valuable original has been lost . . . the problem is too many copies. The old days of a solitary, hand-scribbled manuscript are long gone. Anything worth finding has been found." I sipped my drink. "All that Emily Dickinson stuff," I continued, "finding fascicles of unknown poems wrapped up in ribbons in locked drawers, discovering moldy manuscripts by Shakespeare, that's all yesterday's kind of literary research. Who cares?"

"Ah, this isn't Shakespeare," Lachlan said. He sipped his whisky. "But what you're really saying is that I'm old-fashioned, an academic has-been."

I like Lachlan's smirk when playing cat and mouse games. He prefers to imagine himself as being my elder, a sort of mentorial major professor, even though the difference in our ages is only—exactly—six days. Seeing us together, one's first reaction might be to think, as others have, that I am his younger sister. Which I most definitely am not.

"No," I said, exaggerating the soothing tone of my voice, "but there's no longer a market in old manuscripts. All the facts have been uncovered about all the major authors and their work, all the theories cemented into place. But just for conversation's sake, what do *you* think is contained in this lost manuscript that fascinates you so?"

"Haven't the faintest idea."

"Well, would you say that James Nugent is someone famous?" I asked.

"No, unh-uh. Not at all. Unheard of, you might say."

"A notable, talented writer?" I asked.

"I doubt it. He might be fair, but probably not good. Otherwise, we would find more of his stuff in the Colorado literature collections."

"Let me sum up, then," I said, taking a deep sip. "You want to give up your next sabbatical leave, or vacation, to go questing after a long-lost manuscript, possibly non-existent, with an authorship certain to be second-rate or worse. A manuscript you know nothing about."

"That's right," he said.

"I sometimes have serious misgivings about you, Lachlan," I said, finishing my drink and standing up. "Do you ever nod off with your forehead against the computer screen? Causes brain damage, some say."

"Come on and have another drink, and we'll figure out how to start looking for Nugent's manuscript."

"No, you don't," I said, putting my hand over the shot glass before he could pour it full again. "One shot of Irish whisky is quite sufficient for me. I need to stay sober enough to do my grocery shopping this afternoon."

"Get married and you'd have a husband to do that for you," he said. "Besides, who's waiting for you? Big hurry?" As he mentioned marriage, the mirth left his voice.

He was right. He also knew that I have too much curiosity. I couldn't just walk out without hearing his manuscript theory. The only warm bodies waiting for me to come home were Persian and alley. I sat down again.

"Your point is taken. So, what is your idea? I can't leave this way."

The little droop that I now saw in his face made me feel suddenly sorry for him. He needed to talk. He needed something to cheer him up again.

I leaned back in the chair, deliberately crossing my legs so as to give him a long, slow glimpse at my Hanes. Lachlan always seemed to appreciate that particular view. He never did anything about it, but he liked it.

"Well," he said, smiling at my face while gazing at my knees, "we start with Enos Mills, that grand old nature writer of Estes Park and the Rocky Mountains."

"Do you think he could have seen the manuscript?" I asked.

"Nope." Lachlan tapped his finger on Buchholz's ROCKY MOUNTAIN NATIONAL PARK: A HISTORY. "But he arrived in the park ten years after Nugent's murder, and he either heard about this manuscript or he read about it. It was still important enough that someone still remembered it. Mills didn't get around to writing his history until Nineteen Oh Four. Thirty years had gone by. And this manuscript was still common knowledge?

"Think about that confined little community at the turn of the century. Petty jealousies, backbiting, competition, and gossip. And this manuscript . . . they probably suspected that it had something interesting in it. Maybe something incriminating."

"I'm starting to think I should accept that other drink," I said. Lachlan raised the bottle almost before I could snatch the shot glass away. "No! I'm joking! You know, Mountain Jim Nugent was supposed to have had a romance going with the Englishwoman, Lady Isabella Bird. Maybe she took it because of something he had written about her. Maybe she wanted it because she was sentimental. Either that, or wanted to protect her reputation."

"Nope," Lachlan said. "That theory won't work. She was long gone by the time Griff Evans shot Nugent. But what if we went to Ireland and looked into the archives of the Earl of Dunraven's descendants? We might just find it there." He lifted the Jameson's and looked at the label. "Or we might find where they make this stuff."

"That's fine," I said. "The two of us just abandon classes and pick up and go to Ireland together. No problem with that idea. Well, listen, Lachlan, I really do need to go to the grocer's and select some carrots."

"Then there's the motive for murder," he said.

Dammit, he *knows* I adore murder mysteries. The man

just doesn't play fair at all.

"You think that's why he was killed . . . for the manuscript? Because it gave away some village secrets?"

"*That's* the beautiful part of it!" Lachlan said. "We don't know! If his killing was just another case of two citizens blasting away at each other, even if there have only been four or five homicides in the last hundred years up there, that wouldn't be interesting. But the missing manuscript . . . now *that* makes the shooting interesting, don't you think?

"That's why I've been reading your library material," he pursued, "and everything, so far, indicates that somebody used Griff Evans to kill Mountain Jim. We have the means and the opportunity, which is to say that we know it was a shotgun and that it happened when Jim rode up to Griff's cabin. But where's the motive?

"Here's what I have so far. Evans might have been angry because Jim was paying attention to his daughter, Jenny. Or, Lord Dunraven might have put Evans up to it because Evans owed him, and Mountain Jim was a threat to the whole land steal plot. Theodore Whyte, one of Dunraven's men, might have been the one to get Evans drunk and convince him that Jim was out to murder Haigh. Even this man called Brown might have been involved. Don't you think it's odd that he was riding alongside Nugent, and yet he wasn't wounded or even particularly startled when Evans cut loose with that doublebore gun? And damn' odd that of all the witnesses, he was the only one to vanish. He also seems to have been the one who told people about some shotgun pellets going past Nugent and hitting a steel tire and bouncing back. *That* ricochet, my dear Doctor Palmer, is very important. It's supposed to explain how a man could get wounds in the front and in the *back* of his head from the same shot.

"What if," Lachlan went on, his eyes dancing with the excitement of playing detective, "what if this whole thing was a Dunraven plot to get rid of both Nugent and Evans? What if Brown was paid to bring Mountain Jim to the Evans cabin, and then paid to disappear? What do you think of that scenario?"

"I don't know what to think, Sherlock," I replied, "except that, if the game is afoot, you may chase it all by yourself. Seriously, though, where do you think you would find the legendary manuscript? In Estes Park?"

"If not there, I don't know where. But I've got a feeling that if we find it, we find the man and the motive behind Evans. Maybe the manuscript *is* in Ireland."

"Well," I answered, gathering up my pages and moving toward the door, "at least the number of plumbing fixtures in hotel rooms can be ascertained." Damn. I had just uttered another periodic sentence. Perhaps he hadn't noticed. "Thank you again for your input. I owe you a drink."

"Correction," he grinned. "It is lunch that I am owed."

Lachlan might have lost his tenure years ago, except that he was an entertaining teacher and his students liked him. Most of the faculty liked him. And he got lucky and got published—serious articles—a few times.

But there he was again, off to dig up some old manuscript by some old nobody. And probably do nothing with it if he did find it. He just wasn't interested in contributing to the *corpus* of academic knowledge. But I'm not saying that we need to retire Lachlan. Frankly, I *like* sitting in his office on a Thursday afternoon with the door closed, sipping Irish whisky out of college souvenir shot glasses. No, I'm certainly not saying we should get rid of him.

When asked, I merely suggest that he should be more closely watched.

The next day, David Lachlan McIntyre resumed walking to campus. He usually drove half the distance, parking his truck at the athletic field to avoid the necessity of a parking permit, the price of which he considered exorbitant. He could purchase a very good pair of walking shoes every year for the cost of a parking permit.

Whenever a new intrigue fermented in his brain, he either swam laps or made himself walk. It gave him time to organize his strategies. He called it part of his methodology. His method was to spend two or three weeks worrying about procedure. He planned a research scenario. He carefully laid out a logical sequence of investigations. He compiled a bibliography. And then one day he climbed into his pickup with an auto club map and went, happily speeding toward whatever venue he imagined held the key to his hidden treasure. That was the methodology of McIntyre's, in its entirety. His primary guide and support was not systematic method, it was serendipity. That, and a genius for making informants out of total strangers.

As he walked, he pondered two immediate questions and several of the far-reaching sort. One far-reaching question was, of course, whether the supposed manuscript had any literary merit. McIntyre had seen colleagues unearth long-forgotten diaries and journals of pioneers which they presented to the world as overlooked specimens of great literature. These had an unfortunate habit of turning out to be either spurious, suspicious, or sophomoric. If McIntyre found new material, bearing the name of James "Rocky Mountain Jim" Nugent, the odds favored it turning out to be all three of them.

Could such a manuscript still exist, after all these years? Among the European pioneers, families scrupulously preserved an ancestor's writing; diaries and letters were kept as treasures along with the family photographs, each new family generation speaking of someday having them copied and published.

People then were far less encumbered with piles of paper than today, and more apt to give over some trunk or cupboard in the storage room to the keeping of little ribbon-bound gatherings of handwriting. Houses stayed in families for generations. Jewelry, gowns, furniture, hats, silverware, glassware, even hardware such as padlocks and harness were all handed down and handed down. So, too, the writings of the ancestors. If Uncle Harvey had ever written a book, one could be ninety-nine percent certain that somebody in the family had kept it and handed it down.

Westward migration frequently required discarding the family heirlooms. But as they settled into new houses with empty attics, Westerners lost no time in resuming their accumulation of that clutter known as the family heritage. The literary portion of it might be no more than a complete set of *National Geographic*s thought to have potential value, or it might be an unpublished masterpiece or historical document. If ever in the family, chances were that it would still be in the family. But where?

McIntyre was already convinced that someone had purloined this particular packet. All other possibilities were mundane and, therefore, unthinkable. Nugent had burned it; vermin had nested in some of it and banqueted on the remainder; Nugent had sent it to a publisher without the obligatory return postage; or it had never existed in the first place.

The first thing to do was to prove that it had existed. Then he would review the possibilities, all of them. In his mind, as he walked, there was no doubt that he would find solid evidence that it had existed. He would discharge all other reasons for its disappearance and would take up the culprit's trail.

So, McIntyre mused as he strolled down familiar sidewalks, *Enos Mills is our first source of information.*

Chapter Two

Spring term was over at last. The examinations were graded, semester grades had been posted, and the campus was almost deserted. I was at my computer, composing politically inoffensive comments concerning a new book, MOCCASIN TRAILS AND **MAN**-IFEST DESTINY: A RE-EXAMINATION OF CONESTOGA CULTURE SHOCK. Bloody tripe. The journal editors wanted my assessment of this recent outpouring of revisionism, and they wanted it on Monday.

A voice in the doorway broke my concentration. "Still at it?" he said. "Haven't you heard that all work and no playing around makes a dull Jack? Or, in your case, Jill?"

Lachlan was leaning against my door frame, walking stick in hand and khaki field trousers girding his loins. He also wore a leather jacket and the annoying smirk of a professor who has his semester all wrapped up and filed away.

"Book review," I answered. "I do not know why I ever let editors talk me into writing book reviews. I absolutely hate them."

"Editors, or reviews? Either way, I concur. I just turned in my grades," he continued to smirk, "and I'm free as the proverbial cockatoo. Want to go for coffee?"

I hated him, too.

"Sorry, I just can't," I said.

But I wanted to. Strength, lady, I told myself. Have strength, stay here, write the words they want to hear. No harm in being pleasantly conversational, however. "And where are you flying off to, with your newly fledged freedom?"

"I told you . . . to have coffee. Where the hell do you buy blue jeans that tight?"

I looked down at myself. I like tight jeans and Western boots because they make my legs look longer.

"What you really want to know, you lech, is how I get into them." And I hurried on to another topic. "What I meant was . . . what are your future plans? I see you've whittled yourself a new stick."

Lachlan stroked the glossy finish of the long staff. "Lilac," he said. "Probably the toughest wood you can find around here. Last week I was tempted to try it out on some bicycle spokes. The little twerp came shooting out of that sidewalk next to Smith Hall and almost ran me down. One of these days I'm going to go amuck and start jousting with those ten-speed transgressors. One good poke. . . ." He demonstrated a jab that would, indeed, take a cyclist out of the saddle. "But you changed the topic." He smiled. "We were talking about your jeans and my future plans. I'm heading up to Estes Park to look for old Mountain Jim and Enos Mills."

"Oh, so it's that simple for you, is it?" I gave him the raised eyebrow of haughty incredulity. "Just drive into town, ask anyone if they've seen James Nugent and his manuscript, and leave with it under your arm? I fear, Lachlan, that you are in for a disappointment."

"Want to come along? I'll wait while you fix a picnic lunch."

"Disappointments two and three for you. I simply can't go anywhere unless I first finish this bloody book review. And no picnic."

"Alone again!" He sighed. He slumped down the door frame, knuckles to forehead, trying to look like a dying Hamlet. Instead, he looked like Petruchio with a migraine. "Alone, alone . . . ," his voice faded along the hallway.

I resumed my assault upon the pile of academic offal before me that now looked more than ever like tripe.

McIntyre knew, of course, that a drive to Estes Park would not produce the manuscript. He needed to discover what kin, or friends, or creditors might have inherited Mountain Jim's belongings. He needed to search libraries and museums throughout the region for accounts of Nugent's life. With great luck, after months of work, he might find a scrap of Nugent's writing. If he could even prove that it had ever existed. So far, the only thing McIntyre had to go on was Enos Mills's statement. The question was if Enos Mills was dependable?

The cañon road up Devil's Gulch swept to the right, curved left, arched right again, and straightened itself out. In a few hundred yards it began twisting again, all the while climbing steadily. Near the top of the cañon, the curves abruptly became steep hairpin turns. McIntyre's pickup truck lost momentum at first, then growled into second gear, and negotiated the first and second switchbacks. The grade increased. First gear, a scant ten miles per hour, doubling around the third and finally the fourth switchback. Second gear the rest of the way.

At the top of Devil's Gulch the road flattened out, pointed straight across the valley into a breathtaking sudden vista of Long's Peak. Long's loomed like a granite pyramid flanked by jagged gray ranges, effectively closing the valley all across the western side. By contrast, the park it dominated laid green and smooth. Open fields of grass freckled with groves of pine and aspen sloped gently toward brooks whose meandering bends reflected the columbine sky.

Behind the park-like meadows, however, the mountains of the Front Range stretched away from Long's Peak in that formidable wall, two miles high at the Continental Divide. A gray rank of broken stone teeth leaning into each other, the barrier of the Rockies overwhelmed the diminutive park huddled at its base. In those open pastoral fields, one was effectively imprisoned by the mountains.

Long's Peak had the most daunting parapets and towers of all the Front Range mountains. It was so high that its summit had a view of distant Kansas and a panorama stretching from Colorado Springs and Pike's Peak all the way north to Cheyenne. From there, Isabella Bird had seen tiny lakes on the western slope of the Divide, calling them "links of diamonds showing where the Grand River takes its rise to seek the mysterious Colorado . . . and to lose itself in the waters of the Pacific."

Few people from the valley went there. Even among Estes Park residents, only a small percentage had made the climb to the summit. Perhaps they preferred being hemmed in; perhaps they didn't want to be up there where the village was only a dark speck cowering in a comparatively small clearing.

Coming into Estes Park in the year 1874, stopping on any high vantage point, one would have seen the Thompson River's liquid silver ribbon from where it flowed down out of the Front Range, crossed the grassy park, and vanished on down the cañon. And one would have seen a smaller stream from the south joining the Thompson. At that confluence stood the earliest cluster of human structures ever to blight the park's pristine beauty. It was Griff Evans's place, consisting of a fairly good house that had been purchased from the first settler, Joel Estes, a ramshackle barn he had thrown together from native timber, and two guest cabins—one-room affairs with gaps between the logs, crude doors slung on leather hinges, and windows that closed by means of a piece of canvas fixed to roll up and down over the opening.

Nearby had stood other log buildings, mostly pertaining

to R.H. Windham Thomas Wyndham-Quin, fourth Earl of Dunraven and Mount Earl. There were differing accounts as to the appearance of these buildings; an early sketch showed a large cabin with two added wings, making it a five or six room structure. Behind this cabin the sketch showed a smaller one, evidently for overflow guests or for some of Dunraven's employees.

Accounts also differed on the matter of dates. It was probably during an 1872 hunting trip that Lord Dunraven had been relaxing in a Denver drinking establishment and met Theodore Whyte. The earl was thirty-two, a landed aristocrat, and rich. Whyte, an Englishman from Devonshire, was a one-time trapper, a one-time miner, and a full-time self-promoter.

That year, Whyte led Dunraven to Estes Park to shoot bear and elk. The next year, 1873, the earl returned. He had decided to buy Estes Park, and Whyte eagerly agreed to handle details. Together with some Denver bankers and lawyers and a few other English aristocrats they set up the Estes Park Company, Ltd., locally known as The English Company. And then began to steal the park.

Jobless men in need of ready cash were not difficult to find among the foothill settlements. The Estes Park Company recruited dozens of such men to file homestead claims on one-hundred-and-sixty-acre parcels that they soon sold to the company for approximately $5 per acre.

Two existing homestead claims stood in their way. One was the Griffith Evans place. But Griff was apparently in awe of the English lords with their money and titles and fine clothes; he assisted the company in every way he could. The other obstacle, down in Muggins's Gulch, was the shanty and acreage of James Nugent. Nugent knew a tinsel show when he saw it, and he was seeing it all over his hunting grounds.

Genuine English lords and ladies came and went, but two would-be aristocrats stayed and worked on the acquisitions all winter. One was Theodore Whyte, who had begun to dress in English riding costume with high patent leather boots and all. He led hunts across the fields and fences, complete with hounds. As Lord Dunraven's agent and manager, he browbeat the servants and intimidated investors. More than one traveler wrote that Whyte was a most pretentious and abrasive self-styled gentleman.

The other man, Haigh, was more mysterious. He was English. He liked slaughtering game, gambling, heavy drinking, and women. And while he spent considerable time in Estes Park, neither Dunraven's autobiography nor the account by Dunraven's physician, Dr. Kingsley, told anything about him. Isabella Bird might have met him during her visit to the park.

Abner Sprague, who wrote "An Historical Reminiscence," heard about Haigh, from William Brown, one of the few witnesses to Nugent's shooting. According to Brown, Lord Haigh had met a "woman of the town" while entertaining himself in Denver. He wanted this woman to join him in Estes Park, for obvious reasons; however, for reasons that were not so obvious, Haigh was reluctant to travel back to Denver to get her. Instead, he paid James Nugent $100 to go. After "a week or ten days," Nugent returned. Without the Denver woman. She would not spend the summer with Haigh, Nugent said, for all the money in Colorado. Haigh called him a thief and liar. Nugent tucked the muzzle of his rifle against Haigh's ear and offered him the opportunity to amend his opinion, which Haigh did with all possible alacrity.

Nugent's picturesque shanty defiled a little meadow several miles east of Estes Park, on the other side of Park Hill, at the foot of Muggins's Gulch. Both roads into Estes Park converged at Muggins's Gulch and then followed the Park Hill route into the valley proper.

Undocumented histories tell of Kit Carson, standing on Park Hill in 1840, choosing a site for the cabin he and his partners would build in 1851. Carson left soon after, looking back from Park Hill for the last time. Joel Estes came next, in 1859, with the family belongings loaded on two pack horses. Some years later his son's wife wrote: "We kept well, enjoyed the climate, had plenty of fun, were monarch of all we surveyed, had no taxes, and were contented as long as we stayed."

In 1866 the Joel Estes family stood on Park Hill, looking back at the valley they were leaving. Monarchs or not, the winters were lonely and cold, and there were neither teachers nor ministers or doctors for the new children. Joel Estes must have known deep melancholy, seeing the last of his cabin and the last of the park that was, however briefly, the Estes kingdom.

Mr. Michael Hollenbeck next paused on Park Hill for his glimpse of paradise, but the charm was short-lived for him. Only a few months after he had bought the Estes claim from Joel Estes, he sold it again to a Mr. Jacobs, who in turn relinquished it to a character known only as Buckskin.

Hollenbeck, Jacobs, Buckskin, all took their turns at pausing on Park Hill to look back at the kingdom that might have been before turning their faces toward the foothills and great plains below, where there were more people and better crops to be harvested.

Most melancholy of all must have been the sight of Griff Evans as he departed the beautiful valley forever. He had become owner of the Estes claim and kingdom in 1867. He had enjoyed playing host to visitors and had looked for the day when people would come to Estes Park to build churches, stores, a post office, a school, ranches, and summer homes.

He ruined his dream in 1874, when he raised that shotgun and blasted James Nugent. The congenial little Welshman became a celebrity, a curiosity, a Western character who had "got his man." Temperance lecturers pointed to him as an example of the evils of alcohol. British ladies and gentlemen, staying with Dunraven, viewed Evans from a distance; he was not invited to *soirées* at the Dunraven Ranch.

Two years of deep-browed gloom in paradise, and then, in 1876, it was Evans's turn to pack his belongings, hand his land title over to Theodore Whyte, and slump over the hill toward lower elevations where he was not so widely known. Did he linger there at the Park Hill summit, and look back? Did he again imagine Mountain Jim and William Brown riding across the small stream and up to his cabin door? Did he wonder whether, at the crucial moment, he could have greeted Jim with an open hand rather than with a load of buckshot? Or had fate made inevitable the time and the spot for that mortal conjunction?

As he left the valley for the last time, perhaps Evans stopped on Park Hill and listened to a far off sound of hammering. Imported workmen were erecting The English Hotel, a fine European-style building with all the modern conveniences. When it was completed, elegantly dressed people would stand on its porches of an evening, looking down the valley at a collection of sagging, crumbling log shacks with dried-out sod roofs, the remains of Griff Evans's own tourist accommodations. Whether it was the sound of hammers or the light breeze rattling the aspen leaves that was the valley's final salute to the departing murderer cannot be said. But he did listen to the valley, Griff Evans did, as he took the back trail eastward.

★ ★ ★ ★ ★

McIntyre parked the pickup at a gravel pull-out near Lake Estes to visualize how the valley had looked before the reservoir was built. From this spot in 1874, instead of a lake he would have seen a meadow with meandering mountain streams and herds of deer and elk wandering miles of greensward punctuated with thickets of willow and chokecherry.

He had copied an 1870's photograph showing little more than a buggy track curving down from the Evans place and fording the stream. From the Dunraven site, its stone foundations now buried beneath the dark waters of the reservoir, another two-rut track led downstream and turned to climb Park Hill.

Somewhere out there under the water was the exact spot where Mountain Jim Nugent had fallen. Buckshot had smashed through the bridge of his nose, through his cheek, through the upper part of his left arm. A chunk of lead had entered under one ear and buried itself in his brain, yet he lay conscious, spurning the aid of the detested Englishmen who wanted to carry him to the Dunraven lodgings, asking, instead, if someone would help him to lie down in a nearby grove of trees.

James Nugent no doubt thought that he would draw his last breath there among the aspen. *Did he think about his manuscript at that moment?* McIntyre wondered. *Had he finished his book? Had he exposed the land scheme before being ambushed? Did it incriminate The English Company, and had he somehow succeeded in putting it beyond their reach?*

McIntyre wrote notes and made a sketch, then drove up Fish Creek Road to look at the last remaining Dunraven building. Afterward, supplying himself with a cardboard cup of steaming hazelnut coffee and a scone from a mini-mart café, he drove up to park at the overlook on Park Hill.

On the edge of the parking area, he found a spot on the low stone wall to sit with his back against an ancient ponderosa pine. There he perused the sum total and grand result of his morning research—a few photocopies of library documents, including Enos Mills's history of Rocky Mountain National Park. Before long, a deep scowl wrinkled that photogenic brow. His coffee had gone cold, but that was not what caused the frown; he was seeing serious problems with the Mills material, material that he had hoped to use as his starting point.

The basic problem was clear—as an historian, Mills was a clumsy amateur. Born in Kansas in 1870, he was four years old and six hundred miles away when James Nugent rode into that double-barreled load of blue whistlers. Mills arrived in Estes Park in 1884, ten years after the murder, at age fourteen.

The year 1902 marked a turning point for Mills with a publication in *Outdoor Life*. Fired with success, Mills decided that, like his idol John Muir, he was a born naturalist and writer. Despite his lack of education and training, he went on to publish more than a dozen books. The account of Nugent's shooting was in his 1905 volume, THE STORY OF ESTES PARK AND A GUIDE BOOK, and was reprinted, slightly revised, in his 1924 book, THE ROCKY MOUNTAIN NATIONAL PARK.

There, with his back to the pine, McIntyre scowled over his coffee. In the first place, Mills's account was written thirty years after Nugent's shooting. In the second place, Mills had relied on hearsay, much of which he had not bothered either to substantiate or document. McIntyre had already found a half-dozen flaws in Mills's narrative.

"Meddling parents with a lovely maiden in the background may have started him on his reckless way," wrote Mills, repeating some thirty-year-old gossip, the sort of thing

Victorian biographers used to flavor their character sketches. Many a man of good looks and an individualistic life style had his exile blamed upon misdeeds with maidens. One might think of Byron. Mills offered no evidence for his assumption that Jim had engaged in "reckless" living full of "debauches." And probably had none.

Besides repeating old gossip, Mills turned chronology upside-down by transposing the Boulder *News* article of November 14, 1873 with the one from the October 17 issue. Apparently it had not occurred to Mills to wonder why Nugent had given a share of his trout to the newspaper editor, but it should have; Nugent had made his living by trapping and hunting and fishing for the markets in Boulder and Denver, and there was no money in giving it away.

When McIntyre put the articles in correct order, they made more sense. In October, the notice about Nugent's writing a book was a teaser to readers, a plug in advance. A month later, Jim came back with a gift of fresh mountain trout. A reward for the support of the *News*? Maybe the editor had had friends in the book publishing business. Maybe he had gotten the trout in return for reading the manuscript. Maybe, McIntyre mused, that manuscript was still in the archives of the Boulder *News*, if such still existed.

The strangest part of Mills's history was his version of Mountain Jim's hand-to-paw struggle with a bear, the fight that had left Jim blind in one eye and terribly scarred all over one side of his face.

Jim and the bear had run afoul of each other in 1869 near Grand Lake on the other side of the mountains. According to the Mills version, Jim was ripped and torn, blinded and battered, his scalp nearly ripped off, and an arm dislocated, yet he still killed the brown bear. Then he managed to drag himself onto his mule and ride into the Grand Lake settlement where his bloody appearance frightened "the few settlers, who were expecting an Indian raid."

The astonishing thing was that Mills could have been ignorant of Judge Wescott's significantly different version.

Joseph L. "Judge" Wescott was among the Grand Lake settlers. According to Wescott, it was a grizzly, not a brown bear; moreover, Jim's revolver and knife did *not* kill the brute. After the fight, Jim's dog ran to the settlement for Wescott, who dragged Jim back to his cabin on a crude travois. Jim's mule did not appear in this version; it was Wescott himself who "dragged him through the sagebrush and carried him across the outlet. How he managed to do this alone, even he could hardly understand. But with superhuman strength he got the stretcher across the river, up the farther bank, and into the cabin."

McIntyre had found this version in Mary Lyons Cairns's GRAND LAKE: THE PIONEERS. Cairns also had written that Wescott had tended to Jim's wounds and broken bones, and nursed him back to health.

Wescott had arrived in Grand Lake in 1867. He became postmaster, then justice of the peace, thus the honorific judge title. He died in 1914. Mills had known him; in fact, a chapter in ROCKY MOUNTAIN NATIONAL PARK was "The Story of Grand Lake," in which Mills had discussed Wescott's rôle in settling the valley. Mills also wrote about Mountain Jim's trips to Grand Lake. For all Enos Mills knew, it might have been Wescott who had Jim's manuscript.

McIntyre also had a problem with Enos Mills's ambiguous rhetoric. He studied a passage from ROCKY MOUNTAIN NATIONAL PARK:

Evans told the writer that he shot Jim for insulting his daughter. But incidental remarks of Evans to the

writer concerning the affair did not harmonize with the studied assertion. A claim is made that there was a woman in the case—a woman to whom the man behind Evans and Jim were paying attention. . . . It does seem that Evans was only an agent when he did the shooting, but his hatred for Jim and the hatred of his backer, the land unpleasantry, and whisky all combined in causing Evans to do the shooting.

McIntyre knew there was no reason to doubt that Mills could have spoken with Evans, who was probably living in Lyons, Colorado at the time Mills wrote his book. But the juicy allusion to Evans's daughter is more gossip, romantic and sensational, but not very logical. If Evans actually had said this, why hadn't Mills asked him for particulars? Instead of interviewing his source for details, Mills just got some "incidental remarks." Using them as his evidence, he then formed the "other woman" hypothesis. A woman capable of provoking murder would probably have been noticed in Estes Park, yet McIntyre had found no other mention of such a person. Unless, McIntyre pondered, it was the Denver tavern trollop found in Sprague's story. If so, did Mills mean the man *behind* Evans to be Lord Haigh? By *behind* had he meant that the man was just standing behind Evans as he pulled the trigger, or that he was a motivating force? Did easy-going Evans really express *hatred* for Jim?

Mills's account added gossip to gossip. The bit of infamy—"Give him another . . . he's not dead yet."—was uncorroborated. Had he gotten it from a newspaper report? Was it in Jim's own report of the incident? Equally libelous was Mills's repetition of the rumor that Jim's "attending physician was hired to put him out of the way." A reliable historian either cited a source for such a remark, damaging as it may be to reputations, or dropped it like a pyrotechnic tuber.

McIntyre's pen drew a big circle around an illustration in his photocopy. It was a sketch of the park with a long cabin in the foreground. Underneath the picture was the legend—**MY HOME IN THE ROCKY MOUNTAINS**—with the annotation *From a Sketch* in italics. Any reader would infer that this was Mills's cabin and his sketch. After all, it was his book. However, in the library McIntyre had seen other books that called it the Griff Evans cabin, or the Dunraven cabin. Both were possible, since Evans sold his holding to Dunraven. One thing is certain. It was not Mills's cabin, and the only way it could have been his "home in the Rocky Mountains" was if he had stayed with Dunraven when he had arrived in the valley. But by 1884, the Dunraven hotel, called The English Hotel, had been built behind the site shown in the picture, and the sketch would have shown it.

Besides, McIntyre already knew that the sketch was made long before Enos Mills had come to Estes Park. It was by Isabella Bird. Bird's pencil drawing of the Evans house in which she stayed in 1873 was in her book, A LADY'S LIFE IN THE ROCKY MOUNTAINS. Enos Mills clearly lifted it for use in his own book. *But was it plagiarism,* McIntyre asked himself, *or just amateurish bookmaking?* Either way, it was more evidence that Mills was not a dependable source.

McIntyre flipped to the place where Mills had made allusions indicating that he had tried to have a correspondence with the Lady Isabella:

. . . Jim was a picturesque and interesting fellow and might easily delight a young lady author without her falling in love with him. I cannot think that Miss Bird was in love with him, but she may have been. She refused to write anything concerning her Estes Park ex-

periences for this book.

A number of things, however, would indicate that Miss Bird was deeply interested in him. During the closing years of her life she declined to write anything concerning the region and apparently avoided any discussion of it.

McIntyre leaned once more against the ponderosa and gazed out over the broad valley. *Fascinating,* he thought to himself. For the moment he dismissed Mills's fallacy of assuming Bird was interested in Jim just because she avoided discussion of it, or at least avoided discussing it with Mills. Still, imbedded in the ambiguity of the words "cannot think . . . but she may have been" and in the deliberate vagueness of "a number of things" was a strong suggestion that Mills had written to Bird about her Estes Park experience. Could the Bird archives contain an Enos Mills letter? How had she replied when she declined? Was her reply among Mills's papers? *Fascinating.* So she "apparently avoided any discussion" of her Estes Park experience, did she? The use of *apparently* sounded like Mills's leaping for another conclusion.

Still, McIntyre mused, tipping the cardboard cup to get the last cold drop of coffee, *something about Bird's refusal is troubling.* She had written so much about Mountain Jim, both in A LADY'S LIFE IN THE ROCKY MOUNTAINS and in letters to her sister. Why would she have refused to do so at this late date?

McIntyre began his next train of thought. Mills would have composed his letter in 1903 or 1904, since the book appeared in 1905. Isabella Bird died in October of 1904. The last thoughts of her seventy-two years had been focused upon the disposition of her papers and her money and plans for a stone clock tower at Tobermory, a village on the Isle of Mull off the Scottish coast. The tower was to be a memorial to her sister, Henrietta. She had lived in a Tobermory cottage during most of the years in which Isabella had done her traveling. It was to Henrietta, in Tobermory, that Isabella had sent letters from Estes Park, the letters that later became the basis of A LADY'S LIFE IN THE ROCKY MOUNTAINS.

In failing health, Isabella had been anxious to dispose of her estate among various charities—for she had no heirs—and to put her instructions for Henrietta's memorial into trusted hands; it is unlikely that she would have expended time and energy on a reply to Mills's invitation to revisit the long dead past. The very rudeness of it must have amused her, if anything. Here was a young, unschooled American writing to one of Great Britain's most respected and prolific travel authors to ask if she had been in love with a Rocky Mountain fur trapper thirty years previously.

McIntyre tossed the cardboard cup into the trash can. He could attack Mills's credibility all day, but he still could not dismiss that one mesmerizing question.

"Come on, Enos," he said to the valley below. "Where did you hear about Nugent's manuscript, for God's sake? Why didn't you find it?" Neither the mountains nor the valley gave back an answer.

McIntyre started the engine and drove slowly down the cañon's twisting road.

Chapter Three

"Hank," he yelled, "over here!"

Lachlan's ebullient greeting carried through the coffee shop, causing two summer students to look up from their espresso conversation and one from her studies. I do wish he could use my title, or at least my correct name, when shouting at me in public places.

He already had his coffee in front of him, in a thick white porcelain mug. When I asked if he had ordered for me, he waved in the direction of the coffee urns. "Take your pick," he said. "Sabrina will put it on my bill. They have five flavors today, three of them your unleaded kind. The bran muffins are in that Plexiglas humidor thing on the counter."

I brought my decaffeinated Colombian Supremo and low-fat organic poppy seed muffin to the table where he sat. The high ceiling, brass fans turned lazily, stirring the air ever so slightly. There was a long counter and a display case of dessert cakes, most of them containing enough calories to stun an elephant, behind which the attractive owner and her equally attractive manager laughed together while manufacturing reaming cups of latté and espresso. I could see why this was Lachlan's favorite spot: it offered coronary-grade caffeine, lovely women to smile at him, and comfortable chairs.

"So," I said, arranging my plate and mug on the table and drawing up the other upholstered chair, "on the phone you indicated that the trip to Estes Park was less than productive."

"You could put it that way," he said, pushing my plate

aside to set down a stack of photocopy pages. I leafed through them; the margins featured liberal amounts of his ink markings.

"Look at these and tell me what you think of Mills's writing," he said.

I studied Mills while Lachlan went back for another refill and another big smile from the blonde manager. It did not take long to appraise what the photocopied pages had to offer.

"It's not terribly useful as solid historical data, I'll say that much. However, it flows right along in a lively kind of way. Rather nice in places."

"Nice?" he scowled at me.

In return, I gave him my sweet cheery little don't-take-it-so-seriously smile.

"Does this mean the end of your search for Nugent's missing manuscript?" I asked. "If your obscenities in these margins are any indication, you appear to have less to go on now than you had before."

"I don't know," he said. "What about you? Did you find anything else while you were digging around for Dunraven information?"

"No, nothing that would pertain to lost papers. Or even to our friend Rocky Mountain James. Did you read Isabella Bird's account of him?"

"Yes. I turned that book inside out, too. I'd love to find the letter Enos wrote to her the year she died. Or the one she replied with. But neither one would have been likely to say anything about the Nugent manuscript. She had left Estes Park months before he was shot, and Mills didn't get there until ten years later. But I don't know. It's all too vague, too little to go on. Damn it. I was really hoping to prove that Mills had been the last person to see the manuscript, and he didn't even tell us where he heard about it. We don't even know if there's a needle, let alone which haystack it might be in."

Poor baby. Resorting to farmyard clichés. I could see it was time to boost his spirits. With the scent of a good chase in his nostrils, Lachlan can be irrepressibly cheerful. But let him lose that spark, and he resembles a bloodhound listening to Bach.

"Well," I said brightly, letting my eyes flash at him, "let's take these scraps you have found and see what kind of stew we might concoct from it. Some of it shows potential. For instance, you might write to Isabella's publishers, John Murray of London, and ask about her letters and so forth. And while awaiting an answer, I think you should attempt to resolve this matter of Mountain James and the bear."

"The bear? Why?"

"Think about it," I said. "In order to look into this discrepancy, you would have to drive over to Grand Lake Village. And, of course, you would be forced to stay there several days to find anyone who might remember this Judge What's-His-Name. Didn't you once tell me that there was good fishing over there? And who knows? You might actually discover the source of the judge's version. It would be good for a magazine story, at least. A weekend in Grand Lake Village would be far better for you than haunting the empty hallways of the Liberal Arts and Social Sciences building."

Lachlan swirled his coffee thoughtfully. I could see that the idea of getting out into the woods had caught his attention. So had I. I was leaning forward on my elbows as I spoke to him, and caught him glancing down my shirt cleavage. The resuscitated gleam in his eye was due either to that, or to the idea of going fishing. It is so hard to tell with D. Lachlan McIntyre.

"A few days at Grand Lake," he said. "Not a totally bad

notion. There's a little café in the village where the pancakes are the old-fashioned kind, industrial strength. It wouldn't even be expensive . . . I'll sneak into the trailhead parking lot on the North Inlet trail after hours, and sleep in the camper shell on my pickup. So, you want to come along?"

Had Lachlan indicated that he intended to stay at the splendid old Grand Lake Lodge with its wonderful dining room, where one can enjoy brandy on the balcony while watching the sunset on the lake. . . .

"Sorry," I said. "I don't sleep in trucks."

McIntyre sat on the tailgate of his pickup, poured himself some coffee from the thermos, and looked across the lake. A pair of tall sailboats in the distance raced each other, their masts leaning and white sails stretched full. Gulls soared above the water like predatory sailplanes. Colorado's unhindered sun made a pattern of scattered diamonds on the surface. Shadow Mountain, across the lake, wore a black thrust of spruce forest, deep and dense, an ominous rising bulk between the blue water and the silvertip peaks beyond. Over it all was an azure sky where scudding puffs of cloud mimicked the racing sails below.

He tried to spot Columbine Creek on the other side. To his left, the stream from Grand Lake now carried water into Shadow Mountain Reservoir. Judge Wescott's cabin once stood beside that stream and, just below the site, the sagebrush plain now beneath the reservoir. Columbine Creek was somewhere over there. McIntyre picked up his book. It was Mary Lyons Cairns's account, GRAND LAKE: THE PIONEERS.

It was in the summer of 1868, the year after Joseph L. Wescott settled at Grand Lake, that Jim came riding up to Wescott's cabin on his white mule, accompanied by his little dog and his pack mule. Wescott, no doubt lonely, made him welcome, and the two planned to do some trapping and fishing together.

The next morning, Jim crossed the outlet to Grand Lake, went over the Sagebrush Flat, and stopped near the little stream now known as Columbine Creek to catch grasshoppers for fish bait. Glancing up, he was startled to see a mother grizzly with two cubs. Slowly and cautiously, he began to back away, when his little dog foolishly barked at her. Little dog? Then it couldn't have been Ring, Nugent's dog described by Isabella Bird as having "the legs and body of a Collie, but a head approaching that of a mastiff."

Not important. Whatever dog it was, in Cairns's version it "rushed back to Wescott's cabin" to lead Wescott to the bleeding and unconscious Jim.

McIntyre set out to explore the dirt roads on this side of the lake. At the site of Wescott's cabin, on the other side, there were nothing but summer cottages and condos. Now he hoped to find a road that would lead up to a panoramic view of Shadow Mountain and the reservoir.

One road finally came to a dead-end at an old cabin. In the yard sat a faded 1978 Power Wagon. *A kindred Dodge spirit,* thought McIntyre.

The owner of the Power Wagon turned out to be a long-time native of Grand Lake. He was busy raking pine needles into little piles, but was glad to answer McIntyre's questions as he raked. McIntyre asked where he could find a good vantage point from which to see the whole lake.

"Whole lake, eh?" the old-timer replied. "Let's see. Y'could go back about a mile down this road, take the road where you see Spencer's mailbox, turn at his gate . . . to the left . . . and that'll bring you up on top of the hill. Takin' pictures, are y'?"

"No, not really. I'm trying to get an idea of how far Judge Wescott had to drag Mountain Jim."

"Wescott? Hell, he died years ago."

"I'm thinking of writing a book about the area."

"Oh, a writer. You from around here?"

McIntyre told how he had grown up on the East Slope of the same mountains. Typical of him, it was less than an hour before he and Walt Johnson were sitting on a log together, chatting away like lifelong chums. They complained about taxes and politics and weather and deer hunting and, finally, tourists.

"Dang' thing about tourists," Walt was saying, "is that they clog up the damn' highways and drive all the prices sky-high. Hell, durin' the summer the cost of a six-pack seems to go double around here."

"I know what you mean," McIntyre replied. "Speaking of which, I happen to have one in the cooler. Don't suppose I could talk you into a can of beer."

After the popping of the tabs and the slurping of the foam, resulting from riding in McIntyre's truck, and after the traditional male exchange of viewpoints as to which is actually the best beer, the conversation went back to the high cost of living.

"The price of campgrounds has gone up, I notice," McIntyre said. "I got run out of the North Inlet trailhead by some snotty little summer ranger who told me to go to Arrowhead Campground. Arrowhead wants ten bucks to park my truck and sleep in it."

"Hell," Walt said, "park yourself right here. What the hell do I care? Better yet, park down by that ol' ramshackle garage of mine. There's an electric light by the door, and that ol' outhouse is still usable."

McIntyre didn't hesitate to take up Walt's offer. And

when the six-pack was gone, he was on the road to town to get more. This wasn't going to get any research done, but McIntyre had one other gift besides the gift of gab—he could always sense a story, especially when it sat down next to him and snapped open a beer.

He first drove to Spencer's mailbox and on up the hill to take in the view, and then went into Grand Lake Village for a hamburger. After eating, he strolled the board sidewalks, ambled down to the boat docks to admire a classic old mahogany ChrisCraft, paused to listen to one of the street entertainers rendering John Denver tunes—rendering was a highly appropriate term—and finally stopped at the small liquor store on main street for a bottle of bourbon. And another six-pack.

At eight thousand five hundred feet above sea level in the Colorado mountains even a midsummer sunrise found the dew still frozen. Chilled air frosted the long, black, pine shadows and the blue shadows of the peaks. Hours after sliding up into place above the mountain summits, casting bright corridors of light through the forest, the sun finally began warming the ground and the grass.

McIntyre peeled himself free of his plum-colored sleeping bag, looking like a pupa in boxer shorts getting rid of a purple carapace, shivered into stiff jeans, then got into the cab to move the pickup out of the shadows. Ice water grass between his toes made his feet wince.

Satisfied that he had the tailgate pointed straight into the rising morning sun, he drew on his fleece cardigan and broke out the breakfast necessaries: gas stove, coffee pot, can of coffee, package of bacon, frying pan, eggs, granola, and some thick slices of bread. Before the sun had gone much higher, the aroma of boiled coffee and fried bacon drew old Walt to the pickup like a lodestone. He perched on the tailgate, accepting a mug of coffee with one hand while filching bacon with the other.

"Feeling OK this morning?" McIntyre asked.

"Oh, sure. Takes more than runnin' into a Beam to make this ol' head hurt."

"I wish I could say the same," McIntyre said. "Jim hit me pretty hard. Got a screamer of a headache."

"You're the guy threw the cork away," Walt said.

"I guess so. Hey, tell me something. Somewhere after I lost the cork, did you tell me you *knew* Judge Wescott?"

"Nope. It's a guy knew a guy who knew a guy kinda deal. A long time ago, I kinda did what you might call keepin' company with a woman, back before I figured out that all women go crazy on you sooner or later. Her ma was born here, back in Eighteen Ninety-Eight. And her ma was a kinda unofficial records keeper for the county. That ol' county clerk's office we had . . . when was that thing built? Eighteen Eighty or somewhere around then . . . anyway, didn't have no place to store records."

"So she still has these records?" McIntyre asked.

"Hell, no! She's dead. Give the legal stuff over to the county to deal with. Thing is, there was this woman Wescott had cookin' and housecleanin' for him in his ol' age, and, when he kicked the bucket, she cleaned out lots of his old books and papers and such. Give the papers to Meg, see, 'cause she had a place to keep 'em. The daughter's got 'em now."

"Meg?" McIntyre laid more bacon into the sizzling grease of the pan and checked the hardness of the eggs. His head still hurt, and Walt's non sequiturs were no help. "Meg was the mother of this woman you know? So there was this housekeeper, then Meg, then her daughter."

"Sure. But y'want the granddaughter. She's got the stuff. Let me tell y', the local history outfit, they don't even know what she's got. She don't like 'em."

"This is the daughter of Meg?"

"For a writer, you don't listen too good. This here's Meg's granddaughter. It was her ma that put things right, though. Nice and tidy. That's why we never ended up livin' together, see? She's a weird fanatic about keepin' stuff straight. Back when they was drillin' that tunnel through the mountain an' buildin' the reservoir, she used t'go up there and collect dynamite boxes. Those good wood ones, you know? Can't get good wood boxes any more, not any more. Plastic or cardboard, mostly cardboard. Can't find a peach basket, either. Apple crates outta wood, all gone. Just cardboard."

"So what did she do with all the dynamite boxes?"

"I'm tryin' t'tell y'. She put the judge's stuff in 'em. All arranged by date and tucked up in them folders . . . I tell y', she was weird for being neat."

"And now the daughter has them?"

"Well, that follows, don't it? I mean, she's dead. Got one of them brain things, aneurysms or somethin' like that. Any more coffee in that pot?"

The sun went on rising up the blue sky, and the morning was suddenly warm. The odor of coffee and bacon gradually gave way to an incense of sun-baked pines. McIntyre cleaned his pans and stowed the breakfast gear while Walt polished off the toast and bacon.

"Ever see any grizzly bears around here?" McIntyre asked.

"Not in a hundred years, nope. Why?"

"I came across a story about a grizzly mauling a man over here. Enos Mills wrote it. . . ."

"Enos Mills," Walt snorted. "Not many people around here have much use for that nabob, I'll tell y'."

"Anyway, he wrote about this bear. . . ."

"Is that the story of Charlie? Charlie Rogers or Royers or somethin' like that. Kinda long before my time. Seems he and a bear waltzed around once, tore him up good."

"This was Jim Nugent. Rocky Mountain Jim?"

McIntyre told Walt the two versions of the bear incident, pointing out that the bear had changed species between one story and the other. And what McIntyre wanted to know was whether Judge Wescott had written a version of the story himself. Mary Lyons Cairns had to have gotten it somewhere. Maybe the judge had it in a diary or notebook.

"Dunno," Walt said, wiping his fingers on his jeans. "Tell y'what . . . I'll go find me a cleaner shirt, and we'll just drive over there, and see if this little gal knows whether ol' Judge Wescott wrote it down. But a grizzly? Maybe, but I don't think so."

The granddaughter of Meg Tyler, the keeper of the Wescott archives, Glenda was one of those women who other women envy, admire, and hate. She was McIntyre's age and very pretty. McIntyre was hard pressed to keep his bourbon-battered brain cells on his research.

"Here is another box of things dated from Eighteen Seventy," she cooed in her throaty voice. "You might look at it when you've finished with that one."

"OK," McIntyre replied. He was sitting on a high stool next to a workbench, rifling the large envelopes from a wooden dynamite box. The storeroom was light, airy, and dry; the papers were completely free of mold and decay.

"So far," he said, "all I've found are letters about building sawmills and civic improvements. Here's a whole stack of weather records, including how high the lake level was."

Glenda's stocking feet took her noiselessly out of the

room, and soon she returned with a tray bearing a teapot, cups, and an assortment of cookies.

"I'm so sorry Walt had to leave," she said. "Would you care for some tea? I have Earl Grey, or there's Wallingate. Oh, and herbal, of course. Somehow you don't look like a man who drinks herbal tea!" Her laugh was enchanting.

"Sometimes I do." McIntyre smiled. "Thanks. Walt made serious inroads on my breakfast this morning."

She laughed that enchanting laugh, again. As there were no seats in the storeroom other than the stool upon which McIntyre was perched, she stood with her little *derrière* pressed against the bench, the taut curve of her jeans almost touching the document McIntyre was examining. Glenda took another folder from the wooden box, and the two of them remained that way, making a serious search for information. McIntyre found his attention divided.

Two hours went by. McIntyre offered to pay for a lunch in the village; instead, Glenda led him outside to her rustic table on a flagstone patio all hedged about by cedar and spruce, and there she brought him chicken salad and tuna sandwiches, cold creamed cucumber slices, watermelon, and lemonade.

He spent the afternoon alone in his search. At day's end he invited Miss Archives to dinner, but she had a previous dining engagement. McIntyre had another hamburger, split a six-pack nightcap with Walt, and the following morning, after indulging in a stack of café pancakes, he was back at it.

Glenda was wearing a sundress from Distractions of Hollywood, but fortunately for McIntyre's labors she merely floated in from time to time on her petite bare feet to see how he was doing. And to offer him coffee, that he accepted.

And suddenly there was a sealed envelope. It was the old-fashioned legal size, of very heavy paper, yellow from age. It was still glued shut. It was addressed to **James Nugent, Esq. of Muggins's Gulch, Estes Park**. It had neither stamp nor a return address.

Glenda had gone to the village, leaving McIntyre the run of the house in case he needed anything. He went to the kitchen and turned on the stove burner under her tea kettle. The hundred-year-old glue softened grudgingly, but soften it did. McIntyre extracted a folded sheet of paper, undisturbed since 1874. The penmanship was broad and bold in the old style.

June 10, 1874
James Nugent:
No doubt you think yourself quite the public servant, sir, and live in hopes &c that your scribblings shall make you a person of fortune and reputation never minding other reputations unjustly or shall I say DISHONESTLY spoilt and ruined by it. We have law yet in this Territory of Colorado and by the living God, sir, I shall see it brought down upon your head for LIBEL should you publish any version of this trash that you have caused to be put into my hands. Persons of our community here will speak against you as a single voice supporting their Justice of the Peace in whom they place most implicit trust. Of your version regarding the incident with the bear I have no need of defense, as you were delirious and undoubtedly drunk most of the time of your recovery and remember little that occurred and wish furthermore to take all credit onto your own person for killing the bear, crawling to safety &c.

As to this alleged record of my military service you say you have "rescued" from Mr. Dunraven's own office drawers and intend delivering to me &c. and no

doubt expecting reward. My reply to you is that my personal history prior to settling this valley as a pioneer is no man's business but mine own and should you proceed to publish what scandal you think you may know from these military records of yours, by God, sir, I will come and shred & burn them and this manuscript before your eyes and BE WARNED THAT I ALSO HAVE FRIENDS who live on the eastern side of these Rockies and who can shoot and will if I but say the word. You think yourself clever posting a copy of your libelous trash to your English friend, but what good can that do when you lie cold with a bullet in your heart.

My suggestion to you is that you leave off writing any history of our region and stick to your traps & bottle until such time as you know your facts and who your enemies are.

The letter was signed in an angry scrawl: **J.L. Wescott, J.P.**

For several minutes, McIntyre stood in that sun-flooded kitchen reading the words over and over. The date corresponded with Nugent's shooting. But the letter had not been delivered. Had Wescott heard what Griff Evans had done, just as he was preparing to post his letter, and so stuck it away until he could learn more? Or had he taken it to Estes Park personally, only to return with it upon hearing the news?

More importantly, the letter was evidence of the existence of another copy of some sort of history. Clearly, Nugent had sent or given Wescott something, whether a manuscript or a portion of a manuscript. Maybe it was nothing more than Nugent's own account of the bear story for which he wanted Wescott's corroboration of facts.

But what about the references to libel and Wescott's military history? What was in Nugent's writing to make the judge so angry? It seemed apparent that Nugent had acquired private information about Wescott's mysterious past.

The question was why would such a thing have made Wescott irate? Mary Lyons Cairns had quoted from letters by Harriet Proctor Boyle, one of several children who had hung around the judge. "He was never known to tell anyone where he came from, his age, or anything connected with his life prior to coming to the lake; and if anyone was so ill-bred as to ask him personal questions, they were simply dropped from his list of friends."

Cairns also reported that facts of Wescott's life prior to coming to the lake in 1867 were sparse, indeed. The only information he seemed to have given anyone was that he had been in the Union cavalry and had been mustered out after the Civil War because of "inflammatory rheumatism." He showed up in Hot Sulphur Springs, approximately fifteen miles from Grand Lake, to try the curative waters. According to one story, he had been so ill as to be carried in a hammock slung between two pack burros.

McIntyre went back to the storeroom. When his hostess returned, he would ask to copy the letter. Meanwhile, he would keep digging. There was now a possibility that whatever Nugent had sent Judge Wescott was still in one of the boxes.

The very next folder he opened held not a manuscript or another letter, but an antique photograph. According to its label, it was Judge Wescott with his Civil War rifle. McIntyre looked closely. The photo, dim and indistinct, was of Wescott as an old man. The background suggested mountain scenery. The rifle butt rested on the ground near Wescott's foot. The barrel reached all the way to the man's slumped shoulder. A long bayonet was affixed to the right side of the barrel. Wescott had told people he was a Union cavalryman. *I wonder,* McIntyre thought, *if anyone ever asked him why a cavalryman would carry an infantry rifle, complete with bayonet? It would also be fascinating to find out how a cavalryman would get rheumatism.*

"Find anything?" Glenda inquired with her gay little smile, peeking her head around the storeroom door, upon her return.

"Maybe," McIntyre replied. "It might be a dead-end, though. When you and your mother organized all this material, did you run across some kind of history narrative? Pages out of a manuscript? They would have been in someone else's handwriting, not Wescott's. I found a letter by Wescott, never delivered, and it talks about a document Nugent sent him."

"Oh," she chirped brightly, "that could be the Sprague essay!"

"Sprague essay?" McIntyre repeated. "What does that mean?"

"Well," she said, depositing her packages next to the door, "Abner Sprague was an Estes Park pioneer. Mother found several pages in among the judge's things that weren't his handwriting. I don't recall why she assumed they were written by Sprague. She put them into a big envelope and wrote Sprague essay on it. It used to be in that box labeled other."

"Used to be? Do you remember what was in it, what it said?"

"It's down at the Grand Lake Historical Museum now. But I've never opened the envelope. I do remember Mother saying it described a horseback ride across Trail Ridge from Estes Park to Grand Lake. Oh, and some gobbledygook about Lord Dunraven's takeover and Wescott's military service."

McIntyre's mind went into high gear. Meg had seen something among Wescott's material, something to do with crossing the Front Range, which Mountain Jim had done many times. It also had to do with Wescott's past. This had to be the manuscript referred to in Wescott's letter.

Glenda slid her pert bottom into McIntyre's pickup to show him the way to the museum, although he already knew where it was. It was an old log building, two stories high, overlooking the public beach and boat rental docks. Local history aficionados had restored the covered porch and painted the trim and chinked the logs, and for all of its age the antique structure had quite a sturdy and business-like look to it.

Unfortunately for McIntyre and Glenda, it was also closed for the afternoon. Nonetheless, they walked around the building, trying each door and peering in at each window in hopes of catching some attendant's attention.

"Oh, there!" Glenda said, drawing McIntyre by his sleeve to look through a window. "See that file cabinet there in the office? That's where the Sprague essay is."

"How do you know?" McIntyre asked.

"Because it's part of a book project, and the files are kept in that file cabinet. Except that the man working on it hasn't been well . . . he hasn't been up from Arizona for the past two summers."

"And what's the project?"

"He's a retired engineer, or something like that, who's doing a history of Trail Ridge Road. He wants to collect first-hand accounts by people who crossed the Front Range on horseback or on foot. Or in cars, once the road was finished. Mother remembered the Sprague essay and let him borrow it. I was in the museum one day, about three summers ago, and ran into him. He told me that he appreciated having it, and offered to take me into the back office to show me that he was keeping it in a safe place."

I'll bet he did, McIntyre thought. *I'd do the same.*

Rather than return home, McIntyre and Glenda voted unanimously to spend the evening sampling the gourmet delights of the village and whatever entertainment offerings might be found after sunset. They dined on well-done steaks and cheap, red wine in a noisy, blue-collar place called Bob's; they strolled the streets and toured the consignment art gallery. Dessert was a cherry sno-cone for him and a chocolate-covered strawberry for her, purchased at the hole-in-the-wall sweet shop. They topped off the evening at the Boardwalk Saloon, drinking Coors from long-neck bottles and watching the dancers tripping the country/western fantastic.

And somewhere in the evening, a conspiracy was born.

Above the din and music and stomping of the Boardwalk dancers, McIntyre spun his web of words, telling Glenda about the mysterious manuscript and his eagerness to lay hands upon the envelope with the Sprague essay. But he didn't want to walk in and ask for it at the museum, since to do so would invite all kinds of curiosity.

Perhaps, he suggested, tipping his fourth long-neck, in the morning they could go to the museum again. She might distract the attendant long enough for him to slip into the office and get a look at the papers. Once he knew what it contained, he would figure out how to get a copy.

"What fun!" She smiled. "A secret mission! But why not just ask Missus Jones for a copy? She's a nice lady and would be glad to make a copy for you. Especially if you told her what it's for."

"That's what I want to avoid. Walt told me that the historical society doesn't know about your boxes of Wescott's material."

"No, I don't think they do. Grandmother didn't trust the historical society, and we've just assumed that she . . . and the judge, I guess . . . didn't want the material turned over to them."

"Then we can't be answering questions about why I know about this Sprague essay and what I'm doing looking into Judge Wescott's life and times. See?"

She saw. Besides having good looks and intelligence and a willingness to commit larceny, the woman had a natural talent for McIntyre's variety of literary scholarship.

Chapter Four

Professor McIntyre and his new henchwoman parked up the street from the Grand Lake Historical Museum and waited, since they were early, and it would attract attention to be the first ones there. They watched as an older woman unlocked the door, swept the front porch, set out a rack of postcards, and went back inside. Glenda identified her as Mrs. Jones, local history buff and chief guardian of the collection.

At about nine o'clock a slim adolescent female appeared. Glenda said she was the daughter of Mrs. Jones. She went into the museum and did not come out. Glenda ventured that she was probably helping her mother with the cleaning and straightening up; the girl also filled in as a tour guide on busy days.

At five minutes before ten, a tourist couple came walking down the street, paused to make a videotape of the exterior, studied the postcard rack, and walked on. No one else arrived to visit the museum.

McIntyre had enough of sitting. "Let's go," he said.

Glenda went first; they had agreed to separate. In a few minutes, McIntyre walked across the porch and pretended to be interested in the postcards and free brochures. He entered as if he had nothing better to do, made his voluntary donation at the desk, and began to stroll around. He looked in display cases at Grand Lake memorabilia and studied the neatly arranged photographs on the wall. He pretended to take a few notes—an excuse to linger about.

He heard someone moving around upstairs. It had to be

the daughter, since Glenda had engaged Mrs. Jones in conversation at the front desk. That was a problem, the daughter. While the open office door could not be seen from the front desk, anyone coming down the stairway could certainly see in. If he was discovered in the office, should he pretend to be lost? Across the doorway sagged a faded velvet rope with brass ends and a sign—**Private Please Stay Out**—hanging on it. It would be hard to argue that he hadn't seen it.

McIntyre looked up the stairway. He couldn't see anyone, but the daughter was up there dragging chairs across the floor. If she kept at it, he would be able to tell when she stopped. He would probably hear her on the old wooden stairs, too. He decided he would chance it.

He left the rope dangling by one end and made sure that the lettering on the sign faced the wall; he might be able to say that he had found it that way. He listened to be certain that Mrs. Jones and Glenda were still chatting, and his ears were strained from trying to keep track of the little noises upstairs.

The file cabinet was not locked. Nothing obvious in the top drawer. The second drawer was stuffed with books, pamphlets, file folders, but no large envelopes. The third drawer, however, yielded the prize. An old brown envelope of the type manufactured during the WWI paper shortages. Across the front, written in an elegant hand, were two words: **Sprague Essay**.

McIntyre quickly slid the envelope into his waistband behind his back and made sure his light windbreaker covered it. All that remained was to get out of the museum unchallenged, find a photocopy machine, and make a copy. He would leave the original with Glenda; she would hang onto it in case the ailing Arizona historian came back, or she could find a means of returning it to the museum. But since it *was* from her collection, she didn't have to do anything about it. It was natural and legal for her to be in possession of it.

The Flattop Mountain Manuscript
[James Nugent's title for the chapter:
"Thwarted by Snow on the Great Divide"]

Universally in the frontier territories there may be found a variety of specimens of foreign scoundrels, largely originating in the British Empire, assuming unto themselves proprietorship of vast cattle ranges, monopolies of the gold and silver interests, and rulership of enormous estates of timber and water. So saturated is our territory with their corruption and thieving methods that what I have called the "Estes Park Land Steal" seem commonplace. Indeed, some see the Irish Lord Dunraven's efforts as practically benign in nature, inasmuch as he does not intend the valley to profit him in the monetary way but rather to give him the pleasure of exclusive sport with the rifle, gun, and rod.

The plot which he and his lieutenants intend to carry out in completion of their American kingdom, however, promises fair to grow and spread like rot through the timbers of a sturdy ship, infecting it from keelson to topmast in the fullness of time. Across the Great Continental Divide from Estes Park lies Grand Lake settlement, a fresh and innocent community unaware of certain machinations moving down upon it to incorporate it and its natural wonders, its wild game and scenic marvels into the general land steal.

Grand Lake, possibly the largest body of water in these Rocky Mountains, surrounded by virgin forests and unexplored mountains appears doomed to exploitation and seizure by these illegal English interests. Should the Estes Park Land Steal manage to cross the divide and conquer the Grand Lake valley through the same simple and surreptitious means as were employed in the acquisition of Estes Park, then our friends of the British Empire would effectively hold the keys to both the front and the back portals of the Great Divide.

Armed with evidence of the plot, I resolved to make the long trek to Grand Lake and lay my facts before the most influential citizen of that valley beyond the Divide in hope of enlisting his aid or, at the least, frustrating and delaying efforts of the Estes Park Company in recruiting him to their own ranks.

I had set out from the park, my notion being to confront Judge Wescott of Grand Lake, gaining his ear either through diplomacy or threatening force, with my knowledge of a conspiracy betwixt himself and Dunraven's henchman Theodore Whyte, demanding explanations inasmuch as Dunraven's motivations had a direct and essential bearing upon my own options—either to remain in the park or to remove myself farther into the mountains and take up new lodgings along the Grand River.

Riding through the dark forest, I was scarcely overjoyed by the prospect of the wind-blasted open wastes of ice and snow that awaited me above timberline. What, I questioned myself aloud (much to the amusement of my laboring steed, I am sure), could Dunraven and his sportsmen friends want with such inconquerable mountains as these? Surely they had easier game and more of it in the valleys. Timber had they in plenty, within wagon's reach. Of water there is always a surplus in the park. Here, in higher and more rugged country, was nothing for them but scenery—and such scenery as is better enjoyed from the removed perspective which the park offers than in close proximity where spruce trees conceal the farther view and what is seen as a jutting peak from afar is seen closely to be another cliff to around which to detour. Vista, in mountain perspectives, is all.

There is little gold to be found here, and less silver. The winters here are deep and harsh; the westerly winds which bring welcoming warmth in the winter to my own eastern side of the mountain are cold blizzards on the western side. Southerly winds, too, bring fierce storms to Grand Lake. The west slope has thicker forests, and less of the morning sun's warmth.

Thus it was on a fine cloudless May morning that I took to the trail where once the Arapaho warrior trod. I elected to reach Grand Lake by way of the path known as the Warrior's Trail—the other two routes across the mountains known as the Squaw's Trail and the Dog Trail. The Warrior's Trail leads first among the crags and then along the treeless tundra above timberline finally to make its descent down through verdant forests to the lake in these mountains. Spirit Lake, the Arapahoes dubbed it. By white men it is called the Grand Lake due to its association with the Grand River.

Snow lay everywhere along the ridges above me, in the vast vertical valleys, in the crevices of granite and the ledges. It was likely, I knew, that the snow on top of Flattop Mountain, up on the Continental Divide, might be more than my faithful mount could negotiate. My long experience, however, in crossing the Divide informed me of a possibility of thickly crusted snow—the effect of the spring sunshine and freezing nights.

Ere I had reached timberline with its unimaginable vistas of mountain, crag, and gorge, I found myself overcome by the sublime beauty of nature's verdant works. Here were dense forests of spruce, fir, and pine, impenetrable for a mounted man, with deadfall and low tangled branches creating formidable barriers to passage by a man afoot. Were it not for the narrow trail of the ancient people winding through the trees, there would be no possible way to negotiate the mountains. Here the ground is steep; to slip off of the narrow pathway would mean a long and rapid slide into one of the river cañons, themselves naught but hellish gorges through which ice cold tumults of water roar and rush across sharp broken edges of rock.

Down below, the aspen are in full luxuriant leaf where around my cottage can be heard the songs of the bluebirds, the jays, the spring robins, and wrens. Farther up, having added what I estimate to be two thousand feet to my elevation, I find the aspen a lighter color and of less impressive leaf, but so brilliant in their yellow-green garb that it becomes almost painful to the eyes to gaze upon them. Here are no mere acres but hundreds of acres of the white bark trees straight as pillars supporting a Greek temple, the dark "eyes" up and down their trunks seeming to watch the traveler pass by.

Another increase in elevation and we find ourselves seeing snowfields lying still in the springtime forests, the grass bent and brown from the weight of their winter's burthen, and the aspen appear bare and shivering in the light breeze off of the glaciers above. No leaf to cover their twigs, no green to offset the stark whiteness of their bark. We have indeed ridden back into winter.

The horse kicks his steps in the snow, the steepness of the slope increasing. All seems lifeless here. No leaf, no animals leaving their winter den, no sound of birds. Only the heavy breathing of my mount and the plop plop of his hoofs sinking through the crusty snow. It has drifted and mounded into miniature mountain ranges, so much so that I doubt at times where the trail is although I know this trail well. Where in the summer months I would see long flat stretches of easy trail, I now see hills and heaps of snowdrifts.

I begin to doubt that we will make it over the divide, and the farther we go the more certain I am that the downward trail on the western slope will be quite thoroughly choked with snow, that being the side of heaviest timber and heaviest precipitation. But if *I* cannot succeed in reaching Grand Lake, neither can Dunraven's representatives. Irish lords and earls may "walk on water," yet even they cannot walk through chest-deep snow.

Progress has lately arrived in the Rocky Mountains in shape of a postal service, and so my documents can travel from Longmont to Denver City, thence by stage road to Granby Village, and by horse carrier to the Grand Lake settlement. Thus will my awareness of Dunraven's designs upon that remote community pass unto Judge Wescott that they might be forestalled by exposure.

I am aware that there are those who will accuse me of theft, even though what I set out to convey across the Flattop Mountain trail were public records. I have invaded no man's privacy; I merely went to Dunraven's cottage at the invitation of Dr. Kingsley, who one day told me that he might be able to perform surgery upon my damaged eye and restore it to the light again. The two aristocrats, Dunraven and Kingsley, were expected momentarily but did not return.

Waiting in Dunraven's office, I could scarcely avoid seeing there, upon his table, a record of those to whom he had paid money for land patents in the valley. Payment accountings from The Estes Park Company as recorded in county filings show two dozen names this May alone; here is $1500 paid to James Harris for his 160 acres, to Henry Brown a similar amount, to James Dunn $1000 for his 160 acres in the valley, and so forth. Not one of these gentlemen on the list resided in Estes Park, but they were all brought there from the slums and saloons of Denver City to be land claimants for Dunraven's Estes Park Company.

My certainty that a similar scheme is being laid to gain control of the Grand Lake valley and all mountains in between comes from my discovery that day of a second document beneath the record of land transfers. Here was a letter from the Department of the Army, specifying that a certain pioneer settler of Grand Lake had, indeed, served in the U.S. Army during the War Between the States. But not as a cavalry officer; rather as an infantry enlisted man assigned to clerk duties with the Quartermaster Corps and subsequently punished by being assigned the duty of digging drainage ditches and latrines for the Washington fortifications. Not a record a man need be ashamed of, but adequate blackmail material for Whyte and his henchmen.

Look at the statement found in these records!! American democracy! Here is a common man, forced to conceal his past, forced into lies, for wanting to serve President and country, yet managing with nothing more than his freedom and his own intelligence and ambition to become settler, landholder, and even justice of the peace in one of our American frontier communities. A man who has "pulled himself up by his own bootstraps" sans family, sans funds, sans friends.

Those who claim land through the selfsame democratic means, however, and pass it off to a great lord for a few dollars and a bottle, they conspire to deny the opportunity to legitimate homesteaders. And here is our aristocrat, with generations of family and inexhaustible wealth at his disposal, able to gather up vast acreages at a whim.

Dunraven, Whyte & Co. have exhibited remarkable forwardness. They clearly intend recruiting Grand Lake settlers now, to extend the Dunraven hunting grounds, his private game reserve, right over the spine of the continent and into the Grand Valley itself.

I pause for lunch, near the timberline. Seated upon a large rock jutting above the tops of the forest I eat and marvel at the vistas to the east. I can see lakes unspoiled by the buildings of man, tall virgin tracts of timber, long rivers running out of the mountains, extensive parks, towering peaks. So many valleys and rivers and parks. All that verdage and water and land. It is clear to see the extent of Dunraven's ambition. If the man has his way, this "park" in which three or four cities could be built, in which a hundred farmers could make their crops and graze their cattle, will be a single game park for a single man and his English friends. Someday settlers will come, and may well find that one man owns the roads, the trails, all the building sites, all the grass, all the logging woods, and controls all the water.

My mount stands, head down, nearby. He seems exhausted, and I do not think we will be continuing from here over the pass into Grand Lake. Another day will have to do. We still, fortunately, have some time. Horse and man both gaze upward at the tundra where here and there amongst the deep drifts of snow can still be seen the Arapaho monuments, stackings of granite rock as high as a man's head, by which means they kept to the path as they made their way across the open treeless ground. Near one of the monuments, a year earlier, I had picked up a flint arrowhead which some luckless hunter had no doubt lost in the grass as he let fly at his quarry an ill-aimed arrow. That memory puts me in mind of another experience with Indian arrowheads, an experience which formed the most incredible and intense experience of spiritualism which I have ever known.

Chapter Five

McIntyre announced himself to one of the dean's three secretaries, a fashionable streamlined blonde with a painted smile and condescending voice. She whisked him into a waiting room and parked him there with nothing to read but back issues of *The Journal of University Administration*. Eventually she reappeared.

"Dave?" purred the streamlined voice. "Dean Rolman can see you now."

McIntyre's neck turned angry red. He kept on reading the journal, ignoring her until she approached within firing range.

"Dave?" she repeated.

He turned on her, his eyes as cold as brown eyes can be. She almost took a step backward. He rose from the chair, every muscle tightened.

"How many times have I been in this office since you began working here?" he asked.

"I don't know," she began, still cheery but wary. "Perhaps six, ten? I really can't say."

"You call him Dean Rolman"—McIntyre's thumb pointed to the inner office—"but I don't rate such formality? Refresh my memory . . . when exactly did I ask you to call me Dave as if I were your boyfriend or one of your work-study helpers? Do we know each other that well? Maybe you think we've slept together."

The blonde flushed to a deep red that did nothing at all to complement her dark roots. "Well, the Dean and Norma both refer to you as Dave, so naturally I assumed. . . ."

"Wrong assumption all the way 'round," he clipped. "First, only my fishing buddies use my first name. Second, I expect office help to accord professors full professional respect and formality. So until *I* tell you otherwise, it's Professor McIntyre."

He brushed past her and went in. The dean was pretending to study a memo set squarely in the center of his empty desk, but McIntyre knew he had overheard. No way not to.

"Hello, Rollie."

"David! Good to see you. Sit down, sit down! Coffee?"

"No thanks. I got a message that you wanted to talk about my sabbatical application."

"Yes. Well, how are things going in the English Department these days?"

"OK, as far as I know. Same old stuff going on."

"Well, that's good, that's good. Heard anything about your last book? Sales going well?"

"Yeah, it's pulling in a couple of thousand a year. About what you'd expect from a textbook."

"Well, great, just great. I hear good things about it." Dean Rolman went to the buffet to pour himself a cup of coffee. "And have you been doing any fishing here lately?"

"No," McIntyre said. "It's a bit early yet. Rivers are still high and roily. Not much good for fly fishing."

"That's right, that's right. You know, someday you and I just have to go out and do some fishing together. We've been saying that for . . . how many years now? And by golly, we just ought to do it, just do it one of these weekends."

"Any time you're ready," McIntyre said.

"That will be great, that will be great," Dean Rolman said. "Well, now this project of yours looks very interesting, very interesting. You want to go to England, is it? Or is it Ireland?"

"Probably just London and Edinburgh, for now," McIntyre said.

"Yes, well it sure looks interesting. This manuscript you think you are after, that's pretty exciting, let me tell you. And you think you've got a lead on it, too. Now tell me, uh, David, do you think the library's Special Collections branch will have an interest in acquiring this manuscript? I understand they have some good funding over there. They might help you out, you know. Might be very interested."

"It's a little early to talk about selling them a manuscript, since I don't even know if it exists. But, yes, they might buy it for the college. I don't think they are about to pay me to go look for it, though."

"Never hurts to ask, you know. Never hurts to ask."

"Speaking of asking. . . ."

"Oh, you want to know about your sabbatical request. Now, you know, David, not all of these can be funded. No, indeed. Darn it, you know, I bet for every ten I get I can only find funding for half. You had to wait for your first one, as I recall."

"So you're saying that you're turning it down?"

"Now you know it isn't me, David. That's not it. There's a few people in line ahead of you, for one thing."

"Oh, come on, Rollie! I know who's in line ahead of me! Crazy Charlie Dorospki, who wants to go look up his family roots in Greece. And Victor, hell, he wants to go to Venice just to be with his wife because she's going to be there studying art. He doesn't know any more about Venetian literature than *I* do, for God's sake. We both know he'd be better off staying here by himself."

"Now, I can't get into particulars about that," Dean Rolman responded. "Besides, when you leave campus, it increases the load on other professors. If you had a grant, that would be different. If we could use a grant to hire some temporary instructors to replace your student production hours, that would be different. Fill in for you. Frankly, David, you have a problem because you are so popular. If you go, we'll have a hard time making it up. Not to mention the disappointed students."

"Do you know how many are disappointed when they get their grades from my class?" McIntyre was getting warm along the back of his neck again. "And if we put your student credit hour production argument alongside your waiting list theory, it looks as if some teachers get rewarded for crummy and unpopular courses while I have to stay here in the salt mines because I'm so damn' good at it. Is that it?"

"A dean would like to be good to everyone. You know that. If I could, I'd let everybody go wherever they wanted. But I have to watch the number of student hours. That's our bottom line."

"How about one semester instead of the whole academic year? One lousy semester. I know it's only been five years since the last one, but Roberta got two sabbaticals in five years, plus a semester of academic leave, *and* a semester with reduced teaching load."

"That was when she was organizing the Shakespeare Festival. She had to travel and plan . . . oh, she did a lot of work on that. And we make money on it, we make money. Besides, it was easy to cover her classes."

"More logic? OK. I have to run, I guess. But let me suggest that you reconsider this. I'm only asking for one semester, but, if I dig up some grant money or some other way to afford it, I'm going to ask for academic leave without pay. And you'll have to approve it. It's in the FACULTY HANDBOOK . . . full and associate professors with tenure and ten years service can take unpaid leave whenever they want to. So you can fund me for a semester, or fund my replacements for a whole year."

"David, I admire a fighter, I really do. But that leave application will have to go through your department's executive committee, and from the looks of their comments about your sabbatical application they are pretty cool about the whole thing. I got the feeling from the letters that they are pretty lukewarm about this idea of running around looking for hidden manuscripts. Pretty lukewarm."

"I wouldn't doubt that."

"What I'm saying is that they might not give you leave, either."

"I hear you. But I have to try."

"I wouldn't stick my neck out too far, if I were you." The dean stood and stuck his hand out across the polished walnut desk top. "My hands are tied, you know. Tied. I have to answer to the board of regents, and in the final analysis they're business people who are already suspicious of professors who only work three or four hours a day and take the summer off. Every time I grant a sabbatical, I hear from at least one of them about what a waste of time it is. They treat the sciences a lot better . . . over there you could get a sabbatical to study how to grow carrots in the space shuttle. Sciences get it all.

"Regents want the school to be Princeton or Stanford or Yale. They really put the heat on us, really put it on. But you've got a really interesting project here, David, really interesting project. And listen, if I can be any help to you, any help at all, you just let me know. Just let me know."

McIntyre had his hand on the door frame when he looked back at Dean Rolman. "I'll let you know," he replied. "I'll let you know if I ever think you can be of any help."

The streamlined blonde secretary leaned into her computer screen with sudden interest as McIntyre strode past her desk, and she did not look up when he slammed out through the door.

The walk back to his office helped calm McIntyre down. He passed a few familiar faces who smiled and greeted him, and stopped a moment to talk to a student who had missed several classes. At the office, he helped himself to a cup of the departmental coffee, reminded himself for the tenth time that he needed to contribute to the coffee fund, and picked up the phone. The Grand Lake number rang three times, the machine picked up the connection, and McIntyre grinned when he heard Glenda trying to disconnect the answering machine while saying hello at the same time. He could just picture her juggling the receiver and pushing buttons.

"David McIntyre," he said.

"Hi! How are you doing?" Glenda greeted him.

"Fine, thanks. I just wanted to thank you again for your help."

"Did it really help? Are you going to get to go to Scotland?"

"I'm working on it, you might say."

"You know, David, I got to thinking about the judge after you left. I would sure hate to be the one to mess around with his reputation, such as it is. Know what I mean?"

"Sure. I'll be fair. Everybody in this case has a reputation at risk, though. Dunraven, Nugent himself, Evans . . . all of them. In fact, I feel sorry for Evans more than anyone. He had to go through life as the killer of Rocky Mountain Jim, and it probably was a story that followed his family, wherever they ended up."

"Did they leave Estes Park?" Glenda asked.

McIntyre could picture the bright eyes and the eager look. He loved the quick enthusiasm she showed in even the simplest of questions. "Yes. Right after the death, or within a few months of it. Sold the place to Dunraven and headed out for points unknown."

"Parts unknown."

"OK, *parts* unknown. Are you an editor as well?"

Glenda laughed her silver ringing laugh. "No," she said. And then: "Listen, do let me know if you go to Scotland. And I hope you're planning to come back to Grand Lake."

McIntyre took his turn to laugh with what he hoped was a light nonchalance. "First chance I get. You take care. Don't steal any manuscripts!"

"Same to you, Professor," she said. "'Bye."

" 'Bye." McIntyre put down the phone and stood at his window gazing westward toward the Continental Divide. Whatever had happened between Mountain Jim and Griff Evans, he was willing to bet that he would find a woman at the bottom of it.

Chapter Six

Friday afternoon. My day of the week, during the summer break, to visit my office and deal with the week's accumulated mail. Most of it I merely threw away; the remainder took only an hour to answer and file. As a reward for being tidy and diligent, I decided to indulge in something forbidden—a chocolate bar from the vending machine.

This particular road to sin took me past the English offices, and Lachlan's was the only open door. He sat there, looking like the lone survivor of the semester exodus.

"And have you taken to living in your office now?" I asked, poking my head in.

"Hank! What brings you to my academic doorstep? You're supposed to be on vacation, not haunting the hallways."

"Do I hear one cooking pot observing soot on the other?" I said. I could see him wince at the mangled idiom. "After all, you should be on vacation, too. I'm surprised to find you here."

"Where would I go? Home? I've been there. Fixing rain gutters and toilet floats and building rose trellises. . . . all the things you'd expect a research writer to be tending to. Things I managed to put off all winter."

His desk was immaculate. Not a stray scrap of paper, not a loose pencil, nothing that had not been neatly filed away or arranged in a drawer. Many professors live in academic disorder, with ancient student essays stacked in one corner, old exams yellowing away in slumping, sliding piles on the tables, books opened and left face down in the mess, dirty coffee cups with stubs of pencils in them, unopened mail tossed onto the top of the file cabinet. But not our Lachlan. He was by nature a man who liked formality and order, a real Virgo. His piles of student papers were current and neatly ordered by class. His books were in alpha order on the shelves.

Sometimes he went even further. He put away all files, shelved all the books, and even put his pencils out of sight in a desk drawer. This clearing of the decks meant but one thing. D. Lachlan McIntyre was preparing for another campaign. It was his signature behavior.

"C'mon in," he said. "Shut the door."

"Why not," I said, pretending to be enchanted by his sophisticated invitation, "what have I to lose?"

He leered at me with arched eyebrows. I leered back. From the card file cabinet he withdrew the green bottle of Jameson's and the souvenir shot glasses. "I'm really glad you dropped by, because I want to ask you something. Join me?"

"Oh, oh! You're offering me a free drink. Trouble?"

"Didn't get my sabbatical."

"I'm hardly surprised. You weren't even due for it."

"Yeah, but Rolman still could have cut me some slack. I get so damn' sick of these administrators, pretending that they are *our* representatives, our buddies in academe, then yelling that their hands are tied by the regents. How the hell can they be the drum majors with their hands tied behind their backs?"

"So what are you going to do?"

"I have no idea. I've e-mailed everybody I know in Scotland and England, begging for lecturing jobs. But their universities are on vacation, too, and they don't have any money, anyway."

"Any chance of grants?" I asked, sipping the peat-tasting whisky. "Did you look into the NEH fellowship program?"

"Too late to apply. Besides, I don't exactly have the wholehearted support of my administration. I suppose I could just take out a personal loan and finance my own trip, except for the high interest rates."

"You might put your truck up for sale. You won't need it over there."

"Sell my truck? I don't think so."

"Well, don't ask me to loan you money. Not after buying myself a house. I wouldn't loan you money anyway, not for such a harebrained idea. The dean sees it as a blue-sky scheme, doesn't he?"

"In a nutshell, yes. I even showed him these photocopies of Nugent's writing." Lachlan took a file from his open attaché case. "Right here, at the start of the essay, look what Nugent writes . . . 'Thus does what I have called the 'Estes Park Land Steal' seem commonplace.' And here at the end of it . . . 'That memory now puts me in mind of another experience.' This is classic Nineteenth Century personal narrative style . . . the casual reference to a previous chapter, the contrived transition into another chapter about another experience. It all points to the existence of two more chapters. At least. That's what had me all excited the other night, when I got back from Grand Lake. I wanted to show it to you right away."

"Oh, yes." I cleared my throat the way my mother used to when she wished to express icy disapproval of my behavior. "And while we are speaking of the evening in question, Gordon sends his greetings. He said to be sure to say hello to you next time I see you."

"Gordon?" Lachlan looked quizzical. "Oh! He was the guy . . . I mean, he was with you in the living room when I. . . ."

"Yes. The *guy* who was there when you knocked once and burst in like a fireman answering an alarm."

"I'm sorry about that, Hank. It was the excitement. I could hardly wait to tell you what I'd found at Grand Lake."

"Next time . . . do wait."

"Hey, at least you both had all of your clothes on!" Lachlan said.

"Yes. Well. The thing is, Lachlan, that Gordon didn't exactly understand our relationship. He still doesn't, in fact. If you know what I mean."

"Hell, Hank, I don't understand it, either. It's been a puzzle to me for ten years now. Why should Gordon be entitled to some sudden epiphany of comprehension? But I see your point. I was just excited."

"Humph," I said. "Well, the next time you get excited, make sure you call me first." That didn't exactly sound right. So I added: "Actually, I'd prefer that you call someone else first."

"I apologize. But would you do me a favor and take a copy of this piece? While you're researching your history, you might find a way to verify it. Dates, writing style, that kind of thing."

"I see," I replied. "First you steal documents, and then you want me to authenticate them for you, while you cavort through the mountains with a little filly who wears low-cut sundresses."

"Nah. She's just not my type. Very nice, but just not my type."

"I understand. Platonic. Thrown together by larceny. But look, Lachlan, returning to your manuscript for a moment, what prompts you to assume that Nugent gave it to Wescott? *If* it is Nugent's. If this is your famous lost manuscript, why, it's only a journal fragment, a diary, a few pages about a man riding a horse across the Divide in early spring."

"Think," Lachlan said. "Why would he have given Wescott a copy of a journal about crossing a mountain?

Because it *isn't* a journal."

"Of course, it is," I said. "He said right in it . . . I was crossing the mountain and the day was such and such . . . exactly like a journal."

"No, that's not what he said," Lachlan said. "It sounds like a journal, in places, but its part of a book he was writing, a history about his mountain experiences in Estes Park. Just like Enos Mills did twenty or thirty years later. This is a *chapter*. It's a chapter of a personal narrative."

"I see. And you can substantiate that?"

"In the first place, it looks like dozens of other Nineteenth-Century travel and history narratives. The style reminds me of Dunraven's own two-volume book, PAST TIMES AND PASTIMES. It even reminds me of Isabella Bird's style. No, this was not just a personal diary. This was part of a Victorian-style narrative of history and travel. Nugent was a well-read man. He was writing stuff just like the stuff he read, with romantic, wordy descriptions of scenery, over-emphasis of personal peril, emotional reactions to the sublime power of nature, all of that."

"So why would he have given it to Judge Wescott, especially in unfinished form?"

"I think Nugent was going over to Grand Lake to corroborate the bear story. I think something else happened during that episode with the bear, something that alienated Nugent and Wescott. It's too coincidental that neither account mentioned the other man."

"I see your point. But why would he be going over the pass to see Wescott, if they had become enemies?"

"Ah! Ask yourself a different question. Why would Nugent have been writing about Dunraven and Whyte and Haigh? If Dunraven and company had uncovered something about Wescott's past, why would Nugent have wanted to tell Wescott about it?"

"I suppose you've figured that out."

"Yes. Nugent was hoping to get Wescott as an ally. He was resisting Dunraven's takeover. He was afraid that the take-over was going to spread up the Thompson River drainage and over into Shadow Mountain and Grand Lake valley . . . one huge Irish shooting estate. But Wescott had clout. He had friends in Grand Lake and Granby and Kremmling and Hot Sulphur Springs. If Nugent could have set Judge Wescott against Dunraven, it would have been a big victory.

"Or there's the other alternative. If Dunraven could have won the judge over, it would have given him a lock on the northern Rockies. He would have controlled the eastern access, while Judge Wescott controlled the Grand River access on the west side. Together they could have monopolized stagelines into the mountains, got hold of the mail service, everything. Nugent needed to drive a wedge between those two."

"I see. And the manuscript would do it. But what about Wescott's reaction? The letter that was not delivered?"

"Oh, the letter. Wescott didn't react according to Nugent's plan. Nugent misjudged the judge, you might say. Instead of getting mad at Dunraven, Wescott wanted to kill the messenger. Nugent."

Lachlan finished off his drink and took out another file folder in which there was a photocopy of a page from the *Grand Lake Prospector*. "Look at this," he said, handing it to me.

Local Items June 21-28

Joseph L. Wescott is back in residence this week. His week of hunting, although an odd time of year for it,

netted him a net loss when upon his return he discovered that otters had broken into the cages wherein he keeps his trout alive and fresh at the edge of the lake. In addition, friends informed him that he chose to take to the woods during the best week for fishing we have seen in two years or more.

I handed the sheet back to Lachlan. "So?" I said.

"Look at the dates, historian. That's when Jim Nugent was shot."

"You've already theorized that it was coincidental. In your scenario, that's why the judge brought the letter back unopened."

"I think Westcott went over there, without telling anyone where he was going, to deliver the letter and rip up the manuscript and maybe even find Dunraven and give him a piece of his mind. What if he got there and found the tension running pretty high between Evans and Nugent? Or Haigh and Nugent? Maybe Judge Wescott figured he could instigate some kind of shoot-out that could bring bad publicity to Dunraven's whole scheme of a private hunting preserve.

"The judge might have worked it out like this . . . if he could convince somebody. . . . Evans, Haigh, Whyte, whoever . . . to shoot Nugent, they would have to go to Longmont or Fort Collins to stand trial. Nugent would be dead, Dunraven would be implicated, and he . . . Wescott . . . could just hang around a few weeks, try to grab the blackmail documents, and scurry back over the Divide."

"Funny, Lachlan, that you of all people would think of grabbing documents."

"Shut up." He smiled. "You remember the confusion about who was in the cabin and who was outside, during the shooting? What if it was the judge inside, getting Evans liquored up and telling him how much Lord Dunraven would like it if he were to shoot Rocky Mountain Jim? As a justice of the peace, he might have even told Evans that he could keep him from being arrested for it. Evans was Lord Dunraven's toady . . . he would have done anything to stay in the Irish aristocrat's good graces. Besides, there was Evans's daughter. Jim had been paying attention to her. Oh, there's all kinds of things the judge could have said to provoke Evans. Then at the crucial moment, he could have slipped out the back way and have been in Muggins's Gulch, stealing the manuscript, while everyone else was running toward Evans's cabin to see what had happened."

"So," I said, "let's sum up. You've convinced yourself that there was a chapter about the Estes land steal, and another one about spiritualism?"

"I'm sure of it. And the judge's letter has another important clue in it. Wescott as much as said that Nugent had sent a copy to some English friend or friends. Who could that be except Isabella Bird, the one person whom Nugent felt he could trust? Isn't it natural that he would have sent her the manuscript?"

"Well, I will say this much, Lachlan. If you went to England or Scotland or wherever and actually found that copy, it would save you considerable trouble. You might even be able to steal it."

"Thanks," Lachlan said, "thanks a lot. At least, you didn't accuse me of wanting to go to Scotland just for the fishing."

I stood up and opened the door. As an afterthought, I turned toward him. "Thank you for the drink," I said. "And, David. . . ."

"Yes?" he said, startled that I had used his first name.

"Bring me back a salmon?"

* * * * *

Walking home, McIntyre stopped at the hardware store for a new toilet float and some sandpaper. He started to hand the clerk his credit card, then thought better of it, and took out cash. He had just gotten the card balance paid off, even though it had taken a garage sale and a manuscript consulting job to do it. He had also won a small cash award in a short story competition, and that helped, and, by God, he had the thing paid off. Zero.

He went out the door, studying the gold plastic. What did he have, ten thousand dollars worth of credit on this thing? Maybe it was five thousand. What would it cost just to fly to London, check out the publisher, fly to Edinburgh, check the archives or whatever, and fly home? He could eat at pubs, stay in cheap bed and breakfast places, use the tube and the trains, instead of renting a car. And he could always volunteer to teach summer session next year to pay it off. Put it all on the card, and have it paid off within a couple of years at the most.

That's a nice bit of irony, he thought as he walked. *I'm tracing a man who bartered with animal pelts and fresh trout, and I use a piece of plastic. How the world has changed.*

Chapter Seven

When the phone rang, I was right in the midst of a major domestic decision—should I turn in early, or make popcorn and watch the all-night movie channel?

"Hello?"

"Hank?"

"Hello, Lachlan. What's up?"

"I'm going," he said. "To England. My travel agent had a client who was trying to get rid of a round-trip ticket to London. I made him an offer, and he took it. So, Thursday morning I'm on my way!"

"Sounds like fun," I said, and I meant it. I was envious. "So, shall I assume you have uncovered a lead as to the location of the missing manuscript?"

"I've got two leads now," he said. "Let me read one of them to you. It's a letter from Isabella Bird to her sister. Listen to this. . . ." He read the letter.

1 December 1873

In the afternoon Lyman and I rode to Mr. Nugent's cabin. I wanted him to read and correct my letter to you, giving the account of our ascent of Long's Peak, but he said he could not, and insisted on our going in.

I read my letter aloud—or rather "The Ascent of Long's Peak," which I have written for *Out West*—and I was quite sincerely appreciative of the taste and acumen of his criticisms on the style. He is a true child of nature; his eye brightened and his whole face became

**radiant, and at last tears rolled down his cheek when I
read the account of the glory of the sunrise. Then he
read to us a very able paper on spiritualism which he
was writing.**

"How about that! It's the spiritualism chapter, and she apparently expressed interest in it. What if he later decided to send it to her, after she had gone? What if he figured he might as well send her the whole manuscript while he was at it? She had a publisher to show it to, John Murray of London. She was the only cultured person he had seen for years, and probably one of the few he could talk to. She might even have been his ticket to England, if he had decided to leave the U.S."

I wedged the handset between my chin and shoulder so that I could unwrap the popcorn packet. I set it in the microwave. "Go on," I said. "I'm listening."

"It gets even better," Lachlan said. "I was reading Dunraven's PAST TIMES AND PASTIMES, and guess what I found?"

"Nugent's fingerprints?"

"Cute. But, no. Dunraven had a section on spiritualism. He told how he went to Malvern for something called Doctor Gully's hydropathic cure in Eighteen Sixty-Seven and met a medium named D.D. Home. Got very interested in spiritualism. In fact, it seems he believed in what he called 'the survival of intelligent personality after physical death.' Listen to this . . . 'It may be possible for a human being to abstract from the consciousness or sub-consciousness of other human beings of whose intimate lives he is in ignorance information as to their past history and present circumstances.' "

"So?" I asked, walking into the other room so I could hear Lachlan over the noise of the popcorn.

"So? Don't you remember my idea that Nugent could

have been using his writing as a way to enlist Wescott's help? Why not have done the same with Dunraven? Nugent was out to get Dunraven *and* the Estes Park Company to let go of the park, but he was not stupid. In fact, Isabella thought he was extraordinarily intelligent. What if Nugent found out about Dunraven's interest in spiritualism? What if he had given this essay, this chapter, to Dunraven to read?"

"So now you think the famous desperado of Estes Park was a diplomat?"

"Why not? Dunraven himself called Jim extraordinary, and said that he had heard Jim swear in both Latin and Greek, and Kingsley said that he was without doubt an educated man. Consider this . . . Jim had written a spiritualism essay for his book. He discovered the coincidence that Dunraven had some interest in the topic. He knew that his book couldn't be published for another two years, at least. So Dunraven wouldn't have known about the other chapter, the one exposing the land steal. Jim just copied out the spiritualism chapter and gave it to Lord Dunraven, probably with a flourish. Lord D. said something polite, such as expressing some desire to keep it or perhaps send it to Doctor Home. So, unless there was a shipwreck or something, *that* copy could have ended up in the Dunraven archives along with his other journals about his American experiences."

"Does this mean you are going to Ireland as well to look into the Dunraven archives, if they exist?" I asked.

"No. Can't afford it. As it is, I'll barely have enough time and money to check with Isabella's publishers and look in the London and Edinburgh collections. But I did write a letter of inquiry, and I left it with Joel at the library. He said he would try to find out whether there were any Dunraven archives and would forward it for me."

"What about Tobermory?" I asked. Lachlan had loaned

me his copy of Evelyn Kaye's biography of Isabella Bird, AMAZING TRAVELER, and I was rather intrigued by the relationship of the two Bird sisters who had had a cottage at Tobermory. Henrietta Bird lived there while her sister traveled the world and wrote her letters. "Wouldn't Isabella's letters and things be at Tobermory in some museum or library or something?"

"Not likely," Lachlan said. "If I find a reason to go there, I'll try to fit it in. But I looked up Tobermory in Fodor's guide, and apparently it's only a few dozen buildings and a dock for the fishing boats. Half the people, which isn't many, probably haven't even heard of Bird."

"Very well," I said. "Stick with the dusty city archives, then. Oh! I meant to ask whether you had resolved the matter of the bear story?"

"Not important, it turns out. Nugent did wrestle with some kind of bear, that much is certain. The animal ripped Jim's face and left a huge ugly scar running right across his eye. Let's see, I have Isabella's letter here. . . . yes . . . here it is. She said that one side of his face was 'repulsive' but went on to say that the other side 'might have been modeled in marble' and that he had 'large grey-blue eyes, deeply set, with well-marked eyebrows, a handsome aquiline nose, and a very handsome mouth.' She goes on about his mustache and 'tawny hair' that hung to his shoulders in curls and ringlets."

"Gracious. How terribly romantic!"

"It gets better. To her, Jim seemed 'a chivalrous gentleman' with a refined accent and language that was 'easy and elegant.' She wrote about his 'genius' and his 'chivalry' and 'magnificently-formed brow and head' and 'cultured tone of voice.' And, remember, Isabella wasn't all that easily impressed with people."

"So why did he tell her this story of the fight with the bear and leave out all mention of Judge Wescott rescuing him?"

"And *vice versa*," Lachlan said. "Wescott also told the story, and *he* changed it, too. I don't know. But I don't think it has any bearing on the manuscript."

"That's disappointing," I said. "Your little burglary with the fair Glenda should have come to more than that. Well, my popcorn is getting cold, so I'm going to hang up. If I don't see you before you leave, Lachlan, have a safe trip. I wish I were going along."

"Do you want to?" he asked. "What would Gordon say?"

"Don't worry about it," I said. "I couldn't go, even if you *were* serious. So have a good time. Send me a postcard of a burly Scotsman in a kilt. Oh . . . and Lachlan?"

"Yes?"

"Don't forget my salmon."

McIntyre looked up at the clock and set his watch to 10:13 A.M., London time. It seemed like mid-morning, yet it didn't. He retrieved his bag from the Heathrow luggage carousel, shuffled along in the boustrophedonic customs queue in the airport's cavernous basement, made his declaration—"Nothing to declare."—and looked around for the way out. **TAXIS** said one sign, with an arrow pointing upstairs. Too expensive. **UNDERGROUND** said a second sign, pointing off toward a subway station. Too complicated, especially after a tiring plane ride. **BUSSES** a third sign said, with an arrow pointing down an antiseptic-looking tunnel that was lined with ceramic tile the color of leftover tapioca. A bus would do fine.

Eventually, after what seemed like a mile of twists and turns, the echoing square tunnel turned into a set of steps to the surface. McIntyre was facing a nondescript glass and concrete cube with the London Airbus logo on it. Red double-deckers plastered with advertising were lined up across the street. Shiny little black taxis seemed to be everywhere. A light drizzle was falling.

McIntyre drew a deep breath. He was in London.

For the first time since he had rushed to grab the shuttle to Denver International Airport, had rushed to get his bag checked, had rushed to catch the flight, had rushed to change planes in Washington, and had joined the rush and crush to get off the Boeing 717 and down to Heathrow's baggage maze, McIntyre had nowhere to rush to. His room at the Kensington Plaza Hotel was reserved, so he had no need to hurry. Across the corner, as the British say, he saw a shop that sold coffee, tea, books, and magazines. That would do nicely.

And so it was that McIntyre had this trip's first cup of Earl Grey tea. And a scone. He savored both of them dramatically, lovingly, letting the tea scald slowly across his taste buds, sinking his teeth gratefully into the scone, inhaling to get the taste and texture and aroma all at once. There was something about English tea that made it taste different in England. English tea in the States lost part of its essence. McIntyre once said that it was like drinking Mexican beer in Mexico. You can get it in the U.S., but for some reason it tastes better in Mexico. This London cup of tea was given an even more unique savor by the atmosphere of the shop, with its magazines and tobacco and new and used books. In the stagnant air hung the tang of leather bindings and old paper, of cavendish and Turkish, and that bright, plastic aroma of new magazine covers.

There was a pay phone at the end of the counter, and an empty stool. McIntyre sat down, studied the telephone instructions, and looked in his appointment book for the number of John Murray, Publishers. It was a wrong number.

"Do you have a phone directory?" he asked the young

lady behind the coffee bar.

"What district?" she asked.

McIntyre looked blank. "I don't know," he replied. "I'm new in town." His ingratiating smile had no affect on her. "I was hoping to telephone the John Murray publishing company."

"Just a minute," the sour face said. She vanished through a curtained doorway into a back room. McIntyre noticed a man sitting at the counter nearby who seemed unusually attentive to all this. He wore rumpled trousers, a checked shirt with old-fashioned wide necktie, and a tweed jacket that had seen better days. He had a full sweeping mustache and wore the ubiquitous cloth cap. He looked as if he could be a bookstore owner. Or a wholesale gin salesman. A self-employed London tour guide, perhaps.

The woman came back with the number written on a piece of paper. "That's Murray's," she said.

"Thanks." McIntyre smiled. He got no smile in return. After getting a second cup of tea, he dialed the number. He glanced in Mr. Cloth Cap's direction. He was sure the man had moved to a nearer stool.

The voice answering the telephone was precise, carefully modulated, and warm with that particularly polite charm that must have been invented by British women. McIntyre proceeded to introduce himself with as much formality and dignity as he could. He mentioned a few John Murray book titles that he happened to own. She asked about his flight from America; he said it had been long but without incident. He remarked that London was having rain; she replied that it was good for the lawns and trees after the three weeks of drought. He mentioned having read Evelyn Kaye's book on Isabella Bird; she remarked that Ms. Kaye had arranged a year in advance to study the Murray archives.

"She was quite industrious, you know," the gracious voice with the educated accent went on. "I believe she was on our doorstep each morning, when the receptionist arrived, and worked straight through until tea. And is it our Miss Bird that brings you to London, Doctor McIntyre?"

McIntyre's spirit withered. So, the last American scholar allowed into the Bird papers had been methodical, polite, and industrious. She had stayed several weeks and had made a good impression. Here *he* had come, unannounced, no credentials, virtually ignorant of what he wanted or what was in the collection of letters and papers, more or less expecting to dash into Murray Publishing, rummage around for a hypothetical manuscript or clues leading to it, and dash out. *Good job,* he thought to himself. No wonder some of the English didn't have any use for most Americans.

Meanwhile, McIntyre noticed that Mr. Cloth Cap's teacup was empty, but he was pretending to drink from it anyway, staring off into space over the bar as if totally oblivious to the phone conversation going on.

"By coincidence," McIntyre said, "I was hoping to see the Bird collection myself."

"Oh? And what is your interest in Miss Bird?"

"My interest is actually in James Nugent." And then, although he knew better, he blurted it out. "I'm acting on a theory that Nugent sent a manuscript to Isabella, possibly hoping she would leave it for Mister Murray to read."

"Nugent?" the voice said. "Hmm. Oh, you must mean the Rocky Mountain Jim fellow she met in Colorado. No, there's nothing by him in our collection."

McIntyre's jaw clenched, and his eyes winced. He had just blown any chance of browsing through the archives. The woman, polite and refined though her voice sounded, was giving him the brush-off.

"At any rate," she went on, "I'm afraid the Bird archives are closed at present. Missus Murray supervises their use, and she is on a fortnight's holiday."

Two weeks, McIntyre thought. *Two bloody weeks.* Here he was, less than twenty-four hours out of Colorado, and half of his research plan was already in the dumper.

"Of course," the woman on the phone said, "you are most welcome to visit us and have a look around. I'm sure that you would find it interesting."

McIntyre tried to keep the jet lag and the disappointment out of his voice. "Yes, I'm sure I would," he said. "Well, suppose I come at ten or so tomorrow morning? You might have to give me directions."

"We'd be delighted to see you. Where are you staying?"

"The Kensington Plaza Hotel," McIntyre said, wishing it was a more ritzy place now that he had heard this voice on the telephone. "On Gloucester Road."

The formal friendly voice told him how to catch the tube at Gloucester Station, take it to Piccadilly Circus Station, walk toward Harrod's on Knightsbridge, and find Albermarle Street. McIntyre made notes.

And his notes got him there. The next morning found McIntyre in the depths of Gloucester Station down under London's sidewalks, then on the speeding underground train. He left the train, when it pulled into Piccadilly Circus, climbed the stairs up into the hazy London daylight, and asked a bobby to find Harrod's. Or Albermarle Street. The bobby knew both.

McIntyre felt much improved, following his deep sleep and the hearty breakfast of eggs, sausage, fried tomatoes, and toast. The same breakfast one always got at any English hotel or b&b. He was not as discouraged as he had been the day before. Perhaps the Murray archives were closed to him, and had nothing of Nugent's in them—the adventure was the thing. As the walked along the sidewalk, drinking in the atmosphere of London, he experienced the adrenaline rush of being somewhere new, looking for something unknown.

But McIntyre did not recognize the adventure when it walked up to him. It happened just outside the publishing house. He did recognize the man; it was Mr. Cloth Cap. McIntyre thought he had glimpsed him earlier, lounging at the corner of Albermarle Street, but he had disappeared. Now he appeared again, sauntering along from the far corner up the block.

McIntyre's brow wrinkled in curiosity. Cloth Cap suddenly grinned, his yellowish teeth shining under the sweeping mustache, and touched the bill of his cap with one finger.

"We meet again!"

"Yes," McIntyre said carefully. "So it seems."

"Corrigan's me name," said Cloth Cap, "Otis Corrigan. Antiques and rare books is me line. And you, you'd be an American, I'm guessing."

McIntyre shook hands. "David McIntyre," he said. And he said nothing more for the moment.

"The coincidence, it never struck me until just this very moment," Otis Corrigan said, "but I do believe we are both intending to visit Murray Publishers. I'm hoping the ol' boy is to home."

McIntyre muttered something, by way of seeming cordial, and together they mounted the steps and entered the tiny reception area.

Murray Publishing was lodged in one of the narrow four-story buildings that present a solid two-hundred-year-old front along Albermarle Street. The reception area had once been a stair landing and a wide hallway; it now had a glassed-in office for a receptionist, a few Queen Anne chairs for visitors, and several shelves displaying Murray's latest publications.

McIntyre went straight to the young woman behind the glass, who took his name and relayed it by telephone to someone deep in the interior of the old building. While awaiting an answer, she made pleasant conversation.

"So," she said brightly, her eyes giving McIntyre her full attention in a way that made him feel ten—make that twenty—years younger, "your interest is in our Isabella Bird material? She traveled a good deal, I understand. Mind you"—her voice dropped to a conspiratorial whisper—"I've only read the one book, the one about her American adventure. I've only been working here a few months. But I know that we've published a half dozen or more of hers."

"I won't tell anyone you've only read one of her books," McIntyre whispered back, and smiled. "She did always manage to come back to England, though. Well, Scotland, actually. After her father's death, she and her sister had a cottage on the Isle of Mull. And then after Isabella married, she lived in Edinburgh."

The young lady's eyes never left his face as he talked. "And so your investigation will take you to Edinburgh and to the islands?" She chuckled at what she had said. "The Hebrides, I mean! Not the other islands!"

McIntyre smiled broadly. "Not the Shetlands or Orkneys, then? No, I may get out to Mull. The village of Tobermory, in particular."

"Oh! I've never seen . . . excuse me a moment." The telephone was buzzing. She picked it up, and her large dark eyes now gave the handset their full and undivided attention.

During all of this chit-chat, Mr. Corrigan remained midway between the reception booth and the door, taking feigned interest in some book jackets thumbtacked to a poster board. He did not volunteer to step forward and give the receptionist his name, which seemed rather curious to McIntyre, especially if Corrigan had an appointment.

She came out from behind the glass partition and led the way up the stairs. McIntyre was pleased to follow—the receptionist had one of those figures that fashionable clothing stores like to call trim, encased in a clingy narrow skirt and silky blouse. Her high heels were also well to McIntyre's liking.

Corrigan followed McIntyre. She led them into a pair of rooms joined by a wide doorway. The rooms were furnished and decorated in excellent taste, from the airy windows and the Persian carpet to the restful wallpaper and magnificent collection of graceful desks and armchairs. However, the first thing McIntyre noticed was that there were books everywhere. Bookshelves were built into the walls. Bookshelves capped the doorways and ran down the sides of the doorways. Bookshelves with glass doors stretched from the mantle of one of the antique fireplaces clear up to the ceiling that had to be fourteen feet high.

The ceiling was an ornate affair in white plaster with a gold chandelier suspended at the center of a carved oval, framed in carved moldings. The two fireplaces were carved, too, as were the top moldings of the bookcases. Wherever there was a space between bookcases there was a portrait in it. Some of them were authors McIntyre recognized: Southey, Byron, Coleridge, Wordsworth, Shelley.

It was a sitting room straight out of the Victorian era, from the expensive wallpaper and elaborately carved moldings to the Queen Anne and Chippendale furnishings. McIntyre stood and turned slowly around, openly gawking. When he finally let his eyes come to rest on one of the bookcases, behind the glass door he recognized first editions of the same authors whose portraits hung on the walls.

He turned to say something to Mr. Corrigan, but the man in the cloth cap had disappeared through the connecting doorway into the next room. McIntyre thought he heard a scraping noise, like a piece of wire against brass. Rather a sharp, disagreeable sound. And then he thought he heard the click of a cabinet door being either opened or shut, and he started for the doorway. But he was interrupted.

A large man entered the room, a man in the most business-like business suit McIntyre had ever seen. It was brown, with stripes. Under the jacket, a fully buttoned vest stretched over an ample stomach that had seen many a pint. McIntyre couldn't imagine anyone wearing such a suit except to the office. One certainly wouldn't wear it for social occasions. The man had a business smile to match his business suit, a stiff smile. He had obviously acquired the ability to keep the entire upper row of his porcelain teeth showing as he spoke, no matter what lip movements his words required.

"How do you do?" he said. "I am Phillip Pontis. Mister Murray's assistant. Missus Kent tells me you are interested in the Isabella Bird material. Did you see her books in this cabinet? We have all of the editions, of course. In fact, Mister Murray . . . two of them, now that I think of it . . . conferred with Miss Bird in this very room."

And on this very furniture, McIntyre thought. He considered introducing himself, but Mr. Pontis seemed rather uninterested. Or disinterested. "How interesting," McIntyre said. "I gather that the Bird archives are closed at the moment, however."

"Sadly, yes. If only you had given us some warning, perhaps as little as a fortnight, we might have arranged for you to examine the papers. Have you seen them before?"

"No," McIntyre admitted. "Although I have read the biographies by Anna Stoddart and Pat Barr, of course, and they have rather specific lists of the letters and so forth."

"Missus Kent mentioned your interest in Rocky Mountain Jim?"

"Yes," McIntyre said. Now for the part where he would start to sound stupid. "I'm working on a theory that Jim Nugent had written a manuscript, which he subsequently might have mailed to Isabella Bird. Naturally, he would have expected her to show it to Mister Murray."

"And you hoped it would repose in our collection, of course."

"I admit it would be a minor miracle. But, yes, I did have hopes."

"I can assure you that we have no such piece. Every scrap of paper has been catalogued, you see. When would that have been, do you think?" Pontis was bored, but polite.

"About Eighteen Seventy-Three or Seventy-Four," McIntyre responded. "Of course, mailing it from Colorado could involve a great deal of risk. Maybe it never arrived."

Mr. Pontis looked meditative for a moment. His smile did not dim, but his eyes looked thoughtful. "She may have been in residence at Tobermory during that time," he said. "Surely the mail there was almost as undependable as in Colorado in the Eighteen Seventies. As a matter of fact," Pontis sniffed, "Miss Bird did comment in at least one letter that she did not trust the mail carrier who brought the mail to Tobermory. The boat would leave it at Craignure, you see, and a man would walk it all the way across the island to Tobermory. It was a common bit of folklore that he would lighten his burden, so to speak, by disposing of heavier objects along the way."

McIntyre started to ask Mr. Pontis about possible evidence that Isabella Bird had shown Jim's material to John Murray—Murray's diary, for instance—but at that instant there came a sneeze from the other room. The sound was muffled, but definitely a sneeze.

"I say!" Mr. Pontis headed for the connecting doorway. "I didn't realize you had a companion with you . . . we must ask him to join us." He stopped in the doorway, and McIntyre could clearly see the man's neck going red and rigid. "What in hell are you doing there?"

McIntyre got to the doorway in time to see Mr. Otis Corrigan standing at an open cupboard, leafing through a leather-bound volume.

Mr. Pontis turned on McIntyre like a lion. "I'm sure I don't know what your game is, but your confederate well knows that he is not welcome here. I ask you both to leave. Immediately! Do not be too surprised if I decide to ring up the police and have the both of you investigated!"

"You have it wrong," McIntyre began to explain, but Mr. Pontis advanced on him, the ale-rounded belly now assuming the look of a battering ram.

"It is *you* who are in the wrong, acting as an accomplice to distract me while this man . . ."—he pointed, with his clenched fist, at Corrigan—"this man helps himself to valuable editions. Out!"

Corrigan had already replaced the book and was scuttling sideways toward the door, keeping a defensive eye on Mr. Pontis while checking to be certain his escape route was not blocked. McIntyre, unable to find anything useful to say, also headed for the door. Between the bulging belly and the threat of London police, he quickly decided that the best course would be to leave Murray Publishing for now. He could always come back alone and explain when things had calmed down.

McIntyre hit the sidewalk at the foot of the steps in full stride. His hands were trembling, his heart pumping. Of all the things McIntyre disliked, one of the things he disliked most was being flummoxed to the point where he couldn't think what to say. His face was red, and he felt hot. He had fled Murray Publishing like a kid running from a busted window.

He thought of going in the direction of Harrod's, where he had seen a sidewalk coffee shop. Coffee was just what he needed at the moment. And he thought of Otis Corrigan, dealer in antiques and rare volumes, and looked in the other direction just in time to see a figure in a cloth cap and rumpled corduroy vanish down a side street.

Chapter Eight

When it came to moving quickly, McIntyre had an advantage over poor pudgy Corrigan; his long daily walks to campus kept his legs in top shape, and Colorado's altitude gave him excellent lungs as well. McIntyre dashed across Albermarle Street and then, rather than going in direct pursuit of Corrigan, turned to his right and headed for a small intersecting street paralleling the one Corrigan had taken. Hitting his full stride, McIntyre emerged on the other side of the block of buildings and looked to his left. At the entrance to the next street Corrigan appeared again, walking in a hurry, and panting as he walked. He turned up the street.

McIntyre had hoped to have Corrigan walk right into him, but it wouldn't matter. He smiled and started out again, making two long strides to each one of Corrigan's. He caught up with him just as they reached the opening of one of those narrow little alleys that some comical London map-maker had dubbed a *street*.

McIntyre grabbed his nemesis, taking the man's arm in both hands, spinning him into the close passageway. He had him up against the wall before Corrigan knew what had happened. McIntyre's blood was still pumping; his face glowed with anger. Wisely, Corrigan did not try to tear away. He stared into McIntyre's face, stunned.

"Now," McIntyre said between short breaths, "what the hell was that scene back there all about?" He shook Corrigan's arm for emphasis.

"I didn't mean harm!" Corrigan replied. "Honest! I was

popping up to see Mister Murray, same as you. Just visiting, as you might say. No harm intended."

McIntyre used the hot glare he reserved for students when he caught them handing in plagiarized material. "Now let's have the truth," he said. "Don't make the mistake of taking me for stupid, Mister Corrigan, or whatever your name is. There's a lot of things people take me for, but one of them isn't stupid. You knew I was going there, and you used me to get yourself in. And obviously the man there knew you. Just as obviously, he didn't want you in his sitting rooms. And I don't mind where you go or what you do, because it's none of my damn' business. What I *do* mind is people trying to use me." McIntyre twisted Corrigan's arm savagely. "I mind even more when I get my damn' research ruined by some damn' yahoo like you screwing up my relationship with a source. So I'd like a damn' explanation, if *you* don't mind."

"Now really, old . . . uh, Mister McIntyre, was it? I'm a researcher, same as you. But me and the folks at Murray's, well, we had a bit of a falling out as you might say. They just don't like me for some reason."

"And you're taking me for stupid again." McIntyre was still holding Corrigan by the arm, but his other hand was now balling into a fist. This did not go unnoticed by the man in the cloth cap.

"All right, all right," he said. "Let's not get all testy now. I'm in the business, like I told you. Locating old books, antique items. Mostly in the paper line, like books, maps, letters, manuscripts and such like. It's what I do. Rarities, in the literary line. Know quite a bit about it, too, if I do say so meself. Now, Murray's, they have all those rare editions kept behind glass. Nobody uses them, nobody reads them. Just sitting there, like in a museum, see? Now here's the straight truth, since you look like a sort of chap who'd understand.

There's this client of mine, engages me to find a certain early edition. So I begins to trace it, don't you know, and as it turns out, Murray's had a contract to re-issue this edition back in Nineteen Twelve. Which fact, in turn, leads me to figure that Murray's had the original locked up in them glass shelves. And don't get that suspicious look to y'. I wasn't out to steal it, no. But I had to account for all the known copies, didn't I? Waste of me time to be scouring London for a book, if I knowed that Murray's already had it. Well, a chance of luck threw you my way, and I took advantage of it. And that's it."

McIntyre relaxed his hold on Corrigan's arm, and Corrigan stepped back, but did not run. McIntyre had seized upon a few such opportunities himself.

"OK, so what else? Why are they mad at you?"

"Oh, that. Well, let's just say that Mister Pontis and I have had our paths cross before. Several times, in fact. In the latest case, I acquired a certain volume that Pontis swore was nicked from Murray's collection. He couldn't prove it, and I couldn't say who I'd bought it from. Her Majesty's government saw fit to detain me for six months over that one." Corrigan fished through his pockets and came up with a package of cigarettes, one of which he stuck in the corner of his mouth and lit. After a few puffs, he smiled ingratiatingly, as if the whole matter was a dim and distant memory between them.

"As I said," he continued, "I mean, I couldn't help overhearing you're on the trail of some material yourself. Perhaps I can put you in the way of something. I'm not without resources when it comes to finding literary things, you know."

"Well," McIntyre said, "I guess I can do without your resources. Most of what I need to know I can find without paying somebody."

"Ah! In that case, I could let you have one free on the house, so to speak, and, if it turns out to be worth your while, you could pay me what it's worth. I've got no set rates, you see, having no office or overhead to speak of. I work on spec', as they say. Now what's it you need? You said Isabella Bird. I know that name. Wrote that American book. Quite the explorer, I understand. Tell you what . . . suppose I make a few phone calls, local ones, don't cost much, don't spend much of me own valuable time, see what's out there, concerning our Bird lady. I call about, see? Call me mates in the trade, put the word out. Maybe somebody's got a book to sell, or a manuscript, or collection of letters, then you and I talk business. How's that sound?"

"Sounds like it could get expensive," McIntyre said. "Besides, I'm pretty sure I'm going to find what I need in the museum and library at Edinburgh. And on Mull."

"Oh," Corrigan mused, puffing on his stub of cigarette, "that's meaning museum pieces. That's something else again. That's like Murray's, only worse. Museums don't like you to handle their valuables, they don't. Some of them don't even tell you what they got. That's where me resources could come in."

McIntyre felt himself starting to warm up to Otis Corrigan. He fought the feeling, however; it wouldn't do to open up and tell him anything. Above all, he had to keep the details of his search to himself. There was no telling who might get ahead of him, locate the missing material once he had described it to them, and then do God knows what with it. Put it in a museum, possibly.

"Just the same, I'll check the museums myself. And my Fodor's indicates that there's a small museum and collection on the Isle of Mull, so I might check there, too." McIntyre waved off the proffered cigarette pack and stopped himself. Corrigan was getting too chummy. And he was telling the man too much. "I hate to turn down your services," he continued, "but I'm afraid I have to. We'll go our separate ways and pretend this never happened, OK?"

Corrigan dropped his cigarette butt and crushed it with his foot, at the same time reaching into his coat pocket for a bent business card.

"At least, keep me card, and give me a ringo jingo, after you think about it. Me sources, the average bloke wouldn't think of."

"Such as?"

"Well, such as a few times when my inquiries showed that a certain little picture or book or letter got posted in the mails, and then went wrong. Never arrived, you know what I mean. So I've got a chum down at the postal service place where the misdirected mails go, and he lets me poke about. Located two different items that way. Or here's another instance for you. Collections you'd never think of. Ever hear of a Nineteenth-Century magazine called *The Pearl*?"

"Yes," McIntyre replied. "Pornography, wasn't it?"

"Right. So a collector bloke, with a sort of slant in that direction, he engages me to find copies. Even Xerox would suit him, nudge. Prurient reasons, you might say. So I'm thinking to meself, who's going to keep pornographic filth on hand where it can be gotten at? Not your libraries or museums, that's for sure. Private collectors, they like to stay private. Censorship Office, I says to meself. And bingo! The whole run from first edition to last. And, of course, I could Xerox them, being public and a bona-fide researcher and all. And there's little things like that all over the city. Records of estate sales. Auction houses what keep old journals and boxes of letters because they don't know how to auction them. Old Aunt Matilde put a letter inside a photo album, and what's that worth?"

Corrigan's growing enthusiasm for conversation made

McIntyre realize that he could go on talking all day. Time being money on this trip, he wanted to get to his hotel, check out before they charged him for another day, then catch the afternoon train to Edinburgh.

"Tell you what, Mister Corrigan," he said, looking at the business card in his hand. "I'm not sure where I'm staying in Edinburgh, but why don't I contact you before I leave for the States. I have two weeks. By that time, maybe you'll have something and we can talk about it. I'll give you a call."

"No place to stay in Edinburgh, then?"

"Haven't decided on one yet. I'll check at the visitor's bureau when I get there."

"Here's one better," Corrigan said, dragging forth a veteran of a notebook and scribbling on a page. "Here's names of three places, see, and any one of them will give you a clean room and breakfast, and for good rates. You mention the Corrigan name, and you'll get the first-class service, too. I'm not saying these are in the best of neighborhoods, but you'll never beat the prices. Off the tourist way, you know."

"Thanks," McIntyre said, "but don't feel bad, if I don't end up in one of them." He had misgivings about being where Corrigan could find him again. "I'll call you, though."

"Fair enough, fair enough." Corrigan extended his hand. "No harm done, possibly some good as they say. Good time had and nobody hurt."

"Good time? I've been tossed out of Murray Publishing, as you recall."

"Oh, that," Corrigan said. "If it'll help, I'll call up Murray's, and set the whole thing straight for you."

"No thanks. I'll do my own explaining. Besides, after having two or three people there tell me they don't have what I'm after, I'm inclined to believe them. I'll look elsewhere, and let them cool off."

"All right, then. I'll look for you to phone me in a week or so. By then O. Corrigan and Company will have just what you want. If I was a betting man," he said with a sly wink, "I'd bet the family furniture on it. Cheers!"

Corrigan walked up the narrow street and out of McIntyre's sight. Forever, he hoped. All he wanted was a seat in the dining car of the Edinburgh inter-city train, where he could relax with a good lunch and a cup of tea, watching the English countryside speed by.

Chapter Nine

On the ancient side of Old Edinburgh, George IV Bridge Street and Candlemaker Row converged at the Kirk of the Greyfriars. Here ancient rock walls guarded a peaceful grassy graveyard. Here was the monument to a legendary dog, a faithful West Highland terrier named Bobby. Any Edinburgh tour bus worth its salt paused at Greyfriars to let passengers snap photographs of the statue of the brave wee doggie and the headstone of unfortunate auld Jock, his pastoral master.

McIntyre had himself paused at the kirkyard of Greyfriars, but not to photograph the headstones and tombs. He had paused to take in the view of Old Edinburgh. Having spent the morning at the National Library of Scotland, with no appreciable results, just as he had spent the previous day, he strolled up George IV Bridge on his way to the Royal Museum of Scotland, taking that route as a round-about way of getting a little exercise.

Greyfriars' north gate gave McIntyre an unforgettable view of Old Edinburgh. It was once Auld Reekie, back when stinking sulphurous coal smoke cloaked the spires of the churches and smeared itself on the castle ramparts. The stones of Old Edinburgh were soot-stained, from the pinnacles and crowning arches of the great monuments, from the knitting-needle spires of the kirks, down to the uneven cobbles that still paved the close byways. On either side of the crooked, cramped streets stood high houses like fortress walls of quarried stone, discolored from generations of wood fires and eons of coal furnaces. Deeply niched, thrifty little rectangular windows eyed each other across the twisting street. Harsh winter fogs, squeezing between the buildings, had not scoured away the stains.

Behind the high old stone walls with steeply pitched slate roofs, McIntyre saw the tapered needle of a stone spire, the heaven-pointing taper of a kirk steeple. It, too, was stained with the black smearing of old carbon and smoke. Over it all, walls and steeples and ramparts, the featureless leaden sky was an oil painting background done in shades of charcoal and gray.

McIntyre heard the whir of cameras and turned to find a small army making a colorful invasion of the kirkyard. Pale red and green sweaters seemed the costume of choice, along with the obligatory tartan skirts of the women and khaki slacks of the men. A grayish shade of light blue also seemed universal in the group, mostly in the women's hair and the faded little porkpie hats of their husbands. The guide, an impressively intelligent young Edinburgh student with a clear Scots voice, was explaining the story of the dog known as Greyfriars' Bobby.

"And following the death of auld Jock, his master, the wee dog would hae nae lad nor lass for anither laird," he said, "but lay upon Jock's grave there for all of his last fourteen years. Ye canna see it frae here, but up at the castle, prompt at one o'clock each day, there's a cannon fired. When wee Bobby heard that, it was off to the pub over the corner there wi' him. The innkeeper fed him, y'ken, and then it was back to his vigil. Ever' day the same for a' of those fourteen years."

McIntyre's exit was blocked by the group standing around the kirkyard gate. But he didn't mind. He was thoroughly enjoying the Scots accent of the young guide. He had plenty of time to get to the museum. It was a quiet, unhurried day. A few of the older people gave him a cheery—"Good morning."—and smiled as if they, too, sensed that in the long sweep of Edinburgh's history it seemed silly to be in a rush.

McIntyre hovered near the group, listening to the guide explain various monuments and tombs, and, as the tour carried them past another of the graveyard's gates, he slipped out and walked on to the Royal Museum.

The guardian of collections turned out to be a woman his own age, poised, excellently competent, polite. And firm. She listened with interest to his story, pursed her lips slightly in a tolerant little smile when he outlined his thesis that someone in Scotland, possibly the Royal Museum, owned a thick manuscript without knowing what it was. When she finally came to understand that Professor McIntyre's methodology consisted of being turned loose to browse through fragile and irreplaceable documents in hopes of finding something he could use, one of her carefully plucked eyebrows—the left one—formed a supercilious arch.

The museum went out of its way to be sympathetic and cordial, she patiently explained, but one could not simply walk in and expect to rummage through the collection in the hope of discovering something interesting. One needed a specific objective, some advance knowledge of the materials, some way to know where in the catalogued mass of items one might begin to search. One needed, in short, to know what one was looking for.

Many scholars used the collection every month, she went on, usually by pre-arrangement. The usual thing was to send a letter listing which materials one wished to examine and to set an appointment so that an archivist could be on hand to assist. Nevertheless, if Professor McIntyre wished, he would be welcome to use the card catalog and even the computer record of the museum's holdings.

The collection turned out to include a few letters by

Isabella Bird, which McIntyre was allowed to read. But they shed no light on the problem of the missing manuscript. McIntyre returned the dark-green document file box to the inquiries desk and turned to leave, uncertain what to do next. As he turned, he recognized a familiar figure, a man who seemed to be watching him and who ducked behind a corner just as McIntyre spotted him.

The cloth cap. And, if he was not mistaken, the rumpled corduroy suit.

McIntyre shot a quick—"Thanks again."—over his shoulder and, nearly running over the two stolid ladies who had queued up at the inquiries desk behind him, almost tripping over a stroller, ran toward the corner where the man in the cloth cap had vanished. Not there. Not at the next corner. McIntyre spun around and backtracked along the corridor. There! The fellow was strolling down a side passage as nonchalantly as a land agent appraising the place for a loan. McIntyre thought the man was pretending to be following signs pointing the way to a special exhibit.

At the doorway to the special exhibit room of the museum, McIntyre got close enough to his spy to get his attention. "Hey!" he shouted, his voice echoing and drawing attention from the other patrons clustered at displays here and there. "What's the idea of following me, Corrigan?"

The cloth cap turned. McIntyre had never seen the man before in his life. His red-faced apology was met with a frigid smirk. The man strolled on across the room and out the opposite doorway. McIntyre, his face still hot, felt deep embarrassment. Unable to look into the inquisitive faces all around him, he peered into the nearest display case. The special exhibit was a collection of photos and articles from the English mail service in the Victorian era, including a lay-out of colorful stamps, various cancellation symbols, maps of postal routes and districts, and photographs of mail carriers and various means of transportation from horses to bicycles. The next display was a wall-size map of England and Scotland, showing how the mail routes spidered out from London and Glasgow and into the surrounding districts.

"Americans find it hard to believe, but in Scotland's larger cities a person could post a letter in mid-morning, and it would be delivered mid-afternoon by the Royal Mail." McIntyre recognized the Scottish burr of that strong, clear voice. It was the same guide—and the same tour group—he had seen at Greyfriars. He recognized one of the ladies who had said—"Good morning."—to him, and returned her smile.

"Y'can see here on the map, though," the guide went on, "that transporting the post t' the outlying areas posed more of a problem for the Royal Mail carrier. Some went by horseback, but it was more common to walk. Out in the islands, mail traveled by rowboat or ferry."

The young Scot was standing now quite close to him. McIntyre had a flash of inspired curiosity.

"Excuse me," he said, "I'm not with the group, but would you happen to know anything about how mail, or packages, would travel from America to one of the smaller Hebrides islands . . . like, say, Mull, for example?"

The Scot smiled hospitably. "As a matter of fact, I would." He pronounced would with an "oo" in the middle. "A clipper or, later on, a steamer would bring it to Port Glasgow. Or perhaps Leith, the port here at Edinburgh." He turned from McIntyre and added a footnote for the benefit of his tour group. "We'll be going to see Leith this afternoon, an' hae our tea there."

"The mail," he continued, pointing to Scotland's west coast, "probably went by mail coach up to Oban, and then by ferry over to Craignure on Mull. If a package should be addressed to some other town on the island, Salen or Lochbue, for instance, it would hae to wait for the postman's weekly trip. He would walk the length of the island, y'ken, dropping off mail as he went."

"Thanks," McIntyre said, "that's very interesting."

"Thank you," said the guide.

The truism it's a small world no doubt originated with travelers who found themselves encountering each other over and over again while on vacation. Part of the reason, of course, was that cities such as Edinburgh had customary tourist routes that made it quite the common thing to keep running into the same *bande* of rude little French students or the same couple with the twins in a double-wide stroller. Thus McIntyre's third encounter with the blue hair group came as no surprise to him.

Since method had availed him precious little, McIntyre resorted to sightseeing and instinct. If Edinburgh mail went through the Port of Leith, and if Nugent's manuscript could have been carried by the Royal Mail, he would visit the port. Besides, the hotel desk clerk had recommended the King's Arms on the stone wharf; the Arms served an incomparable steak pie, and its assortment of single malt whiskies would overjoy any imbiber.

As he stood reading the interpretive signs about the history of the Port of Leith, he witnessed the arrival of a large motorcoach. The AARP brigade. The folks were beginning to seem like old acquaintances of his. The same little old lady smiled and waved to him.

McIntyre saw them again that evening on the esplanade of Edinburgh Castle, attending the twilight piping. This time he nodded and smiled and exchanged a—"Good evening."—with several of them. *Nice people,* he thought.

The next day McIntyre went to satisfy his curiosity about Number 12 Walker Street where Isabella Bird had lived with her husband, Dr. John Bishop, following their marriage in 1881. Fifty years old, McIntyre mused as he stood across the street and studied the building. Fifty years old, and she had traveled all alone to Australia, Hawaii, the Rockies, Japan, and the Sinai. With her sister dead and the little cottage on Tobermory no longer her fixed point and resting place from travel, she had moved into this building as Dr. Bishop's wife. World traveler turned housewife, to all intents and purposes.

The house had a flat front of smoothly dressed stone, rectangular blocks laid together with monotonous uniformity. The entire building seemed a flat, rectangular block of stone, the exterior decoration consisting only of some steel grillwork across the upper story windows and a fence of steel pickets lining either side of a square doorstep. All in all, it seemed to McIntyre, the outside of the house summed up everything Isabella had never had before: dependable surroundings, solidity, security, monotony. Everything a marriage should offer, he thought grimly.

He wondered if this Edinburgh house had been as inspirational to her as the Tobermory cottage, or the cabin she had rented from Griff Evans in Estes Park in 1874. It certainly held no inspiration for him, yet still it had a certain feeling about it. McIntyre took a few pictures, for the record, but nothing about the house seemed especially interesting.

Why, exactly, was he so sure that Isabella Bird was going to lead him to the lost manuscript and to the solution of Rocky Mountain Jim's murder? He felt almost as if he were being decoyed away from the truth, that the manuscript was elsewhere and not connected with Bird at all. Still, he couldn't deny that the search was an adventure; he felt vigorous and thoroughly alive, as sensitive to new sights and sounds as a cat in a strange room. He empathized with Isabella Bird; whenever the lady was sedentary, whether in Tobermory or Edinburgh, she suffered from crippling back pains, headaches, loss of appetite, and general malaise, but let her board a ship bound for California, Yokahama, or Sidney and she became an electric dynamo, sending off sparks of energy in all directions, instantly strong enough to climb a peak, ride a camel, or seize her revolver and face down a fierce Asian brigand.

McIntyre leaned back against the iron fence, regarding the Bishop house across the street. So far he had been going about his project all wrong, yet exactly where it had started to go wrong he couldn't say. He had allowed himself to be shut out of Murray Publishing without even explaining fully what he was after. The National Library and the Royal Museum had gotten rid of him with equal efficiency.

The archives—Murray Publishing, the library, the museum—could only show him the things they knew they had. That was the problem. If Nugent's manuscript was in such a collection, it obviously wasn't labeled with his name or with any designation linking it to Isabella Bird-Bishop or Lord Dunraven. If it were, one of the biographers would have found it by now. It would be indexed.

So. . . . What would an archivist or a librarian do with such an item, not knowing what it was, or to whom it belonged? Somehow, somewhere, McIntyre knew, it existed. He could feel it. He had an instinct, a series of urges, a gut feeling he got whenever he was going in the right direction. The feeling had brought him through on earlier searches in other places. And it would bring him through now. He was supposed to be here, in Scotland, looking for Isabella Bird's long-faded foot-steps. Somewhere there was a complete manuscript, and it was connected with her. It would turn out to be connected to everything he had seen so far.

Time to reorganize. Time to start something different.

A mailman came whistling down Walker Street, breaking into McIntyre's reverie. He gave McIntyre a cordial wave, said—"Good day."—in a broad Scots burr, and went on whistling as he sorted his letters and stuffed them into the brass letter slots of the doors on his route.

Letters, McIntyre thought. Once again he was reminded of something, something he had skimmed over in one of Isabella Bird's letters. Something about mail delivery. Suddenly he remembered what it was. In that long-stride, rapid walk of his he hurried to catch the Edinburgh city bus that would take him back to the National Library.

He soon had the letter again, spread out in front of him on the polished, spotless, maple table next to the document file box. Although it would be merely another Bird artifact to a biographer, he now saw the implications of it. It was a letter Isabella had written to a friend in which she chatted about the weather and the charitable works of her sister, Henrietta, and transportation difficulties on the Isle of Mull.

How I wish the Crown could be persuaded, she wrote, **to take the very logical step of transferring the Tobermory mail to one of the several ferries and supply ships arriving daily from Oban. As it is, we must wait an additional week for it, at times, while our carrier of the Royal Mail trudges it across the island from Craignure. Moreover, the man is known to arrive in Tobermory with alcoholic breath, having paused along the way at the distillery outside of town, and having found more than one envelope arriving in an opened condition, I strongly suspect he fills his lonely walking hours with unsealing and reading various items in his**

bag. Mr. K_____ has also accused this public servant of lightening his load by dropping heavier parcels into convenient crevices along the way. There is talk of establishing a mailboat service from Craignure to Salen and Tobermory, which many residents support wholeheartedly.

When McIntyre returned the green cardboard box to the check-out desk, the librarian gave him another surprise. "This has been a popular item today," she said, and smiled. "A gentleman requested it just an hour or two ago."

"Did he wear a corduroy suit in need of pressing?" McIntyre asked. "A cloth cap?"

"Oh, that's him," she burred in that sweet Scots accent. Then she grinned at a sudden thought. "At first, I thought he'd come in to make us an offer for our used furniture!"

McIntyre stifled a laugh that would have upset the dour-looking patrons there in the reading room. "That's the guy," he said. "Well, thanks."

"Thank you," said the young librarian.

He sat in his room that night, reassessing his plans, going over his maps and tour books. What next? Somewhere, during the day, he had picked up a brochure about distillery tours, primarily in the Highlands and out on the Hebrides.

McIntyre had a friend back in Colorado who shared his enthusiasm for single malt Scotch whisky. A few days before departure, McIntyre had promised to visit at least one famous distillery—perhaps Glenlivet or Glenfiddich—and make a personal inspection of the conditions under which their favorite beverages were created. A man can't be too careful, after all.

And here on the map was a pleasant coincidence—the Isle

of Islay lay only a few miles south of the Isle of Mull in the Hebrides. On Islay were no less than six distilleries. Here was born Laphroaig, the strongest and most medicinal-smelling of Scotch whiskies; here too one found the wellsprings of Bowmore whisky with all the subtle savor of an old overcoat drying over a peat fire, and Bruichladdich. A bartender had told McIntyre that the name Bruichladdich comes from the sound made by a bourbon drinker trying the whisky for the first time.

McIntyre was not deceiving himself at all. He was trying to be nonchalant about this manuscript hunch, playing the rôle of carefree tourist sans itinerary. He tried to make a practical argument, too; cutting short his stay in London and in Edinburgh might be disappointing as far as research results were concerned, but it would save money. He had spent less on food than he had anticipated. The date on his return plane ticket gave him a couple of weeks to kill, and he had more than enough cash and credit to cover some aimless wandering. Like, for instance, to Tobermory.

Of the three postcards McIntyre had bought, one showed a tartaned highland chief posing picturesquely in the heather. On the back of that one he wrote:

Dear Hank,

Here's a picture of me in the heather hills of Skye, waiting for Bonnie Prince Charlie to return. Interesting trip so far . . . thrown out of Murray's, committed assault on a citizen. Wish you were here. P.S. Next chance you get, think how to find out where Griff Evans went after leaving Estes Park. I'm thinking his reputation followed him.

Cheers,
DLM

The second card was of the Royal Museum in London. On the back of this he wrote:

Dear Glenda,

Wonderful country, but I don't think we'd get away with much from this museum. Tried to get you one of the Elgin Marbles, but no go. Too heavy to carry by myself. Tell Walt he'd love breakfasts over here . . . thick bacon, and you get it every darn day with your eggs and fried tomatoes. No big breakthrough yet, but hopeful. Thanks again for what you did to help.

Take good care,
David McIntyre

McIntyre pondered the third postcard, the one showing a sad-looking, little Scots terrier, began to address it, then thrust it into his briefcase, unfinished.

Chapter Ten

The Rover sedan purred along the highway toward Glencoe. At the wheel, McIntyre relaxed to a cassette of Scots ballads as the road rose and fell to the rhythm of the Trossach hills, gently dipping and curving through shades of green fields and purple banks of heather. When he came to the narrow road leading up into Glen Nevis, he turned off and followed it. After a mile or two, he pulled over to photograph Ben Nevis. It sat sunning its stony bulk in the welcome warmth of late afternoon.

He wouldn't have time on this trip to make a climb of the mountain, at least not enough time to make it a worthwhile climb. However, he would be able to explore the Glen a bit, staying in Fort William, then drive down the coast to the town of Oban; there he could catch the ferry to the Isle of Mull. Or Islay. Whichever seemed right when he got there.

McIntyre had stopped in at the Edinburgh Tourist Bureau where he reserved economy lodgings at Fort William. It had seemed like a good idea at the time, a way of insuring that he would have a place waiting for him. The hotel, however, turned out to be a three-story block of industrial concrete more than a mile from the town center. All it offered was a dreary lobby and a restaurant resembling a college cafeteria and two wings of sleeping rooms. All carpeted in drab crimson shag. On the outside of the place, the best landscaping feature was the asphalt car park. There were altogether too few autos in this car park, McIntyre observed, as he pulled in; in this season, and at this time of evening, it should have been packed with cars.

Inside, he found a trio of polite, but bored, young employees, one of whom took his registration while the other two continued their own conversation. He could see one man seated all alone in the lounge, but other than that the hotel seemed as empty as a nudist's suitcase. McIntyre wondered if had missed seeing a sign outside, reading **Quarantined**.

It was a mercy that the carpeting in his room had faded, like that in the hallway and elsewhere; when new, the Chinese maroon paisley pattern must have been unbearable. But the bed was firm and cleanly sheeted, the window opened to a good highland breeze, and the *en suite* bathroom had a shower. Granted, the shower had only two settings—dribble and stun—but it was a shower, nonetheless. After settling in, McIntyre shaved and put on a shirt somewhat fresher than what he had been wearing. He picked up his research folder, so that he would have something to do while he ate, and then went downstairs to supper.

That's what he was doing—reading about Isabella Bird and Lord Dunraven while having a supper of grilled salmon and assorted vegetables—when the tribe of blue-haired compatriots showed up once again. The first geriatric wave poured through the door and into the dining room and headed directly for the buffet line. A second group soon followed, and another after it, as if coming ashore at the Battle of the Breaded Chops. The tables were rapidly filled. Finally there were three stragglers, two older ladies and a gent. The man looked the very picture of a country squire, from his military-like bearing and Monty mustachios down to his slight limp.

The late-coming trio didn't seem to be in step with the rest of the group and didn't seem to know many people. McIntyre couldn't remember seeing them either at Greyfriars or at the museum. With full trays trembling ever so slightly in their hands, they came toward his table.

"May we join you?" the lady in the blue jumper asked.

"Certainly," McIntyre said, standing politely and moving his reading materials to one side. "Rather a large group, isn't it? Ten minutes ago, I think I was the only one here."

"Haven't we seen you before?" the gent asked. His accent was not American. Irish, McIntyre decided. Irish, but with education in England and many years away from the auld sod. Probably in the army. "I have it!" the man continued. "It was at the museum in Edinburgh the other day. Something to do with mail carriers, if I'm not mistaken. Mind handing me the salt, there? Thank you. We are the Holstrands. George Holstrand. My wife Betsy, and her sister Clarise Jensen."

"Glad to meet you. I'm David McIntyre." But he did not remember seeing them at the museum. He was certain, in fact, that he hadn't.

"Well, you've been following us around!" Betsy Holstrand chirped in a good Irish accent of her own, breaking her industrial-strength roll in half and slathering one half with butter. "Let's see, weren't you at the piping demonstration? Of course, you were. Oh, and at that little wharf place. What was that called, George?"

"Leith," McIntyre volunteered. "Mere coincidence. So, what brings you folks to Scotland, besides the Thistledown Tour Coach Company?"

The conversation lasted through the resilient chops and rubbery diced carrots and on into the bread pudding and coffee. Watching the elderly trio trying to cut the meat with dull table knives, McIntyre was glad he had chosen the salmon.

The Holstrands and Miss Jensen did their level best to exchange personal histories with their new American acquaintance, including occupations—McIntyre had been right;

George was retired military, and Irish—the basic lay-out of their homes—George and Betsy were domestic managers on a large estate in Ireland—the general financial condition and marital arrangements of their children, and their own health—his ruddy war wound was a nuisance in cold weather, but the two of them were still frisky.

McIntyre warmed up to the trio and grinned through his second cup of coffee as they went on about their Scottish adventures to date.

"But we're boring you, I'm sure," Betsy said. "Just old, retired fuddies chattering on and on. Since you say you're keen on Ben Nevis and mountaineering, you really should be making the acquaintance of the Bakers over there. They're Americans, too, you know."

"The Bakers?" McIntyre asked.

"Behind you," Betsy said. "The very fit-looking man in the Loden jacket and the woman with all the clanging bracelets. He's always talking about climbing mountains and taking long treks. Why, just before we all got off the bus, he was saying how he would like to climb Ben Nevis. Why don't you go over and introduce yourself?"

McIntyre protested that he was not exactly the sort of man just to walk up and introduce himself. He enjoyed talking with strangers, up to a point. Besides, when he was traveling, he found that some of his most enjoyable moments came from chats with locals. Still, after twenty minutes of smiling and being agreeable with the Holstrands, he was beginning to feel like one of those figurines people put on the rear shelf of their autos. The ones with the bobbing heads.

So McIntyre rose, thanking the trio for the conversation, and excused himself. He walked to the Bakers' table rather self-consciously.

It was actually Lew Baker who broke the ice. "Glad you

came over!" he said, getting to his feet to shake McIntyre's hand as if he were a long-lost, lodge brother. "I've heard that you're out here touring around on your own. And we were just talking about this mountain they call Ben Nevis. You can't by any chance tell me how to get there, can you?"

McIntyre accepted Baker's gesture toward the empty chair and placed his thick accordion envelope of material on the table. "I've got a map here," he said, "just by coincidence." He unfolded it as Baker fished in a pocket for his reading spectacles. "If you take a right turn when you leave the hotel parking lot, you'll be on a two-lane highway that leads to a round-about. I guess you've seen them . . . they're like traffic circles. Go almost all the way around the round-about until you see a sign pointing to Glen Nevis Visitor Center. From there it's just a few miles. Very pleasant valley. Beautiful drive."

As it happened, the tour was to lay-over for a rest in Fort William, but, without a car, the Bakers couldn't even get to town. Quite keen to see Glen Nevis, Lew was. Quite keen. He'd be glad to pay for the petrol and even reimburse McIntyre for a day's car rental, if he would be willing to drive them out into the mountains.

"Now, don't you do it, if you don't want to," Mrs. Baker said, patting McIntyre's knee. "Lew has been a real estate developer all his life, and he'll spend the whole live-long day telling us where they could build more roads and put up condominiums."

McIntyre laughed. "If it gets unbearable," he said, "I could always get even with him by giving him a lecture on literary theory. Guaranteed to send you into a sleepy trance within fifteen minutes." The woman smiled, and her smile had the effect of making McIntyre feel that he was quite an amusing fellow. She went on smiling at him throughout the next two hours of evening conversation in the lounge, and her charm sent McIntyre deeper and deeper into his reservoir of witty anecdotes.

Noon of the following day found the three of them driving along, chatting like old pals. Lew and McIntyre discussed university politics and philosophies of planned city development; Nancy Baker joined in by describing books she had read and places they had been. Nancy's only bad habit—and it was more amusing than irritating—was her innocent way of asking unanswerable questions. "Look," she would say, pointing out the Rover's window, "what kind of tree is that?" Since McIntyre was concentrating on his driving, keeping to the left side of a sixteen-foot wide, winding road, he could see neither her hand nor the tree at which she was pointing. And most likely wouldn't have known the species if he had seen it.

They drove slowly, stopping whenever Lew saw another good vista to photograph. At a picturesque spot where the lane crossed a bridge over roaring falls, Nancy insisted on having McIntyre pose in his new tweed cap. She even adjusted it for him, cocking it at a rakish angle that she said made her think her of Gene Kelly in that musical, BRIGADOON. McIntyre responded with a chorus of "The Heather on the Hill," even though he had forgotten several important sections of the lyrics.

While the Bakers went one direction to get a panoramic picture, McIntyre walked in the opposite direction to get a closer look at a particularly photogenic rowan tree. He came to the end of the road in the heart of the glen, at the head of the hiking trail, and stood there quietly. It was a place of peace. It seemed one of those places in the world that feel as sacred as a cathedral. A flock of gray, fleece clouds broke from the denser fog up the valley and rose until they stroked against the tip of Ben Nevis above, seeming to be the very clouds that had drained themselves to send the small torrents of crashing crystal washing down over the ledges of shale and mounds of heather and gorse.

McIntyre lifted his face to the summit and felt the kiss of highland mist falling lightly on his brow and cheeks. Rocky Mountain Jim Nugent's background was a mystery, but if he had ever lived in country such as this, he would have stopped at nothing to return to it again.

"I'm glad I decided not to hike up there today," he told Lew Baker later. "The drizzle must be freezing on the rocks, near the top."

"But, oh," Baker said, his gray eyes betraying the nostalgia of a mountaineer who has grown stiff in the legs and short of wind, "what fun it would be to give it a try!"

The Rover purred back along the road, following the tumbling waters of the byrne down through forest and across high open moorland. McIntyre was explaining his project.

"So, at least ten years later, the community was still aware of this missing manuscript that James Nugent had been writing. What I want to know is who took it?"

"Cherchez la femme," quipped Nancy Baker. She winked at him, but McIntyre was intent upon his driving and missed it. "Pardon me?" he said.

"Didn't you say that Griff Evans suspected James of trying to . . . what would they call it . . . court his daughter?"

"Jenny, you mean. Yes. Either Dunraven or Kingsley mentioned that Nugent had romantic notions about Jenny Evans. Enos Mills repeated the same bit of gossip. That might be one reason for Evans having been quick to take someone up on the idea of shooting at Nugent."

"No," she went on, "you don't see my point. I mean that

she may have taken the manuscript."

"She?"

"Of course. Think like a young woman, a girl, for a moment. If Nugent had been paying attention to her, and, if she believed he was writing about it, she would have hurried to retrieve it before her father got there. Am I right? Or, if Nugent was her secret admirer . . . this was a young woman of romantic age, remember . . . she might have gone to the cabin and taken his papers in the hope of finding something about herself in them."

"Jenny Evans," McIntyre said, half to himself. "Or could she have been protecting her father? Nugent's book might have contained something linking Griff to Dunraven's land scheme. It's possible. Hmm."

Lew Baker broke in. "But you think he copied certain chapters and gave them to various people? Don't see why he'd go to all that trouble."

"I'm certain of it," McIntyre replied. "There's good evidence. I believe he used copies of his chapters as leverage, as ways either to intimidate the land stealers by showing them what he would publish, or to get into their good graces."

"If you ask me," Lew said, "it's the land. You wouldn't believe what people will do to get hold of title to a piece of land. Wouldn't believe it. Men *and* women. Go to a tax auction sometime where they're selling someone's real estate for back taxes and you'll see what I mean. It's like a pack of wild dogs fighting over a dead rabbit. They lie, they bounce checks, they stab relatives in the back, they move fences and surveying markers, anything. If you want to find out who put Griff Evans up to shooting Jim Nugent, you find out who ended up with title to his land."

They came to the hotel car park. As Lew shut the Rover's door, he smiled. "That was sure a nice day," he said. "Let us pay you back by buying you dinner. Maybe we could talk about this missing manuscript some more."

"I'd love to hear more," Nancy added. "Please join us. We can drive into town and find a nice restaurant."

"No need of that," McIntyre said. "The hotel dining room has Angus prime rib as the special tonight. If there's anything I like, it's prime rib."

Between Lew's long habit of making real estate clients feel important and Nancy's genuine little smiles of curiosity and surprise, McIntyre was kept in the conversational spotlight all evening. They seemed fascinated with stories about his work. Afterward, over drinks in the lounge, McIntyre told them all about his previous literary riddle, the real-life location of Zane Grey's hidden cañon in Utah. When the time came for the question of whether to order a second round of drinks, however, there was a two-to-one vote in favor of going to bed.

"That's what happens when you get old," Lew Baker said. "You'll find out, someday. Can't stay up and drink the night away."

When they parted company, McIntyre made his way to the bar. He asked for a brand of single malt whisky he had never tasted before—it came from Tomintoul—and struck up a light conversation with the bartender. Before long, they were joined by a third man, a refugee from the Thistledown Tour; having dutifully seen his wife to bed, he was looking for a drink before going to bed himself. A four-piece local band was setting up its electric guitars and amplifiers at the other end of the dining room. Local youths were drifting in, and the place began to hum with energy.

"Who's your friend?" the bartender asked him.

"Who?"

"The man who was near the doorway, watching you. The

one who didn't take off his coat. I thought he was going to join you, but he just now disappeared."

"Didn't see him."

"Oh. He sort of hovered there, between the door and the end of the bar. I think he was sitting near that group of people you were with at supper earlier, like he wanted to have a private word with someone. I assumed it was you."

"Not me," McIntyre said. "Nobody knows I'm here."

"Interesting," said the bartender.

"You're pretty observant."

"Part of the job," the man replied. "Spend twenty years behind a bar and you automatically size up everybody. Get so you can spot the ones who'll be trouble, or the ones who might be looking to find their wife with another man. Learn to see the law in plain-clothes, too. Come to think of it, I saw that bloke talking with that taller man, the one with the limp. After you and that other couple had gone. I didn't see him again."

The other American, quietly drinking until now, spoke up. "Taller man? I think he called himself George Holstrand. I thought you would know his name. . . . everyone in this group certainly knows *you*. 'Course, he only joined the group two days ago. He and the two women he's with."

McIntyre's drink stopped in mid-air. "Then how . . . but he knew that I'd run into your tour at the Edinburgh museum. And at Leith, too, now that I think about it. If this Holstrand group hadn't joined the tour yet, how did he know that?"

"Someone on the bus told him, I suppose. Several of the old ladies took notice of you. They talked about you, too. Even my wife had her eye on you. She told me to get one of those tweed caps like you were wearing when you came in this afternoon. She said it reminded her of that actor in that old movie . . . BRIGADOON."

"Gene Kelly," McIntyre said.

"No, no. The old guy. What's-His-Name?"

McIntyre scowled and gestured his glass toward the shelves behind the bar. "I'll have a shot of your Glenlivet," he muttered. "And I might just work my way on down the line to the Laphroaig."

Chapter Eleven

Mystery isn't the right word, said McIntyre's letter to Hank from Fort William, **unless you call it a mystery that there could be so many motives. Nugent's murder opened up a Pandora's box of human nature. With Judge Wescott, we've got a jealousy motive, or maybe a territorial one. With Griff Evans acting on his own—a possibility that most of the written accounts dismiss—we could blame it on paternal fears because he is protecting Jenny. Maybe there was something more sinister behind his relationship with his daughter. Or we could just plain blame it on his drinking, like Isabella Bird did. Then there's the Irish peer, Lord Dunraven, still operating under feudal philosophy, including the idea that he's entitled to all the land he can get, and the ages old strategy of getting one commoner to kill another. We also have his foreman, Whyte, who may have put Evans up to it out of some kind of loyalty to the land company or because of his tendency to ape the aristocrats.**

Then there's this mysterious Lord Haigh—was he really there at the cabin by coincidence, and was he genuinely afraid that Nugent had come to kill him, or was he part of a long-term scheme? It just seems so contrived . . . he dashed in, woke Evans, said—"I want you to protect me."—as he handed him a double-barreled shotgun, and remained right there, close enough to have said—"Give him the other barrel."—or words to that effect. So who was Haigh and what did he owe to

Dunraven? Or, why did he think Nugent hated him enough to kill him?

It's tantalizing to conjecture up a motive for everyone involved. We've got greed, avarice, jealousy, wrath, drunkenness, pride—pick one.

I've also been looking at my own motives lately. Never verbalized them, though. I guess it's mostly the fun of finding out. I'd love to end up with a manuscript that's complete, or nearly complete, and get it published. I'd like to publish my own story of finding it.

This might be a wild-goose chase. One person says to look for the woman involved, and another one tells me to look at anyone who gained real estate from it. But I guess I'm just looking for a manuscript and a story. The thing is, I don't need to publish. I want to see Nugent published. I mean, here he was, a well-read, literate man with enough wit and verbal fluency to impress not only Lord Dunraven but Isabella Bird as well—and she was a published author and educated woman. He cared enough about his book manuscript to have copied out parts of it, by hand, and have given them to various people to read. He longs for approval and encouragement. So what if a reader flies into a tantrum? It's still a reaction. Writers need that. They need someone to read what they wrote. God, I can't tell you the number of times I've sat late at night writing and suddenly needed somebody to read it to.

And so there's Jim Nugent one fine summer day, his manuscript growing. The judge was impressed, Dunraven had probably expressed reserved interest, Isabella seemed as thrilled as a stodgy Victorian lady could seem, and perhaps even Jenny had seen some chapter or other. The newspaper had taken notice of him as a writer and not just a mountain man.

Then out of the blue, there stood Griff Evans with an English shotgun. *Blam! Blam!* If Jim was about to start a new life as a writer, with Isabella as his agent, that blast put an end to it. I feel a sense of incompleteness there . . . I want to get him published. He just ought to be published.

Maybe if the weather's good, I'll stick around here another day and hike up Ben Nevis. Sooner or later, I'm heading for the Isle of Mull to find out whether the village of Tobermory has any records of Isabella Bird.

Take care of yourself,
David

Meanwhile, back at the ranch, my work on early hotels of the Rocky Mountains was leaning in Lachlan's direction. I'd unearthed descriptions of several well-born Englishmen invading Colorado in the middle of the Nineteenth Century, men such as Sir St. George Gore who made a three-year hunting foray into the Rockies accompanied by two dozen wagons, herds of cows, packs of dogs, and hundreds of servants. I learned all about the growth of Colorado Springs as a spa for the wealthy Brits.

I learned there was a distinction to be made when using the term "mountain man." Rocky Mountain James Nugent was not the beaver-trapping, Indian-fighting sort of mountain man; those became scarce after the 1845 failure of the European beaver market. James Nugent was a second generation hunter and trapper, still wearing leather clothes and living a hermit's life but no longer attached to the fur trade.

I will admit it. Whether I was at the Denver Public Library, the Colorado History Museum, or one of dozens of small libraries in small Colorado towns, I usually spent part of my research time looking for that bloody manuscript.

I had one gem for Lachlan when he returned. And it was going to cost him a nice lunch. Possibly dinner. Estes Park's library, a splendidly catalogued collection, yielded a carefully written account by Ansel Watrous. Watrous, a county historian of good repute, extracted his tale of Jim's shooting from court records. What he said might rock Lachlan's hypothesis:

The case was not called for trial until July 14th, 1875, when District Attorney C.G. White, who succeeded Mr. Carr, entered a *nolle prosequi* in the case against Evans and the accused was discharged from custody. It developed between the time of filing the information and the opening of the July term of court in 1875, so it was alleged, that Evans was not guilty of the charge; that the shooting was done by a young Englishman, who had been sent out from England in December, 1873, to look after Lord Dunraven's interests in Estes Park, and who had left the country.

There are several theories as to what caused the trouble between "Mountain Jim" and Evans, but the most accepted theory is that "Mountain Jim" became enamored of Evans' seventeen-year-old daughter and that the young lady's parents disapproved of his attentions to her. At any rate a coldness grew up between the two men, and "Mountain Jim" had been heard in his cups to threaten to do Evans up. After the arrival of the young Englishman, whose name was Haigh, to take the management of Lord Dunraven's interests in the park, the young lady became much attached to him. They were often seen riding together, which stirred "Mountain Jim's" anger toward Evans to the very depths.

Watrous's article told how Mountain Jim had come to Evans's cabin on June 19th, 1874 "in a frightful mood, threatening to kill Evans and Haigh if they dared come out into the open." And then, Watrous reported "this Haigh, it is alleged, stepped to the door and fired the shot that a few weeks later ended the life" of James Nugent.

So here we have, apparently, one shot rather than two. Jim's own account that he was with a man named Brown and that they were riding peacefully past the cabin was not considered. Jim's account of Evans's firing the shots was not considered. And now Haigh, like the mysterious Mr. Brown, was said to have "left the country."

I sat back, after reading the Watrous version, and thought of Lachlan enjoying himself in Scotland. I did not know how to get a letter or a telephone call to him, but had it been in my power to do so, I would have. This new development made it even more important to find that manuscript, and to find it intact. If it pointed the way to the motive, as Lachlan hoped, it would also point the way to the murderer.

The drizzling blear of dawn found McIntyre in the same foul mood that had once earned him a remark on a student evaluation: **Professor McIntyre is a lively and entertaining lecturer. Except for some mornings.**

His evening of Scotch-drinking had left a pounding pain just behind his left ear, and his mouth felt as though a Highland terrier had slept in it. He took extra time to shower and comb his hair, even though the comb's teeth were torture to his scalp. He entered the dining room for breakfast just in time to see the Thistledown Tour bus pulling out of the parking lot and vanishing into the scudding mist. Breakfast did not modify his disposition. There was something unappetizing about the way the grilled tomatoes and runny egg yolks leaked into his bacon and toast.

The drive up Glen Nevis to the trailhead would unnerve any American driver, what with the poor visibility in the rain and the slick roads and everyone driving on the left. After the pavement ended there were fewer autos; McIntyre saw only one, in fact, a green English Ford following him. Long pools of rain water stood in the gravel. Conifers dripped in huddled clusters. Fern beds hung their soaked heads along the road. Through the bowels of the cloud filling the glen, all he could really see was the few yards of gravel ruts ahead of him and masses of sodden green passing by the smeary side windows.

McIntyre parked the Rover at the trailhead and resolutely struggled into his rain parka and rain pants. Into the lumbar pack went lightweight binoculars, the ordinance map of Ben Nevis and surrounding area, two candy bars, and a flask of water.

The green English Ford had parked nearby, but its occupant didn't seem anxious to get out and begin hiking. *Smart man,* McIntyre thought, as he sludged up a trail that was more like a creek. In the best of places, the water merely ran over rock or gravel. Where the trail dipped into depressions of the terrain, it was like walking through a wading pool. And when it got too close to the ferns and heather where the gravel became sod, the muck of the trail sucked at his boots and sent his feet skidding with each step.

After a mile of this McIntyre stopped at a switchback and looked out from beneath the dripping visor of his rain parka. The trail led on along the side of the same soaked slope and up into fog and mist. If he did get to the top, there would be no view to see. And a long slippery descent. He had read in the guidebook that freezing rain and snow were common up near the summit. He turned around.

Coming out of the trees bordering the car park, McIntyre

137

had the final straw. The two autos were still parked there. And the man from the English Ford was doing something to the door of the Rover. McIntyre took out his binoculars and saw a length of wire the man was using to pick the lock. He wore a tan raincoat and a cloth cap, as did eighty percent of the male population of Scotland. Why hadn't he just picked up a rock and bashed in the window with it? McIntyre had left nothing in the Rover except his books and research file on the back seat, but it still made him angry to see someone trying to break in. Damned angry.

He looked about, slipped behind a tree, and studied the twenty or thirty meters of open lot between himself and the cars. The guy would see him coming, no doubt about it. But there was another way around. He could sneak up close, if he got down in the stream bed and worked his way along the rocks. He stripped off the yellow plastic suit—his shirt and pants were wet anyway, from condensation and sweat—and cached it in the ferns. His wet green flannel shirt and dark khakis would blend into the background. He slipped down through the trees, over the edge of the small rocky ravine, and stalked his way along in the stream, being careful where he placed his feet. He was soaking wet, but unnoticed.

Along the way, McIntyre watched for a good stick, and found one, a wrist-thick piece of spruce branch a couple of feet in length, smoothed and polished by tumbling in the stream. When he was near the cars, he peered up over the edge of the ravine. The man in the raincoat was still working at the lock, casting glances toward the Ben Nevis trail from time to time. It was obvious that he was an amateur.

With soaking wet hair plastered down over his forehead and his eyes angry, McIntyre looked like a demented escapee from a mental ward when he came up over the edge of the ravine with his thick cudgel gripped in both hands. The gravel was too soggy to betray his footsteps, and the man had his back to McIntyre, intent on watching the trail at the far end of the parking area.

Six feet away, McIntyre stopped breathing. Four feet. His knuckles were white, his teeth grinding together. Two feet. And McIntyre made his lunge, a hand on each end of the club, putting it over the man's head, getting it tight against his windpipe, pulling back, pulling the man off balance. McIntyre stopped the man's fall with a knee to the middle of his back. The man just hung there, both hands struggling for the club across his throat, gasping for air.

"Looking for something?" McIntyre queried.

He was answered in strangled gasps.

"I'll bet you had the wrong car," McIntyre said. "Probably thought this black Rover was your green Ford." McIntyre put pressure on one end of the stick, twisting the man's head around. He knew this face. It was the same man he had mistaken for Corrigan back at the Edinburgh museum. "I'm going to give you enough slack to talk," McIntyre said, "and you keep your hands as far away from your pockets as you can."

The man nodded and grunted.

"You make one move to step away from me, you let one hand go toward your pocket, and the last thing you'll feel is this stick hitting you right above the ear. Clear?" Another nod and a grunt. McIntyre released the stick and stepped back just far enough to swing it. He felt his blood cooling, the adrenaline subsiding. "You're not much of a car thief, are you? You've been working at this lock for five minutes, at least."

"Not me line of trade, cap'n," came the croaking voice. "Just looking for valuables is all. No 'arm done, none." The voice was Irish, and no mistake. And the look on his face told

McIntyre that he was lying.

"Followed me up here, did you?"

"Well, now, cap'n, if we're starting in to discuss matters . . . a kind of question and answer game as it 'twere . . . we'll need to strike some sort of agreement. You're goin' to have a real time of it, gettin' me all the way down to the Fort William police by yourself. On th' other hand, I'd like to avoid difficulties." He struggled to swallow, but he didn't move from his position in front of McIntyre with his hands well away from his sides. "Suppose we have our little chat, and, if you're happy with me answers, why, you and I could go our separate ways."

"OK," McIntyre said, "if I'm happy. So spill it. What were you after? And don't tell me it was my books. You wouldn't know what they were."

The man bristled visibly at the suggestion that he was ignorant. "Is that right?" he croaked. "Well, I may not be a hoity-toity professor, but I've seen that LADY'S LIFE IN THE ROCKY MOUNTAINS a few times before this. And your book by Lord Dunraven there, that's not exactly new to me."

"Don't move around," McIntyre warned. "You were after my research material? Maybe I oughta whack you on the head anyway, and take you to the police in the trunk . . . the boot. Tell me one thing . . . you know this character Corrigan?"

"Corrigan?" he squeaked. "Corrigan?" The man was not much better at lying than he was at car-breaking. McIntyre scowled and drew back his club. The man winced.

"All right," he said. "Mister Corrigan is convinced, y'see, that you're one of those American professors who come over with all kinds of grants and funds. Been comin' to the isles for years, stealin' away with our works of art and literature."

"So you were breaking into the car to look for money.

That seems pretty stupid." McIntyre was getting his blood up again.

"No, no, not that. Mister Corrigan indicated to me that you might be either carryin' around some kind of manuscript, or might be wantin' to purchase the same. He thought that, if we had a look at your material and could see what you're up to, y'see, we might have a way to do business w' you."

"It didn't occur to you that most of my stuff is in the hotel room?" McIntyre asked.

"Well, cap'n, you might say that possibility has been covered."

"The Irish couple. Holstrand?"

"I'll say no more."

"Well, you might as well know that I don't have any money to buy materials. I thought I made that clear to Corrigan. And if he or Holstrand prowls around in my briefcase, they'll soon discover that I haven't found out anything so far."

"All the better to do a deal, cap'n! I'm certain you can lay hands on the money somewhere. And if I may say so, you'd be well advised to forget this little incident and then go talk to Major Holstrand himself. He may have something for you by this time."

McIntyre scowled and shivered from the cold rain running down his back. If this was Corrigan's way of helping him with his search for the manuscript, he didn't much care for it.

"When I set out to follow ye," the man volunteered, "I thought y'might head for the Fort William museum or the library. Then y'parked the auto and hiked away up the trail there, and I saw me chance to snoop a bit, if I could open the lock without your knowing. Make meself a bit of change for me efforts, maybe."

There was still a lot about it that McIntyre didn't like, but he could see that the man in the raincoat was not going to be much more help. "Where are your car keys?"

"In the ignition," the man replied.

"Then keep your hands out of your pockets. Just slide into that car and drive away. And don't let me see you again while I'm anywhere in Scotland. Clear?"

"Clear as crystal glass, cap'n, clear as glass." The Irish brogue was now becoming theatrical as the man did his best to be obsequious. "I'll just go me way, then."

"Do that," McIntyre said.

The English Ford sped away down the narrow road, leaving sprays of rain water and gravel to settle back again behind it.

McIntyre got into the Rover, not really caring that he was soaking the upholstery. He sat there, forcing himself to breathe deeply while the rush of adrenaline subsided. Then the shaking set in. After it had passed, he managed to start the motor and drive closer to the trail to retrieve his rain gear. He was hungry as hell, the weather had driven him off the trail, and he was soaked to the skin, shivering.

Sometimes, McIntyre felt, he had all the bloody good luck.

Chapter Twelve

As McIntyre pulled into the empty parking lot, he noticed a human silhouette standing in a second-floor window of the hotel. There had been a defector from the Thistledown Tour, and the defector appeared to be watching him.

McIntyre parked and shut off the motor and pretended to be searching for something on the dashboard while he studied the image out of the corner of his eye. There was no mistaking that large, square figure, that military posture. It was Holstrand. He had joined the tour only two days earlier and now had let the bus go on without him. Why? When McIntyre got out of the Rover, the figure in the window stepped back behind the drapes. *To hell with it,* McIntyre thought. *Once I get cleaned up, I'm out of here.*

He showered, put on dry clothes, and packed. His wet clothes could hang in the back seat until they dried. At the reception desk he paid his bill and turned in his key. All was quiet. The morning desk clerk methodically ran McIntyre's credit card through an imprinter and stapled the receipts together. Far down the hallway, a bored maid pushed her humming vacuum cleaner back and forth over the dull red carpet; somewhere off in the dining room there was a clink of silverware being put away and the rattle of glassware. Waiting to sign the bill, McIntyre thought about Holstrand upstairs, watching from behind the drapes.

It didn't figure. Why would Holstrand be following an American professor? First this Corrigan character, then Holstrand, then the joker up at Ben Nevis. And each one of them was Irish. McIntyre took a bag in each hand and walked out to the Rover, where he put them into the trunk. His wet clothes were on a plastic hanger, courtesy of the hotel, which he hung on a hook in the back seat. Now, how would a real tourist act at this point? Take one last look at the hotel? He turned his head slowly, nonchalantly, and looked at the second floor window. No Holstrand. Maybe Holstrand was standing by the hotel door already, waiting to follow him. Or in a car behind the hotel, waiting.

McIntyre got into his car. "You're paranoid," he said to his reflected image as he adjusted the mirror.

How had Holstrand known he had been at the museum and the library? How did he find him at the hotel? Did he and his wife join the tour just to be at the same hotel? It was a stupid idea, but then how many people stay in this hotel other than economy tours? Damned few, that's how many.

McIntyre's fingers drew the seat belt across his lap, and, feeling for the buckle, he touched a small plastic disk on the strap. What was that for? He grinned sheepishly at the thought that had flashed through his head, when he realized it was just a plastic button to keep the belt from sliding through the metal clip. It was not a miniature microphone, not a location transmitter. That really would have been a romantic Ian Fleming touch. Still, these Irish characters had always known where he was. A bug, a tiny transmitter. But they—paranoids love to say *they*—wouldn't have known that he was going to get a Rover from the car rental agency, because he hadn't reserved a Rover. It had been a free upgrade. *But a paranoid,* said McIntyre to himself, *would have thought something was fishy when he got a sedan for the price of a mini.* What if *they* had a Rover already bugged and ready to go?

In a few minutes, David Lachlan McIntyre, Ph.D., was on his back on the grease-stained asphalt, head and shoulders under the rental car, searching the chassis for a bug. A position more fitting a mechanic than a research professor, but there he was. A man of infinite imagination.

He heard a scuffling noise, like a large man slightly dragging one foot as he walked, and turned his head to see expensive British shoes and razor-creased trousers standing next to the Rover.

"Motor problem?" the Irish voice asked.

McIntyre pulled his head out and looked up at Holstrand, standing over him. He looked even more Irish than before, from the tweed deerstalker on his head to the short blackthorn shillelagh he carried in his hand.

The professor got to his feet with an embarrassed grin. "No, just looking for listening devices," he said.

"Ah, I see," Holstrand replied. "You're thinking that's how I knew you were here in Fort William, at this particular hotel."

"Beg pardon?" McIntyre continued to smile, feigning innocence.

Holstrand gazed skyward, stroking the black knob of the shillelagh across the palm of his hand. "Too lovely of a day here," he said, "for dark games of mystery and suspense. Don't you think?"

"So I'm the reason you're here?" McIntyre asked. "That's what you're saying?" The good news was that he felt less paranoid. He waited for the bad news.

"Precisely," Holstrand smiled engagingly. "You see, Professor McIntyre, we have word that you are touring Scotland in search of certain material. Or, should I say, a manuscript?"

"Ah," said McIntyre. "I should have guessed. So, word is out that an American with a research grant is buying old papers. But if I may say so, you dress a bit better than certain other dealers in literary artifacts."

Holstrand laughed. "You mean Corrigan. No, I don't trade in antique articles. Not at all. And before you even ask, I'm not with the government, either. Far from it. Far from it." He used the shillelagh to whack a pebble off the asphalt and into the bushes thirty feet away.

"Nice shot," McIntyre said. "Hooked a little to the left." He leaned against the side of the Rover, hoping he looked indifferent and nonchalant. "I'm curious," he said. "How did you find me here? I didn't exactly have a travel plan on file anywhere."

"Oh, that's easy." Holstrand laughed his toothy laugh again, although his eyes seemed humorless. "Our friend Corrigan."

"Ah," McIntyre said. "Nothing personal, but next time I meet him I would like to beat him to a pulp. Just for exercise. Not that I dislike the man. I just like exercise."

Holstrand nodded. "Perfectly understood, Professor McIntyre, perfectly understood. I dislike dealing with his sort myself. One thing you must never do is to put your trust in him. He can authenticate his merchandise . . . that's not a concern. But if Corrigan says he is keeping a secret for you, it's time to be on your guard. Turn away, and don't listen. But as to your curiosity. Mister Corrigan does have useful connections. He has friends . . . perhaps relations . . . working with the Scottish tourist bureau. And being a modern nation, Scotland has computer facilities."

"Ah," McIntyre repeated. "I see. The minute I stopped in Edinburgh to reserve a room . . . here at Fort William's hostel for the terminally tasteless . . . my request went to a computer and then to Mister Otis Corrigan. And then to you."

"More or less, yes."

"Let me guess. You have a connection with the tour company?"

146

"Indeed. Not terribly difficult to join them *en route*. Pleasant group. Your marital status, in fact, was the subject of conversation amongst some of the ladies. Oh, and the Bakers think rather highly of your anecdotal abilities. I'll add my own recommendation . . . you seem a regular chap."

"I'm flattered as hell," McIntyre replied. "So . . . not that I'm on a tight schedule or anything . . . but what is it you want to sell me, exactly?"

"Not a thing," Holstrand replied. "I'm empowered to offer you something *gratis*. You know," the Irishman went on, "the way you Americans pronounce schedule has always intrigued me."

"Really. And we both know the anecdote about schooling. So what is this present you have for me?" As McIntyre grew more comfortable with the situation, he also grew more impatient to be getting on with it.

"All right," Holstrand said, "the point of the matter is this. I am in the employ of some very private persons, persons quite well placed in the world."

"In Ireland?"

"Yes," said Holstrand.

"Let me guess again," McIntyre said. "Somewhere around Adare, perhaps?" Among other things, the fourth Earl of Dunraven was also known as Windham Thomas Wyndham-Quin, entitled as the Lord of Adare.

"Possibly. The thing is, Professor McIntyre, our mutual friend Otis Corrigan is not to be underestimated in the area of research. As soon as you had told him that you were interested in things relevant to Lady Isabella Bird and Estes Park, it took him next to no time to educate himself on the Dunraven connection. And having done business with my employers before, on a different matter, he surmised that your search would bring you to their doorstep. And they would prefer, as he knows, that researchers not bother them. Not that you would, I'm sure," the Irishman added, "but, when you publish this discovery of an hundred-year-old document, and describe the charms of my employer's ancient castle and seat, it could bring others hammering on the gates."

McIntyre thought Holstrand was overestimating the readership, but he was content to listen.

"More than ten years ago," Holstrand went on, "the family opened its grounds to a young bloke interested in ancient Celtic ruins. After his article and pictures appeared, the place was besieged by strangers wanting photographs. Two of them . . . two, mind you . . . actually insisted that they had the right to visit public ruins."

McIntyre's brow had been growing a furrow. He had no idea what the man was talking about. "That's too bad," he said. "But what does it have to do with me?"

Holstrand leaned against the car, flicking imaginary dust particles from his shoe with the heavy stick. "What I have," he said, "is in all probability a portion of what you are searching for. It's taken me no end of trouble to find out exactly what you *are* after. I even phoned your college and pretended to be checking academic credentials for the British Museum."

"What is this prize?" McIntyre asked. "You must be pretty proud of it, to go to all this bother."

"A chapter, I think." Holstrand replied. "Ancient families, you need to be aware, accumulate tons of books and many thousands of documents. Letters, diaries, financial documents, you name it. My family . . . that is, the family employing me . . . has for two generations engaged a secretary to keep track of it all. But they can't keep track of everything. Documents are put into bundles or envelopes and filed away, and soon no one remembers what they are, except for a few words in a ledger. Ryan grazing agreement, Seventeen Fifty-Eight, for instance.

"Corrigan telephoned. He had a list of what the computer johnnies call key words. The name Nugent, of course, was among them, along with Estes Park . . . from that, I was able to locate a thin manuscript, no more than a dozen pages. I made a photocopy which I am prepared to hand over to you."

"You're saying that it's a chapter, or something like a chapter, written by James Nugent?"

"A cover letter with the document indicates that it is a chapter. And by James Nugent."

"Let me see if I have this straight," McIntyre said. "Nugent gave it to Lord Dunraven in Eighteen Seventy-Three or Seventy-Four. And it's been languishing in the Dunraven archives ever since?"

"Bright boy!" said Holstrand, tapping McIntyre lightly with his stick. "You've got it exactly."

"It's in Nugent's handwriting."

"Presumably. Addressed to the fourth Lord Dunraven."

"Marvelous," smiled McIntyre. "Excuse my Yankee bluntness, but what's the asking price?"

"Well," Holstrand said, gazing skyward in contemplation, "the family is in no need of money. Nor am I. What they ask is a gentleman's agreement . . . you may have the photocopy, letter and all . . . in return, you agree to protect the family privacy and accept without question that this is all that exists in the archives. Bear in mind, the family doesn't have to give you anything, or even talk to you. But they want to be up front, give you their word that there is nothing else, and let you do what you want with the information in the manuscript."

McIntyre was suspicious, of course, but not so much because of the Irishman's demeanor as because of twenty years of freshmen telling him they had searched every source in the library for their term papers. It was experience—no one ever has the whole story, no one ever exhausts every resource. That's what makes research interesting.

"I see," McIntyre said. "But what assurance do I have that this is all of it?"

"My word," Holstrand said. "All I can do is give you the word of myself and my employer. We assure you that the family has nothing else. Nothing else, that is, that you couldn't find on your own. Elsewhere."

That seemed like a damned odd expression. What else might he find that he had overlooked? Given the McIntyre method, it could be anything.

"Why don't we go inside for tea," Holstrand said, "and I'll dash to my room for the material and meet you in the dining room. You can look it over, and I'll answer what questions I can."

"Sounds fair," McIntyre said. "We'll see you inside, then."

The ferry to the Isle of Mull cut the sea swells, her bow splitting them in a steady rhythm of slaps and booms. The engines far below decks throbbed steadily. McIntyre found a place on the top deck where he could be out of the wind in the lee of the big funnel. He leaned on the rail, watching the bow smacking the waves and the sea foam spreading out to either side like white fronds of fern. The ferry's wake was a path of smooth foam-flecked water.

McIntyre was supremely content to be drinking in the mute exhilaration of being on the sea, feeling big engines underfoot, and the surge of the sea. He inhaled a sensation of discovery and adventure as Scotland's mainland shrank astern and the Isle of Mull grew ever larger off the bow.

The sea air made him hungry. Quitting the rail, he went inside to find a table next to a window where he could keep watching the sea slip past the ferry and could see small islands far in the distance. McIntyre bought tea and a scone and spread the Holstrand material on the table.

Something baffling me, he wrote in his journal. **Maybe it's what I'm looking for at Tobermory. So far, I've found fragments sent or given to various people. No mention of giving one to Bird. And Bird does not mention getting one. That's the odd thing; she's the obvious recipient. And their relationship was so intense. There's that long ride they took together, the one she told her sister about in a letter. Jim poured out his heart to her, crying over his wasted life as an outlaw and renegade and general under-achiever. Yet if he sent her his precious manuscript, or part of it, later on, why didn't she mention it somewhere?**

Maybe because she got married. Be awkward to have a big manuscript from a former boyfriend. What would she have done with it? She was a lady of honor, not one to hide things. Maybe send it back or send it away somehow. But not destroy it.

That's the issue. She couldn't have destroyed it. He trusted it to her, probably wanted her to see about publishing it. She wouldn't have left it lying around the house for years. Wouldn't have destroyed it. Wouldn't have hidden it from her husband like it was something to feel guilty about. But then where the hell would she have put it?

McIntyre munched his scone, his pen suspended over the

journal. Isabella Bird probably carried the manuscript off to Edinburgh, if she had it, and there it remained after her death. Maybe she had a safe deposit box in some Edinburgh bank. Too puzzling. McIntyre closed the journal and picked up the copy of James Nugent's letter to Dunraven. The handwriting looked authentic.

August 22, 1873
My Dear Lord Dunraven,

While it could be wished that your purposes in the Estes Park valley and mine could be more in accord and amicable, we nonetheless unfortunately find ourselves at such odds and disjunctures as could be seen as regrettable, esp. considering we are something of the same race, having both ancestors who sprung from the noble races of the isles. Yet in spite of ill feelings, antagonisms, etc., it has been reported to me that you have an interest in spiritualism; I, therefore, herewith send to you a portion of my book in which you may find yourself reading with interest my own adventure with the ethereal world. Perhaps by discovering some mutual topics such as this spiritualism appears to be, we might move toward a truce and understanding in months to come. . . .

The ferry's horn blew a double blast, and McIntyre looked up. They were coming into the slip at Craignure.

"Passengers with vehicles should now return to the auto deck," the loudspeaker advised. "Please return to your vehicles at this time."

McIntyre gathered up his materials, zipped his travel bag, and headed down the gangway, heart racing, eyes bright. He was grinning from ear to ear. The Isle of Mull. Isabella Bird may have hidden the manuscript in Edinburgh somewhere, but the feeling was strong in him that it was here, somewhere on this little island. He trusted that feeling. The hunt was on again, and it was on in earnest.

Chapter Thirteen

The Isle of Mull has three distinct tips, like a craggy triangle. Just a mile off the southern tip is the tiny island of Iona, revered as the site where Christianity began in the Isles. It was there that St. Columba landed in 563 A.D.

If McIntyre were awaiting some sign that his instinct about Mull was on track, he might have found it in the ancient story of another manuscript pilferer, St. Columba. By coincidence, it was a stolen document that brought Columba from Ireland to Iona in the 6th Century. When Columba was still a minor Irish nobleman, he borrowed a copy of the VULGATE GOSPELS, the very first copy to reach Ireland. Columba had scribes make him another copy, never bothering to petition Rome or local church authorities for permission. On behalf of the Church, the High King of Ireland demanded Columba's copy; Columba refused. Hundreds were killed in the resulting fight, an Irish slaughter known as the Battle of Cul Dremme. Penitent, Columba accepted blame; remorseful, he exiled himself from Ireland forever. With twelve followers, he sailed away in a fragile boat, taking a vow that he would not touch land until he came to a place from which he could not see Ireland. It was Iona.

McIntyre landed at Craignure. Leaving the ferry dock, he took the northeast road, pointing the Rover toward the northern tip of Mull and Isabella Bird's village, Tobermory. It was an auspicious day of sun and clear skies. The car purred along gentle hills of bracken and heather and took long easy curves down into groves of shade where mossy stone walls angled off through the forest. Here and there, the bright red berries of a rowan tree punctuated the green canopy. The road emerged onto high flat terrain overlooking the forest and the sea, where a small loch sparkled blue in the sunshine.

From there, the road ran near a high sea cliff. And suddenly he saw Tobermory in the far distance, shining across the bay. McIntyre pulled off the road and reached for his camera. All the buildings were painted different colors—bright blue, light red, sunflower yellow, green, lavender—an artist's color wheel. They were built in a solid wall along a street shaped into a crescent, facing the harbor.

Everything about the picture was serene. At the moment, however, McIntyre could imagine a brutal winter day when towering waves would come roaring into the bay, crashing against the low sea wall, flooding the street, lashing at the shop doors of Tobermory.

A long curve of road along the bay cliff, then a steep descent through more woods, and the Rover rolled into the center of Tobermory, bumping down the cobbled street between village and harbor. On the harbor side was a high clock tower, a square pylon of stone standing at the center of the crescent. The tower's four clock faces were visible from anywhere in town as well as from the anchorage. It looked like a rook, or castle, from a gigantic chess set, made of quarried granite and two stories high. It was the tower Isabella Bird had commissioned as a permanent monument to her sister—and permanent it certainly was. Even if the interior was hollow, as indicated by a small access door high up under one clock face, building the tower must have taken five or ten tons of rock.

Past the painted shops and the stone church, that had become an upscale shop for Scottish items, the street abruptly twisted left and climbed the hill behind the village to the top of the cliffs. McIntyre saw the hotel he was looking for, and more—across the lane was a white two-story cottage with a steep roof of slate. He recognized it from photographs—it was Isabella Bird's cottage. More coincidence. Nowhere, not at Murray Publishing, not in Edinburgh, had he felt so sure that he was in the right place.

The young desk clerk repeated his name in a rolling brogue. "Doctor McIntyre. Aye, we hae your reservation from the tourist bureau in Fort William. I hope ye'll be comfortable."

McIntyre was not comfortable; he was reading the rate schedule. This place was expensive! Very elegant, especially the dining room that he could see through the French doors. But beyond his budget.

"I wonder," he began, uncharacteristically sheepish, "if you could hold my reservation for another hour. The rates are . . . well, frankly, a bit more than I expected. Hate to do it, but I'd like to go down into the village and see if the tourist bureau has anything that I can better afford."

"Oh," the Scottish lad grinned, "dinna think o' worrying about that. We are the dearest place in this whole end of Mull. Let me mak' a few telephone calls for ye, and it's certain I'll find something. Have ye any particular sort of thing in mind?"

"Well, I'm here to do some writing," McIntyre said, "so privacy and quiet would be nice. I don't need period furniture or evening entertainment or anything."

"I'll see what I can find for ye, then. If you'd like t'wait in the bar there, ye'll find that guests get their first glass o' ale free." He winked broadly and grinned.

McIntyre was halfway through his free pint when the desk lad came in.

"I found several vacancies. This one might suit ye, if ye're serious about no entertainment. The McCullochs call it a bed and breakfast, but they really haven't much time for socializing. He's a local builder, y'ken, up early and comin' home tired. Missus McCulloch teaches at the school, so she often has papers to grade in the evening. Ye'll get the run of the house, and a good breakfast if ye're up in time to eat it with the family."

"Sounds like something I can live with," McIntyre said. And thanking young Sean for the assistance—and the ale—McIntyre went in search of the McCullochs.

The McCulloch home was, indeed, in a state of perpetual motion. Mrs. McCulloch had no sooner settled him in his room than the doorbell rang again. Students bearing tardy essays. Then came a crash of the back door; the McCulloch lad, banging in to drop off his schoolbooks and pick up his football shoes. McIntyre unpacked, arranged his books and notes, wrote his day's expenses in his pocket ledger, and set out for a walk before supper.

Where supper was to be, he did not know. But he was likely to find his way to some out-of-the-way pub or restaurant. When McIntyre was traveling, his suppers could be as impulsive as his research methods. Some evenings he would splurge on a restaurant with linen tablecloths and a respectable wine list; at other times he would end up at a greasy pub table with a corned beef sandwich and a glass of stout.

He strolled down the hill and came to the Bird cottage. There was nothing about it to suggest the emotions that once existed behind those thick walls, hiding away from the keening winter winds of the Hebrides. The cottage had no doubt heard the laughter of the two Bird sisters arranging their belongings on the day they first moved in, and the happy sounds of neighbors coming to welcome them. It had also heard Isabella and Henrietta in serious discussion, far into the night, about Isabella's plan to travel alone to Japan. Prayers it had heard, Henrietta's for Isabella's safe return, and finally Isabella's prayers for her sister who lay dying of typhoid. Tears, then, and mourning. And Dr. Bishop's earnest entreaties that Isabella, now alone, return to Edinburgh.

The face of the white cottage betrayed none of this to those passing by. Two precisely placed upstairs windows unemotionally looked out over the harbor far below. Downstairs, two expressionless rectangles of sash and glass shared the front wall with a deeply recessed doorway. A simple box of a building, sans porches, sans eaves, sans decoration.

McIntyre ventured as far as the steps leading up from the road. He had no need to disturb whoever lived there now. His business was with the dead, not the living. He turned, with his back to the doorway, and faced the harbor. Isabella had stood here often. He could feel it. She might have paused here, coming down the steps and heading for the village, leaving her desk and her writing, stretching her painful back.

It was in this cottage in 1879 that she had gathered together her letters to Henrietta, preparing the manuscript of A LADY'S LIFE IN THE ROCKY MOUNTAINS to send to John Murray. How far away those Rocky Mountains must have seemed as she stood looking out over the boats anchored in Tobermory's harbor. How long ago it must have seemed, the stormy day of her emotional ride with Rocky Mountain Jim. Not the ride up Long's Peak. Her letters speak of a more romantic ride up a side valley in Estes Park, a ride during which Jim spent three hours in confession to Isabella, offering up the facts of his wasted life, the bouts of drunkenness and debauchery, the history of bloodletting and rage. It was "told with a rush of wild eloquence that was truly thrilling," she had written.

The handsome, even superbly handsome, side of his face was towards me as he spoke. . . . "Now you see a man who has made a devil of himself! Lost! Lost! Lost! I believe in God. I've given him no choice but to put me with 'the devil and his angel.' I'm afraid to die. You've stirred the better nature in me too late. I can't change. If ever a man were a slave, I am. Don't speak to me of repentance and reformation. I can't reform. Your voice reminded me of _____." Then in feverish tones, "How dare you ride with me?" He made me promise to keep one or two things secret whether he were living or dead, and I promised, for I had no choice; but they come between me and the sunshine sometimes, and I wake at night to think of them.

A less ungovernable nature would never have spoken as he did, nor told me what he did; but his proud, fierce soul all poured itself out then, with hatred and self-loathing, blood on his hands and murder in his heart, though even then he could not be altogether other than a gentleman, or altogether divest himself of fascination, even when so tempestuously revealing the darkest points of his character. My soul dissolved in pity for his dark, lost, self-ruined life, as he left me and turned away in the blinding storm to the Snowy Range, where he said he was going to camp out for a fortnight; a man of great abilities, real genius, singular gifts, and with all the chances in life which other men have had.

Here she would have stood, McIntyre mused, looking far across the sea toward the mile-high mountains where Jim lay

159

buried, his body at rest however much of a troubled wanderer his soul might be. Here she stood with the memories, with the secrets she had promised to keep for him, "whether he were living or dead." Maybe she thought about his manuscript, lying there on a shelf in the cottage, wondering if her soul could ever be rid of its weight.

In the cottage, Henrietta sat and worked at her needlepoint. Dear, gentle, sister. The one who stayed at Tobermory during Isabella's far-ranging voyages, doing her charity work among the poor and the alcoholic of Tobermory, going to church, visiting neighbors for tea, thrilling to each of Isabella's letters.

In a way, Henrietta must have seemed rather a restraint to Isabella, a beloved restraint. With their parents dead and no income of any substance other than that brought in by Isabella's books, the little cottage at Tobermory had to be maintained. An allowance had to be arranged for Henrietta. To that cottage Isabella knew she must return, no matter where in the world her adventures took her. Isabella had other friends; she led the social life of an author, attending parties and literary evenings in Edinburgh and London. She had recognition; in 1892 she would be the first woman initiated into the prestigious Royal Geographical Society.

Henrietta attended no balls, no dances, no literary *fêtes*, belonged only to her church. She was content to wait for Isabella, or Isabella's letters, never dining out with a man unless invited to the home of neighbors and seated with the minister. She was content.

And then in 1880 Henrietta came down with typhoid fever. Isabella received word in Edinburgh that she must hurry to Tobermory. Dr. John Bishop followed her. He remained at the cottage with Isabella day and night, the two of them taking turns attending the feverish and dying Henrietta.

Five weeks went by, and finally the fever took her. She was forty-six.

Isabella went into a period of mourning that at times seemed self-destructive. She had no interest in her writing, in her books, in her travels. Her own health declined. She lost the vitality and energy that had sustained her on her adventures. This gradually passed, as deep grief will, and she took up some of Henrietta's charities; Isabella went to Tobermory cottages where the typhoid epidemic was still doing its murderous work and helped to nurse the sick, took meals to the needy, counseled the families of alcoholic men.

Copies of her newest book, UNBEATEN TRACKS IN JAPAN, arrived at Tobermory, along with complimentary reviews from the papers. She began to come out of the gloom and into the sun. And then Dr. John Bishop proposed. Would Isabella consent to be his wife? In 1881, on March 8th, it was done; she became Isabella Bird Bishop of 12 Walker Street, Edinburgh.

McIntyre walked down the steep street toward the village. In the end, Isabella had let go of Tobermory. She somehow became free of Jim Nugent, free of the cottage and its sad memories. One funeral, one wedding, and that chapter of life was over. One funeral. . . . McIntyre halted in the middle of the street, his eyes staring at the sea but seeing nothing. A funeral. The grave and the coffin. Was it possible?

He walked rapidly with the long-striding excited pace that seized him whenever his mind began to race. Isabella Bird had had two burdens in life: Jim Nugent's secret and Henrietta's dependency. She had loved them both, but, in death, both contracts had been broken, finished. Henrietta would be committed to the earth; her physical remains would be honored and held sacred, but Isabella could go on. But what could she do with the literary remains, the work of

James Nugent? Publishing the book would not have benefited him then. And if it contained secrets of his past, it was probably better off buried.

In a way, Isabella had already memorialized James Nugent in her own book. She had done him good justice, even adding the introductory note about his death at the hands of Griff Evans. Just as she had never had anything but love for her sister, she had never denied James. Nor lied about him. A LADY'S LIFE IN THE ROCKY MOUNTAINS was published, and that was his epitaph. Closure.

Except for that manuscript, that leftover piece of the James Nugent puzzle. If she had brought it with her, or if it had come in the Tobermory mail, could it be that she had buried it or cremated it in order finally to lay James Nugent to rest? Why couldn't the manuscript be in the coffin with Henrietta, both earthly remains, both heavy burdens, laid down together to sleep out eternity? If so, where was Henrietta's grave?

McIntyre stood there absorbed in the possibility. The sound of a small lorry laboring up the hill roused him; he realized he had been standing in front of a cottage with a blue and white **For Sale** sign neatly attached next to the front door. The lorry stopped.

"If y'd care to see inside," the driver said, "the folk in the house two doors down hae th' key."

McIntyre turned and smiled. "No," he said, "nice place, but I'm just a tourist. Staying at the McCulloch house . . . ," and his voice trailed off as he saw that the sign on the side of the lorry said **S. McCulloch & Son, Builders**.

The driver extricated himself from the small cab and took a cigarette from the pack in his pocket. "I'm McCulloch," he said, lighting up. "Son and father. Welcome to Mull."

"Thanks. I'm David McIntyre."

They stood there like that, awkwardly, in silence, McIntyre examining the wall that ran in front of the cottage, and McCulloch finishing his cigarette.

"Man from the mainland owns it," McCulloch volunteered. "It's a tight little place." He pointed, using the two fingers holding his cigarette to indicate a spot high on one corner. "Fixed that corner, two year back. Can't tell it was ever fixed. Old mortar just gave way, some of the rock fell out. But it's tight."

"Any idea what the asking price is?" McIntyre said to be polite.

"No idea at all. Only came up for sale a week since. Not enough time for locals to find out! Maybe y'could call up that number and find out for us." McCulloch chuckled and snubbed out his smoke. "Give ye a lift tae the house?"

"Thanks," McIntyre said, "but I'm out to stretch the legs a bit. I'll just stroll along. See you there."

"Fine," McCulloch said, shoehorning himself back into the little truck. No other cars had come by. The only sign of life at all was a woman down the street, weeding her flowers, and the movement of a window curtain across the corner.

Mrs. McCulloch gave McIntyre the run of the house, and so, when he returned from having supper—at the pub—he followed the sound of the BBC news emanating from the front room. He did not enter empty-handed, however; he was carrying a bottle of whisky that he had bought in the village.

"For the host," he said, placing it on the sideboard. "A Colorado tradition."

McCulloch did not rise from his easy chair, but smiled and offered a sitting handshake. His was the grip of a man who spent many hours swinging a hammer. "Tak' a chair," he said, indicating the overstuffed armchair nearby. "Th' depressing news is just coming on. In fact," he continued, taking up the remote control and silencing the droning British accent, "I think I've had a hard enough day wi'out that. Ye'll find whisky glasses in the cupboard there, and ice in the kitchen if y'tak' it."

Despite the advance notice that McCulloch was not a conversationalist, McIntyre found him both talkative and well-informed. Taking cues from photos on the wall, McIntyre asked about the house, McCulloch's military service, the history of the family and the kids.

"Father built the place himself, startin' wi' an old sty of a cottage and addin' on. Always addin' on. I went away to the service and came home to a house twice the size. It's why the missus got the notion to take in paying guests." He raised his glass to McIntyre in a toast.

"So your father was a builder as well," McIntyre said.

"Oh, aye. Four generations that I know of. And my son might take it up, if he ever takes time t'help me and learn. Right now it's all football and skateboards wi' him. And I don't think he's even discovered girls as yet!"

"It looks to me like a builder in this town would have to do a little of everything," McIntyre said. "I've seen stone houses, concrete block buildings, thatched roofs, slate roofs, timber construction, half-timber, metal siding, everything."

"Aye, and that's just the start. Many's the time I've done repair to foundations, which takes a stonemason, then found the plumbing all agley and fixed it, and ended up glazing windows an' shingling a roof. My grandfather, though . . . that's him in the photo just next to the bookshelf . . . he did only stone work. Didn't like this frame construction at all. Nothing lasts like stone, he used to say."

McIntyre examined a picture hanging just below the picture of the elder McCulloch. It showed several figures standing on the stone pier near the clock tower.

"He worked on the wharf, too?"

"It's called the long pier. Mostly he did repairs. If y'see anythin' in Tobermory and it's of quarry stone, my grandfather probably had a hand in it. He was scarce twenty year of age and still an apprentice when he worked on the tower there."

"And I imagine you've been in and out of every building in town yourself," McIntyre said.

McCulloch laughed. "I imagine I have, at that!"

McIntyre was thinking of one house in particular, the two story white cottage just down the road. "Tell me something," he said, pouring two more whiskies. "Would a builder such as your grandfather or your father or yourself, would you ever happen to find things hidden in old houses? You know, behind walls or under fireplace hearths?"

McCulloch became quiet. He was either thinking or watching the mute face on the television. After a time, he offered McIntyre one anecdote.

"An attic," he said. "People do store things in attics and forget them. I had a job maybe two, three years ago. Y'can see the house from out on our porch. Ceiling sagged. Well, it was the whole roof, it was. Whoever built it had saved a shilling or two on his kingposts and jackposts, and eventually the whole thing started to sag. Had tae g' up there and put in two great bloody beams t'save the roof."

"And you found something?"

"Aye. Rusty ol' metal box. Love letters of the lady's mother, and a few worthless bonds. An' so," McCulloch said, eyeing McIntyre with bemused suspicion, "would y'be here t'search attics and cellars y'sel'?"

Crisis time. McIntyre could now tell McCulloch the whole story and possibly gain him as a valuable source of information. Or McCulloch could then tell the whole village, and McIntyre would find most doors slammed against him. But he had a feeling about this village. Underneath its dour, stern façade, under the crisp attitude toward strangers he had experienced at the pub, he felt a spirit of hospitality and generosity. He could imagine some Tobermory resident, a stranger to him, coming up to him with an Isabella Bird letter for him to look at. He could not imagine, at all, anyone jealously hiding an old manuscript from prying eyes.

And so, again following instincts and impulses, McIntyre poured more whisky and spent the next hour telling the entire story to McCulloch. "Now you have the answer to that question of what I'm looking for," he finished, "and the lesson here is that, if you ask a professor a question, you'll need fifty minutes for the answer."

McCulloch was serene. And somber. Through his Scots heart there still flowed the blood of a highland clansman who in an earlier era would have fought to the death or gone to his grave with a secret, if it meant honoring a bond with a fellow Caledonian. His clear bold eyes looked directly into McIntyre's.

"You've done well t'tell me. And it stays within these walls," he said. "I'll see what I can find out for ye, too. Y'might get a start down at th' museum in the village, though. There's papers of the lady there."

McIntyre let the soft armchair envelop him. The peat taste of the whisky was a warm mist in his mouth. Tomorrow. Tonight he'd read the Dunraven chapter, and tomorrow he'd start digging for the Tobermory manuscript.

Chapter Fourteen

While Lachlan was off sampling Scotch somewhere in the highlands, I was still grubbing about in libraries and museums for information. His interest in Nugent had involved me in the early history of the Estes Park tourist industry, which was at least related to my own research project, so it seemed the natural thing to do to finish filling in some gaps for the both of us.

Gap number one had a familiar name on it: Dunraven. Despite the fame of the Stanley Hotel as a forerunner of resorts, the first full-scale hotel in the valley was established by Dunraven's Estes Park Company, the same outfit that thought up the scheme that James Nugent called The Great Land Steal. Dunraven's name still draws scorn from Estes Park citizens who perceive him as an early-day land thief and snob. But the more I learned about him, the more doubts I began to have.

Born as Windham Thomas Wyndham-Quin, he acquired four titles—he was the fourth Earl of Dunraven, a Mount Earl of Ireland, the second Baron Kenry of the United Kingdom, and Lord Adare. When Nugent was shot, in 1874 the earl was thirty-three years old. For five years he had been married to Florence Elizabeth, daughter of Lord Charles Lennox Kerr; they had three daughters.

Dunraven's association with the Irish village of Adare seemed to contradict his image as an effete materialist. The sources agreed that his lordship had a sincere lifelong interest in the well-being of his Adare tenants. His father, the third earl, had begun restoring the entire village, and Dunraven went on with the work, giving decent homes to the people and providing much needed work during economic hard times. He had regular meetings with the Adare citizens for the main purpose of discovering ways to help them. Yet, in Estes Park, he supposedly became a murdering villain bent upon dispossessing every resident of the valley.

Would Dunraven have ordered the killing of James Nugent? In his memoirs, PAST TIMES AND PASTIMES, Lord Dunraven described Nugent as "an extraordinary character, civil enough when sober, but when drunk, which was as often as he could manage, violent and abusive, and given to declamation in Greek and Latin." I could not picture Lord Dunraven resorting to murder in order to cure Mountain Jim of drinking. Or to make him stop his Latin and Greek declamations.

The writer of PAST TIMES AND PASTIMES comes across as a gentleman of good humor and wit, a sportsman who laughed at his own naïveté in approaching a full-grown bear while armed with a squirrel rifle, or in becoming lost during a winter hunt.

Dunraven's easy-going approach to life can be seen in his reaction to an incident that took place in Denver within a few months of the Nugent shooting. Some rogue with an English accent, it was reported, was drinking and brawling in Denver's naughtier districts. He patronized the ladies of the line and told everyone that his name was Lord Dunraven. When the real Dunraven heard about it, he laughed it off.

Between 1869 and 1876, quite a few Irish and English gentry visited Dunraven in Estes Park. Sir William Cummings came, as did Earl Fitzpatrick. Celebrated artist Albert Bierstadt stayed the summer of 1874, painting the portrait of Long's Peak that came to hang in the Denver Art Museum. Lord Haigh was a guest, and one should not forget Dunraven's physician and close friend, Dr. George Kingsley.

Isabella Bird mentioned three other Dunraven associates in A LADY'S LIFE IN THE ROCKY MOUNTAINS. She wrote of "an intelligent and high-minded" American couple "whose character, culture and society I should value anywhere" and added that there was also "a young Englishman, brother of a celebrated African traveler, who, because he rides on an English saddle, and clings to some other insular peculiarities, is called 'The Earl.' "

This could be Theodore Whyte, a relative of Dunraven's, hired as Dunraven's foreman. Whyte liked to wear English hunting pinks while leading guests on galloping hunts across Estes Park, leaping gates as they went. It was he who recruited the Denver derelicts to file false homesteading claims that would later be sold to the Estes Park Company. The source spoke of Whyte as a cold, calculating, slightly paranoid braggart who liked to ape his English lords.

Isabella encountered another character while staying at the Evans house: "[I]n the afternoon of yesterday a gentleman came who I thought was another stranger, strikingly handsome, well dressed, and barely forty, with sixteen shining gold curls falling down his collar; he walked in, and it was only after a careful second look that I recognized in our visitor the redoubtable 'desperado.' " He was "well informed" and showed "conversational dexterity." None other than Mr. James Nugent, dressed up.

Sitting in the Estes Park library, absorbed in A LADY'S LIFE IN THE ROCKY MOUNTAINS, I suddenly came across a passage that would make Lachlan leap for joy! Isabella Bird described a boy who lived at the Evans ranch, a young man given to lying, stealing, sneaking, and plagiarism. Her account of him was exasperated:

Again, he lent me an essay by himself, called "The Function of the Novelist," which is nothing but a mosaic of unacknowledged quotations. The men tell me that he has "bragged" to them that on his way here he took shelter in Mr. Nugent's cabin, found out where he hides his key, opened his box, and read his letters and MSS. He is a perfect plague with his ignorance and SELF-sufficiency.

And MSS. The abbreviation of manuscripts, plural. Isabella's "tiresome boy" had seen James Nugent's manuscript. Better yet, this shows that Isabella knew that the manuscript existed.

Oh, Lachlan, I thought, *this is going to cost you a very nice dinner, indeed!* And I went on to make two more discoveries that afternoon, two tiny details related to Lachlan's murder theory.

Discovery number one: Theodore Whyte, openly acquiring land illegally for the syndicate, left a paper trail. There is a record of the names of the derelicts who sold their homesteads, the acreage, and the price. One of these was named William Brown, who was paid $500 for his claim. A man named William Brown lived with another of the Dunraven associates. A man named Brown rode with James Nugent to Griff Evans's cabin on that fatal day. That Brown vanished the following day. James Nugent wrote that Brown was "a friend," but it looks as though he was hired to bring Nugent into an ambush.

Discovery number two: Nugent sold his land. If it was some murderous manipulator who got Brown to lead Nugent to the Evans cabin so that Evans could shoot him, what was the motive? Later, writers assumed that the motive was land: Dunraven, or The English Company, was out to gain title to

Jim's claim at Muggins's Gulch, which commanded the only road leading into the park. When I dug up the fact that Nugent had sold his title, and a month before his murder, that particular bit of reasoning seemed to go out the window.

I toasted my little research coup with a frozen daiquiri in a quiet but rather expensive bar. When the tab came, I looked at it with shock. *Lachlan,* I said to myself, *where are you when you're really needed?*

McIntyre was in his room at the McCulloch house. Through the open window he could see the lights of Tobermory and could hear the surf saluting the coast of Mull. He spread out the photocopied pages and began reading. He saw, with smug joy, that Holstrand had given him the document that Nugent had read to Isabella Bird, the one she had called "a very able paper on spiritualism." One and the same.

And this was what had been hidden in the Dunraven archives all these years? Why had they gone to so much trouble to give it to him? True, it had saved him the expense of a trip to Ireland. It seemed to be nothing more than what Holstrand had said—a way to preserve their privacy.

That bothered McIntyre. They had sent Holstrand and the other man to find him and give him a photocopied manuscript? Just to keep curiosity-seekers at bay? It didn't make sense. If he had gone to Ireland, the family could have simply refused to see him. And there was another thing; if he *did* use the manuscript in a book, it would still raise the same amount of curiosity. McIntyre also pondered Holstrand's offhand reference to something that he could find on his own—"Elsewhere." Perhaps he should stop worrying about it and just study what he had been given.

The Dunraven manuscript, again about a dozen and a half handwritten pages, was written as a response to "certain charges" that it was Nugent himself who wanted to exploit the Estes Park valley. Writing from a lofty intellectual height, Nugent sounded almost as if he were talking down to the reader. He used allusions to Byron and other Romantic poets, quoted obscure Latin writers, and constructed a logical argument of Aristotelian dimensions.

Nugent first asserted that he was not a man interested in commercialism and profit. He was, he said, a man of "poetic soul" and Byronic sensitivity. He saw the mountains as no more—and no less—than a kind of dwelling place of all souls of people who have lived there and who have died. A sacred home to animating spirits.

In evidence, he recounted an experience he had while camping alone. It was a ghost story. He camped on the site of an ancient Arapaho hunting lodge, and in the night he actually felt as though he were in the middle of a romantic triangle tragedy, that he was both the killer and the victim of the killer. It was such a graphic vision that he came away quite shaken and convinced that such things as ghosts inhabit the mountains.

Nugent quoted Hadrian Publius, asking in Latin— "Where does the soul go?"—and once again asserted that the mountain wilderness was a spiritual place, "a kind of acoustic shell for the anima" where the right kind of sensitive beings can feel that they are in touch with the departed. "Can any man disprove with finality," James Nugent wrote, "that spirits co-exist with our material cosmos?

One need not believe in a Creator to realize an animating spirit informing all living things, all animals, all plants, all people. Human logic tells us when the temporary body is sloughed away by what we call death the spirit remains near its familiar ground. It does not

migrate to some crowded paradise or beleaguered per-dition, but remains where the body was wont to remain.

This, then, surely is warrant enough for preserving such sacred places as mountains. Let them be a sort of cathedral, freely opened to all men; let them not become a mere playground closed to all but a few.

McIntyre put down the pages and stared out into the night. Was it for this that the Irishmen had followed him halfway across Scotland? Not likely. There had to be something more. Something these Irishmen did not want discovered.

Chapter Fifteen

Two hours before first light, a crash and a gust of frigid air brought McIntyre awake. The unfastened window swung back and forth, dragging the window curtain. Bone-chilling fog poured over the window sill and spread to the floor.

McIntyre latched the window, shuddering not so much at the cold as at the enveloping fog. When he had gone to bed, there had been bright evening stars over the harbor, street lights and house lights in the village, and red and green mooring lights of fishing boats riding at anchor. Now he saw only gray-black mist, as if the old stone house were suspended in fog. He stumbled back to his bed.

He slept again, to awaken later to the smell of bacon and coffee. Half past five. McIntyre got up and put on his old khaki trousers and a thick flannel shirt. He went down the hall to breakfast.

" 'Mornin'," smiled Mrs. McCulloch, bringing juice to the table.

"Good mornin'!" echoed Mr. McCulloch from the stove. McIntyre looked out the kitchen window. The morning that McCulloch pronounced to be good was just a lighter shade of gray than the night had been. You couldn't see ten feet from the house.

"This stuff," McCulloch said cheerily, "will soon lift. Could be we're in for a bit of drizzle, but the fog, she'll lift when the sun starts to warm things up. Now, here's breakfast," he said, putting a plate of eggs and sausages and grilled tomatoes before McIntyre, "and there's starters there on the

174

countertop, if y'want."

"Thank you," McIntyre said. "Looks lovely. You know, I was expecting oatmeal all over Scotland, but everywhere I go it's eggs and sausage and tomatoes. And cereal for starters."

Mrs. McCulloch came to the table with her own plate. "And do ye favor oatmeal, Mister McIntyre?"

"Oh, yes. I like it very much."

"Bless you!! So do my lads! We'll just have some tomorrow, then. McCulloch will be ever so glad not to be cooking those sausages! Tourists seem to expect it, you know."

"I'd like the oatmeal," McIntyre said.

"So, Mister McIntyre," McCulloch said, "and where d'your searches tak' ye today? I know y'want to see the museum, but Missus Owen is over at Skye these few days, and so it's been closed."

"She's to be coming back tomorrow, I hear," added Mrs. McCulloch.

"In that case," said McIntyre, "I think I'll go look for a path I saw on the ordinance map. Apparently there used to be a walking trail from here to Craignure. Postmen used it back in the Nineteenth Century?"

"The trail past Loch Frisa?" McCulloch said with a whistle. "Mon, that's a good twenty mile or more on foot down to Craignure. Maybe more, as it winds a good bit past a deserted village or two. But y'd hae it all tae yoursel' this day, with the damp weather an' all."

"I don't mind the weather," McIntyre said. "I'll just stroll along until I get an idea what it's like, then turn around."

"It's lonely," McCulloch said, "I can tell ye that right now! But I'll be drivin' that direction, so I'll give ye a lift as far as the trail. It's t'other side of town a mile or so."

"I'd appreciate that. I can just leave my car here."

"Ah! I'm forgettin'," McCulloch went on. "Got to do some repairs to Missus Forbes's heat regulator. It's all to pieces downstairs in my shop. Couldn't leave till about ten o'clock or so."

"OK by me," McIntyre said. "I'll do some writing and wait for the fog to lighten up."

"And," Mrs. McCulloch said, "I'll fix up a bit o' lunch into a sack for you."

"Thanks," McIntyre smiled. "Thanks very much."

McCulloch was right; the fog had lifted by ten, giving way to light drizzle. As the little lorry rolled down the main street in front of the Tobermory shops, they could see the spire on the church, the fishing boats bobbing at their moorings, the clock tower, and the sea wall.

McCulloch parked in front of one of the shops and turned off the engine.

"Need to pick up a few bits of pipe an' plumbing," he said, leaning over to peer at the shop, "but I see he's no open. If y'have the time, we might drop in at the coffee shop and hae a cup. Th' old rascal's probably there himsel'!"

"Good idea," McIntyre said. "My treat."

McIntyre had a particular fondness for small coffee shops and tea shops in rural villages, whether in the wheat fields of eastern Colorado or beside a harbor in the Hebrides. This one, Hay's Haven, smelled of rich coffee and fresh scones, of pipe tobacco and damp woolen shirts. It hummed with the conversation of working men, the *clank* and *click* of thick china and steel tableware.

Men smiled and greeted McCulloch, accusing him of idling his day away when he should be getting to work—and, seeing that McIntyre was with the McCulloch, they smiled and nodded at him. McIntyre felt at home. Each man who looked his way smiled and nodded, except one. The longer they sat there at the window table, sipping at scalding coffee and watching for the owner of the plumbing shop, the more certain McIntyre became that one man in particular was eyeing him with outright malevolence.

Not so much a man as a huge boy. Even his red plastic raincoat looked like something a boy might wear to play in the rain, yet his clothes were those of a workman. He was the biggest person in the place, by far. His face, half-hidden by a baseball cap pulled low across his brow, had a childish look. It looked as if he suffered from Down's syndrome. The slight upward slope of the eyes, that deeply attentive look, the gentle shape of cheeks and ears.

This very bulky lad with the childish face was studying McIntyre intently. If it were possible for these even-tempered and sweet persons to sneer, he was sneering at the professor.

"Ah! There's our man!" said McCulloch, nodding toward a figure coming down the sidewalk. "We're saved from the evil temptation o' those scones, not t'mention th' wrath of th' missus should she hear we went straight from her table to the scones of Eveline Hays. C'mon wi' ye."

Soon they had loaded the iron sewer pipe fittings and were off down the road again. Neither of them noticed that the figure in the red plastic raincoat and baseball cap had come out of the breakfast shop and was following on his bicycle, staying far behind them, but keeping the lorry in sight.

"I'll have to get you to take my picture by Isabella's clock tower," McIntyre said over the sound of the engine. "I have a colleague back home who'd love it. But maybe we'll wait until it isn't raining!"

McCulloch nodded.

"I guess," McIntyre continued, "that you've worked on nearly every building in town."

"If I haven't, m'father or grandfather did," McCulloch grinned. "They kept records o' it all, too. As do I. That cottage o' Miss Bird's, for instance now, I could look up for ye ever' time a McCulloch has put hammer t' it."

"That might give me a lead," McIntyre said. "Does it have an attic or a cellar, you suppose?"

"Ver' small attic. Wee thing, and no way t'get inta it but a wee squirm hole up on the outside o' the place. No lady ever crawled in there, I can tell ye."

"Basement?"

"All stone floor, save for a sma' bit o' a cellarage. Might hae been a cistern. Hardly the size o' a closet it is, all stone."

"Could a box, with a manuscript in it, be hidden behind one of the stones, do you think?"

"Aye, could be. Not likely, not down there. Bloody damp. Y'know," he went on, musing thoughtfully, "what y'say puts me in mind of somethin' . . . that bit about the box and stone, I mean." McCulloch slowed down to think, as if the lorry was not going slow enough already. "Hmm. Wouldn't that frost ye? Years ago, mind. Years and years. My grandfather said somethin' . . . or wrote somethin' . . . which was it? Anyhow, y'saying box like that 'minded me o' it. Box and paper inside. . . ."

McIntyre watched as McCulloch's brow furrowed. With his reddish eyebrows wrinkling and unwrinkling, he looked like an Irish setter trying to remember where he'd hidden a ball.

"Oh!" he suddenly burst out. "It was that funny rhyme! The one he said sometimes, comin' down the hill wi' me!"

"Hill?"

"The road from the house to the village," McCulloch said. "We'd walk together down it, past the Isabella Bird place, maybe on our way t'get a bit o' tobacco for him and a wee sack of sweets for me. He'd sometimes start that tune, like a sing-song, y'know. Let's see . . . 'In a wall of rocks, in a snug tin box, papers inside, too high for the tide.' " McCulloch chanted the words to the tune of what sounded like an old Scots air. "Never told me what it meant," McCulloch continued, "just an old man, y'ken, wi' a secret he took t'be fairly funny. Was a mason, as I told ye. Might be the Bird ladies did hae him hide a box in their wall. Too high for tide, to be certain . . . tae get tae that little house, the sea would need tae rise over the roofs of town and harbor beside."

They were well past the shops and the end of the harbor. McCulloch's lorry was chuffing up a steep hill leading into the forest.

McCulloch let McIntyre out at the top, pointing to where the path led off through the trees. McIntyre pulled the hood of his rain jacket over his head and got out. This was probably the dumbest thing he had done yet, slogging through rainy woods and sodden bracken and heather in pursuit of one of Isabella's suspicions about a mailman. And with McCulloch's rhyming clue seemingly pointing the other direction toward the Bird cottage.

Still, he could use a long walk. And time to think. After all, part of the McIntyre method was to roam about, hoping for serendipity to strike. It would constitute a major departure in methodical research—for him—to turn away from this desolate trail through moor and mud where, according to Isabella Bird, a mailman might have abandoned a package of manuscript pages. More than one hundred years ago.

At least those characters from Ireland wouldn't be following him like he was a spy for the I.R.A. Or like it was they who were I.R.A. spies.

His mind now swirled with an image of an old mason sealing a tin box up in a stone wall. McIntyre took a deep breath and went on up the trail. He exaggerated his stride to make it stretch every muscle, looking to right and left for some rock outcropping where a mailman might sit to smoke his pipe and eat his bread and cheese and read mail.

After a meandering mile among dripping pines, the trail emerged into a lonely clearing. The drizzle kept falling. It took all his strength to push through the thigh-deep bracken growing over the path. Some rows of dead saplings indicated an attempt to reforest this clearing, but the soil was probably too sour for it.

When he had forced his way through to the far edge of the bracken meadow, McIntyre looked back to memorize where the trail entered the woods. Someone was standing at the break in the trees, watching. Even at that distance and in the drizzle, McIntyre could see the red plastic raincoat. He looked around. There were no stout sticks this time, none any larger than kindling. Not much cover, either. He was in a planting of trees, uniformly slender, about the thickness of his leg. His own bright yellow rain jacket could be seen for a half mile. There was no underbrush, and there were no handy rocks in the spongy soil. McIntyre got his bearings and struck off to the left of the trail. There was a road in that direction, maybe a mile away. If this came down to a foot race, he would head for the road and just hope that someone was driving along.

The red plastic raincoat left the path, too, and followed him.

He looked all around, desperate to find some kind of refuge now. Over to his right, about as far as he could see, an even brighter splash of red stood out clearly in the green forest, and McIntyre knew immediately what it was. It was a rowan tree, its bright red berries fully ripe. He had read that superstitious people once planted rowan trees beside their doorways in order to keep witches from crossing the threshold. To this day, in Scotland's hills, wherever one finds a rowan, one was likely to find the ruins of an ancient dwelling. Or, if lucky, a dwelling with people still in it.

Moving fast through the trees toward the rowan, and contemplating trying to climb one of the flagpole-like pines, McIntyre came upon a stone, probably a memorial standing stone that had fallen over, lying in the woods like an altar. His first thought was to hide behind it, an idea he dismissed as ludicrous. Then he thought of standing on it, the extra height giving him some kind of advantage. Equally ludicrous.

The red plastic raincoat came closer, so close that he could now see the dark baseball cap. He knew something else about the isles, besides knowing about standing stones and rowan trees—the figure coming toward him, whether a gentle-mannered Down's person or not, was a Scot. A descendant of men who had become legendary for their fury in battle. Particularly in hand-to-hand battle. *Jesus,* McIntyre thought. Then, again, he himself was a McIntyre. His own clan, in ancient days, had wreaked havoc here and there. In an earlier age this confrontation could have been carried out to the skirl of bagpipes and the clash of highland steel claymore and dirk.

Then again, McIntyre thought, letting the rising adrenaline subside again, *we of the Scots blood are also known for our charm. It might be better to try that, as my last defense. Charm.* He hoisted himself up onto the fallen stone and sat on top of it, wearing his best smile. He waited. For the moment a few trees shielded him, so, perhaps, he would have surprise on his side.

The giant boy was surprised. He came along through the trees, his face showing no expression whatever, and, when he suddenly saw McIntyre perched on the rock, his eyes widened until it looked as if he truly did not know what to do next. He hung his head and came trudging on, looking rather like a person just out for a walk.

"Good morning," McIntyre said, trying for a booming, ingratiating tone.

The boy looked up. "G'day."

"I wonder if you could tell me," McIntyre said, "is this the way to Derwaig?" He had no idea where Derwaig was from where they were, but he had seen the name on the map.

"Oh, no." His large, blunt hand pointed through the woods. "This old path? It goes tae houses where no one lives any more. Water gave out, and the damn' Clearances. Those damn' Clearances."

The Clearances? McIntyre thought. *That was over a hundred years ago. And this kid was still carrying a grudge?*

"What about the trail back up there at the clearing? Would it go as far as Craignure?"

The boy looked puzzled. He considered carefully. "Ah think so," he said at last. "Someone said so. Someone."

"Thank you," McIntyre said. "You live around here, then?"

The young man eyed McIntyre suspiciously. "Ah do," he said, emphasizing the Ah.

"I'm an American," McIntyre went on.

"Ah thought so."

"I'm staying with the McCullochs."

A cold gleam came into the gentle eyes. Where they had been more open and inquiring, they now looked hostile. They searched McIntyre's face. "Ah know them," he said.

"I'm just staying with them a few days," McIntyre went on. "The hotel is so expensive."

The boy understood this part. "Aye. It's a place that comes dear. Ah was in it."

"Really?"

"Mother took me there. Tae meet a man."

"Your mother lives there in Tobermory, then?"

"Aye. She's in the real estate. She's the one tae see, y'know."

"The what?"

"One tae see. If y'd be after buyin' that Harris house by McCullochs. Y'shouldna talk tae McCulloch. Talk to mother."

"I see," McIntyre said. "No, I'm not here to buy real estate. Couldn't afford anything! I can barely afford the house I have back in Colorado." The word Colorado made no connection. McIntyre took another tack. "You work in real estate, also?" he asked.

"Nae. Work'd in the fishing, before they gae out. On boat. No fish now, though."

"I see. So you don't think Mister McCulloch knows much about houses?"

"Aye, he does. 'Tis builder. M'mother, she had house tae fix and didna ask him to be the one. Asked anither. What y'think he did, then?"

"No idea," McIntyre said.

"Told th' buyer what's wrong w' house. Told him bad things. House sat there after that, two years unsold."

"So your mother was pretty angry."

"Aye. Fair fashed, she was. Worse, though, was time McCulloch sold a house. Forget 'is name now. Ah could re-member it. McCulloch, he's over tae mainland, finds wealthy man tae buy house. My mother, she could o' sold that house o' his. Says herself she don't go all over w' saw and hammer and do his business now, do she? So what's he doin' takin' hers? Ah'd lik' to know. 'Tain't fair. 'Tain't good."

"I guess you're right," McIntyre agreed. "Well, I'm just here looking for an old book. Might be hidden. I'm David, by the way, David McIntyre."

"Ah'm Hamish," he said. "Ah know you. You're the one askin' questions about that Harris house. You goin' tae buy it?"

"No, Hamish. No interest in real estate at all. Can you keep a secret?"

"Ah can keep a secret."

"I'm looking for a big book, a thick bunch of paper."

"What is it?"

"I'm not sure. But it is old. Lots of paper. Maybe hidden away somewhere, maybe in the rocks."

"Where is it?"

"I don't know, Hamish. Hidden, I think. Have you ever seen any places where something might be hidden? Like a cave, or a crack in the rocks?"

"Big island," Hamish said.

"It's hidden somewhere near Tobermory, maybe. Maybe in that house. Up here on the path."

"Oh, treasure!" Hamish said. "Like the sunk Spanish ship in th' harbor."

McIntyre knew about the Spanish galleon, a survivor of the great storm that laid low the Spanish Armada in 1588, lying at the bottom of Tobermory's harbor. "Not quite," he said. "Just a book that was being written."

"Oh. My mother keeps books. They covers are green."

"Ledgers? Yes. Might be something like that. Maybe a mailman came along here and dropped it. Did you know that they used to carry the mail on foot across from Craignure?"

"By boat. Lorry, now."

"I was thinking he might have dropped this book into a cleft in the rock or something."

"Might have done," Hamish said. "Weather would get tae it, though. Ah need to go now."

"OK," McIntyre said, much relieved. "And if I want a house, I'll come see your mother. First thing."

The giant Hamish hunched his shoulders under the red plastic raincoat. "Don't talk tae McCulloch about houses," he warned.

McIntyre was suddenly aware of someone behind Hamish, someone down by the rowan tree next to an old stone ruin. The figure was studying them through binoculars.

"Who do you suppose that is?" he asked, pointing.

Hamish turned and looked. "Might be th' distillery man," he said. "Saw him before, where th' used to make whisky. Ah don't drink whisky, no, not at all."

"An abandoned whisky mill?" McIntyre ventured.

"Used not to be locked. Ah could go in there. Then strangers locked it, told me to stay away. That man there, Ah think. We go see."

Together they walked toward the spot where the rowan tree stood, but they had not gone a dozen steps before the figure disappeared. What they found at the ruins of the old house was a cellar door, recently reinforced with new wood, locked from within. But they heard someone moving around. Hamish seemed extremely nervous.

"We'll run," he said, starting off at a trot through the woods, glimpsing back over his shoulder. "They've guns. Ah know who they are now. Irish as Paddy's pig, mother says. And guns hurt, and you don't play with them. C'mon."

Running, McIntyre either heard or imagined he heard the rattle and creak of the cellar door being opened. The two of them kept on running, straight down through the trees, until they came to the paved road leading to Tobermory. Hamish went on pounding down the road, heading for his bike, for all he was worth, but McIntyre wasn't up to it. He found a relatively dry boulder alongside the road and sat on it, head between his knees, trying to get his breathing and heart rate back to normal.

He remained on his stone seat, gradually recovering, thinking. Hamish had been right about the papers. If a letter carrier had dropped the manuscript, or had hidden it, this wet weather or the acid soil would certainly have destroyed it long ago. Which left him with only a silly rhyme about a tin box, tin box, hidden in the rocks, above the tide. Until he could figure out that the rhyming riddle meant, his next stop would be the museum of Tobermory. With any luck, the little old lady who acted as docent and hostess of the museum would have returned from her outing over on the Isle of Skye. He pictured a sweet old Scots widow in black, smelling slightly of lavender.

Chapter Sixteen

McIntyre's legs ached by the time he got back to Tobermory, as if he had been running up and down stadium steps. The adrenaline surge had taken its toll on his muscles. His soaked shoes were like lead, his clothes like saturated canvas. All he could think of was a warm shower and some whisky. But tired and wet as he was, he still paused at Isabella Bird's cottage. He looked down at the village, the harbor, the long pier, and the clock tower that was Henrietta Bird's memorial.

He looked toward the Craignure trail. Something told him that the manuscript was nowhere on that trail. There was something else near that trail, something someone wanted to keep private, but it was not the manuscript. But it had been here, at this village. McIntyre was no psychic, yet he knew, he *knew* that Nugent's book had been here, at this cottage. Addressed to Isabella, the package had come, perhaps by boat, but it had come. He had never been as sure of anything. Up on the Craignure pathway, he had said to himself: *It was never here*. But, now, at the cottage, looking down over Tobermory, he knew with equal assurance: *It was here*.

The pier was stone. So was the cottage where Henrietta and Isabella had lived. Virtually every home in Tobermory was stone, and more than half of them old enough to have been built or repaired by the elder McCulloch. Even the McCulloch home itself had been enlarged by the man who sang the silly riddle. There seemed to be nothing *but* stone walls in Tobermory. McIntyre recalled that, in 1773, Dr. Samuel Johnson had visited the place and complained of having his walking stick stolen for timber, there being no trees to speak of and certainly not enough lumber for buildings.

McIntyre felt the presence of the manuscript. He wanted to make a vow that he would not leave until he found it, but his plane ticket was non-refundable, and his money was running low. Wherever his instincts were going to take him, they had better get a move on.

Next morning, McIntyre donned shirt and necktie, practiced his ingratiating grin in the mirror a few times, and set out for the museum. He instinctively knew the museum would be open, that sweet old Mrs. Owen would be back from Skye, feeling a bit of guilt over having left the town's main information center closed so long. No doubt when she saw the nice American gentleman, her first visitor of the morning, she would fall all over herself to help.

McIntyre plotted as he walked. Assume Mrs. Owen to be between sixty and seventy. Maybe over seventy. Born in the 1920s. Her grandmother could have been a contemporary of Isabella's. And the way these enduring old ladies of the isles hang on to family lore, she might know some tales about the Bird sisters. A little of the McIntyre charm, he thought to himself, could lead to details never before published.

Instead of Mrs. Owen's falling all over herself—it turned out the other way around. While opening the museum door, McIntyre was looking at the window display, and he did not notice the raised threshold. His toe took notice, however; it stubbed itself on the old worn stone, and he stumbled inside, falling face down on the floor. "Well, *damn* it!" he grumbled, as gravity won out over gentility. He got up on his knees, and was instantly aware of someone watching him, someone standing halfway up a stepladder in a dimly lit corner.

"I . . . I guess I fell down," McIntyre stammered, red-faced.

"Well, I wouldna mind picking you up," came the silky voice. It was liquid and pleasant, this woman's voice, caressing her words almost provocatively. Crisp, soft words, words warmly wrapped in the sensuous Scots burr.

As he came to his feet, McIntyre let his eyes enjoy a toe-to-top tour of the woman on the stepladder. Black shoes, moderate heels—black tights encasing legs that Lloyd's could insure as national treasures—short tartan skirt—plain white blouse—and a face, if the sudden breathless contractions in McIntyre's chest were any indication, pretty enough to short-circuit a pacemaker. Professor David McIntyre, meet Mrs. Owen.

"Are you all right, then?" she burred.

"Fine, thanks. That's a high step."

"Oh, aye. It is that."

McIntyre dusted himself off. Mrs. Owen took her place behind the reception desk, much to his disappointment. Now he could see less to ogle at.

"And were you wanting to see the remainder of the museum?" she said, opening her guest register, "other than the floor, which you've already had your look at?"

"Hmm? Oh, yes. Yes!" McIntyre fished out a Scottish one-pound note for the admission fee and put it on the desk. He signed the register. She gave him change out of a small drawer, smiled beautifully, and handed him a brochure.

"And you are . . . ?" McIntyre's dry mouth managed to say.

"Fiona Owen." She smiled. "Keeper of relics."

So this is the elderly Mrs. Owen, he thought to himself. *So much for my uncanny instincts.*

Some small town museums are amateur affairs, random

collections of community bric-a-brac. But the Tobermory exhibits had been crafted by a careful curator so that they read like chapters in a book. McIntyre studied them in order, learning local history, geology, geography, economy, and the nature of the people. The enlarged photographs showed the town as Isabella Bird had seen it. There was a photographic display about the author herself, including photos of the cottage, places she had traveled, and the memorial clock tower during its construction.

For an hour or more, McIntyre examined photographs and artifacts. The Isabella Bird display must have been assembled from a large reserve of materials, resources stored away somewhere. The display included two samples of Bird's handwriting, a letter to her sister, and a piece of the Long's Peak manuscript. What other written material might be in boxes in the back room?

McIntyre returned to the desk, where Fiona Owen was opening a week's worth of mail.

"Excuse me," he said. "Do you happen to know where Isabella Bird's sister is buried?"

She gave him a beautiful highland smile. When she answered, he thought her voice had the sensual softness of a breeze touching heather blossoms—the same sort of smile and voice that drove ol' Robbie Burns near to distraction. More than once. "Of course," the voice purled. "Dean Cemetery, Edinburgh. It's the family plot, you know? Isabella is there, too, along with their father and mother. Oh, and Doctor Bishop as well."

McIntyre stared into her deep brown eyes, not at all in full charge of his senses. She asked if he were interested in Isabella for some particular reason, and he blurted out that he was. So he asked if he could see the rest of the Bird material, anything that might not be displayed.

Mrs. Owen was happy to be asked, leading him to a small office and then going off to a storeroom on the upper floor. She was soon back, bearing boxes of letters and photos.

"Here you are," she said. "Take your time."

With a swing of the short tartan skirt, she was gone again. McIntyre did take his time, turning each plastic sleeve carefully to examine both sides of each letter and picture. After two hours, he had found no clue to the manuscript. There were only personal letters about her books and her trips, letters to her from other people, letters from Edinburgh to old acquaintances on Mull. McIntyre read every word from every document dated with a year of 1874 but found nothing worth noting.

He stretched his back, rubbed his leg that had gone to sleep, and looked out the door. Mrs. Owen was working at the reception desk. *Exceptionally pretty woman. And polite,* he thought. She had expressed no curiosity about his interest in Isabella. No questions, quick to help. Now that he took time to stop and think about it, it was almost as if she had known that he would be coming. And what he was coming for. *You're getting paranoid,* he said to himself.

"Well," he remarked, coming out of the office, "thanks very, very much. Very interesting."

"Were you looking for something in particular?" she asked, her deep brown eyes hypnotizing him again. "I could perhaps find something else of interest for you?"

McIntyre's mental warning light went on. "Oh, no," he said casually, "just interested in Isabella's life. I'm from Colorado, near Long's Peak, and I've always wanted to know more about her."

"Really!" Mrs. Owen said. "I've never met anyone who has seen Long's Peak."

McIntyre wanted to say . . . *what about Ms. Kaye and Ms.*

Barr, the two Colorado writers who came to research Isabella? You didn't meet them?

"I took you for a writer . . . or a professor," she went on. "You have that look about you."

Careful, McIntyre thought, and he began to think fast. "Actually, I am a professor," he confessed. Then he remembered one of the displays he had just seen. "I'm thinking of a book on shipwreck legends. You know, fact versus fancy. I heard about Tobermory's sunken Spanish galleon."

"Oh!" Mrs. Owen said. "So you're not looking for Isabella! You were so long with her materials. Well, at any rate, the galleon story is true, you know. It was in November of Fifteen Eighty-Eight that the gunpowder in her hold exploded and sent her to the bottom. Right out there!" She pointed toward the harbor. "The ship was anchored here after escaping from the battle of the Spanish Armada . . . but perhaps you know all of this . . . and MacLean of Duart wanted the guns and armament. Unfortunately for MacLean, or for the Spanish, there was a mysterious explosion, and she went down."

"Fascinating," McIntyre said. "Any attempt ever been made to raise her again?"

"Oh, aye. Many times over the years the salvers have gone after her. Mostly they bring up cannon and iron shot, some pewter plates and such like." Mrs. Owen consulted her wrist watch. She made even such a simple gesture of raising her arm to look at her wrist into a sensuous experience. "Would you like to see the place?" she went on. "They say that the masts were visible at low tide in the Sixteen Hundreds."

"I would, indeed," McIntyre said, glad to steer the conversation away from Isabella.

"It's the noon hour." Mrs. Owen smiled. "Let me walk you to the spot on the long pier where 'tis said they used to see the masts."

How odd, thought McIntyre. *The pier wasn't built until 1790.*

Fiona Owen locked up the museum, and they walked across the street and down the long pier. As they walked by the butcher shop and the pub and the general merchandise store, he could feel the curious eyes upon him. Or on the legs of Fiona Owen. His money would be on the latter.

Once they had come to the end of the pier, she described the shipwreck while McIntyre watched the sea swells, the seagulls bobbing on the lift of the water, the boats rocking at their moorings. She stood elegantly, a light sea wind blowing back her hair and teasing her little skirt back against her black stockings. He murmured—"Hmm."—a few times, in order to sound appreciative, which he was, but not of the shipwreck. After an appropriate amount of time, he made a suggestion.

"If you know a good place to have lunch," he said, "I'd be delighted if you could join me."

They decided on the dining room at the hotel up the hill. It was much to McIntyre's shock and surprise that, while hiking up that steep cobblestone street, he took her hand. Or she took his. It could have been the uneven cobbles that led to it, a natural impulse to steady each other, or she had planned it, or he just couldn't resist the urge. He really couldn't recall exactly who had done it, but they arrived at the hotel hand in hand. Her hand was as warm and light as her voice, as her smile, and felt as if it had always belonged in his.

After lunch McIntyre just drifted. Fiona Owen returned to work, while he floated along from store to street until he got back to the McCulloch house. He went to his room and tried to do some writing, but Fiona was too brilliant in his mind. Sensory memories tingled his fingers and warmed the palm of his hand; he stared at it in mute stupor.

Evening came, and he could not find any appetite. He put

on his parka against the chill sea air and retraced his steps down into Tobermory, ending up on the steps of the museum, that was closed and locked. He went along the empty streets, nodding at the drivers of the two or three vehicles hurrying home, admiring the long shadows of evening stretching out into the harbor. He went out on the end of the long pier and stood staring at the water. The sound of the gulls seemed lonely, the lapping of the water on the stone wall impossibly slow and sad. The sun was down, and a long Scottish twilight was beginning.

In the main street of Tobermory, the pub door slammed. Three burley men came out and started down the pier toward him. McIntyre felt a pang of sympathy for them. At the moment, he was feeling warm and sympathetic toward all of Tobermory and most of Mull. Fishing was poor, and had been for several seasons. All these men had were their boats and their muscles, and with the market depressed and the fishing sporadic they had to eke out a living however they could.

"Look at 'im stand there," said one of the burleys in a thick peajacket, a seaman's cap pulled down low over his brows.

"Aye," growled another, "already reckonin' how to spend those Spanish coins. Hey!" he shouted at McIntyre. "You!"

McIntyre turned, ready to smile and give them a good evening. But the leading man reached out a big hand and fisted it full of McIntyre's parka, twisting it and bringing McIntyre nearly off his feet.

"Y'forget that treasure ship," he snarled. "There's no place here for ye, whether y'buy that house or no. We've been too long watchin' your kind come and strip away anythin' o' value here."

"Sorry?" McIntyre blurted out. "You think I'm after that Spanish galleon?"

"We're the ones wi' the boats y'see out there anchored, and from now on *we* say who's tae dredge up the treasure, y'hear?" The two other men grabbed him by the arms. McIntyre pulled free of the one, but the first man brought back a thick fist and smashed him across the face.

McIntyre punched back, hard, but only caught the man on the arm. He got his left arm wrenched free, almost dislocating his shoulder, and took a step into the bigger man and punched again, this time with more accuracy. The man grunted. A fist smashed into the back of his neck, and stars began to swirl in front of his eyes. He swung and missed. Another smashing blow came to his neck from behind, and everything turned red.

Now he was swinging wildly, his main desire being to stay on his feet. He staggered forward, trying to arrest his fall, swinging at the same time. An arm or fist hit him across the back, and he went down on one knee. A boot came at him, but he twisted and got it in the chest, instead of the face. It knocked him rolling over the stones. McIntyre curled and protected his face with his hands.

"Why don' y'leave, then?" the voice said above him. "And until ye do, y'keep away from the harbor, and y'keep your hands off other men's women." This last piece of advice was punctuated by a vicious kick in the ribs.

After the footsteps faded away, McIntyre lay still, trying to get enough breath to stop the world from spinning. Gradually things went back to their normal dim gray color, and gradually he got up, first to his knees and then to his feet, swaying his way to the nearest piling for support. That was where the policeman found him, hugging the piling and holding his handkerchief to his bleeding cheek.

"Looks as though you got the worst of somethin', " the pleasant voice said. McIntyre looked around. He hadn't even thought of Tobermory having a police force. But there stood a police constable in uniform.

"Yeah," he said. "I guess you could say that."

"Well," said the constable, "these things happen, you know. Men get to drinking and words are exchanged, and the next thing you know I find some bloke bleeding on the sidewalk. What did you say to them, anyway?"

"Not a damn' thing," McIntyre said through his split lip. "They thought I was after the galleon."

"Oh, aye, that would do it. Things have been tight, y'see. Whenever times are hard, the fishermen begin to dream about dredging up gold and silver from the old wreck. They never get a dredging operation organized, y'understand. But they do feel that it's theirs. And would ye be staying nearby?"

McIntyre nodded. "McCulloch's place," he said.

"Let's try to get you there, then," the constable said. "Ye'll be right in the morning."

But by morning, McIntyre was far from all right. His cheek looked as though he were attempting to smuggle a galleonful of marshmallows. His ribs sported a bruise the color of an overripe plum and the size of a number twelve brogan. His left shoulder was full of electric pains that went shooting up his neck when he lifted his arm. His shoulder joint had a new clicking sound. And his neck felt as if he had slept with a brick under it.

There was another man at the breakfast table with McCulloch, a man McIntyre seemed to recognize. He regarded McIntyre with a cocked eyebrow that showed amusement, concern, mockery, or all three. It was the police constable in plain clothes, having coffee.

"Feeling better, are we?" he asked as McIntyre entered the kitchen.

"Worse, I'd say. Your boys play a bit rough."

"Ah, that's mild, what they did t'ye," the policeman replied. "Ye should see them after a football game, all fractures and contusions."

"I'd like to see that. As long as they're the ones with the injuries," McIntyre said. "I suppose you've come to get my version of it or something?"

"No, nothing like that. My day off." He indicated his plain trousers and fisherman's sweater. "Just came t'visit McCulloch, here."

McIntyre poured some orange juice, even though he knew it would sting the cuts inside his mouth, and dipped a bowl of thick oatmeal from the pot. McCulloch poured him a cup of coffee.

The policeman sat back very relaxed in his chair, regarding McIntyre with a curious eye. "So," he finally said, "McCulloch says ye've a very interestin' story t'tell. About a lost book, it seems? Perhaps it'd be a good job t'let me in on it. Let's begin wi' this murder ye think ye're investigating."

Aha, McIntyre thought. *And what side are you on, I wonder.* Still, what did he have to lose? He sipped his juice, winced as the citric acid hit his raw mouth wounds, and began his story.

"It happened in Eighteen Seventy-Four, in Colorado. About mid-morning. A trapper named Mountain Jim Nugent came riding across the open meadow, along with a man named William Brown, and, when they came up to Griff Evans's cabin, Evans stepped out with a shotgun and fired at Mountain Jim. The blast left four or five non-fatal wounds in his face and arm. But one pellet ricocheted from the iron rim of a wheel behind him and entered the back of his head. Six weeks later, it festered in his brain and killed him. Evans turned himself in, but they acquitted him. Brown disappeared."

"If y'don't mind me asking," the police constable said, "how is it a man can fire a shotgun at a man on a horse and miss both man and horse, and still hae a ricochet conveniently hit him in th' head? Have y'considered that your Mountain Jim might have turned t'flee, and the pellet got him in the back of his head that way?"

"It's possible," McIntyre conceded. "Although none of the accounts told it that way. Evans apparently claimed that Jim was raising his rifle from his saddle and was going to shoot him. But it doesn't matter very much . . . Evans was let off. What interests me is who put him up to it. Evans on his own would never have done it. Somebody got him drunk and put the gun in his hands and said . . . 'Jim's on the shoot, and I want you to protect me.' "

"Someone wi' a serious motive, then," said the policeman.

"Exactly. And I think part of that motive, and the name of the prime suspect, could very well be in the book James Nugent was writing at the time. I think he was exposing a syndicate of land crooks."

"And it ends up here in Tobermory, then?" The policeman smiled.

"Yes. I think so." McIntyre was warming up to his topic now. "My theory is that he finished it sometime before he was shot. I think he would have shipped it here to Isabella Bird. They had an intellectual relationship . . . she was probably the only published writer he had ever met. She had expressed interest in his writing . . . poems he had recited on Long's Peak and an essay on spiritualism he read to her in his cabin. And she may have said that she would read it and refer it to her own publisher, John Murray of London. So he mailed it. But he didn't live long enough to get a reply. Three or four months after returning to Europe, Isabella received news of his death."

"Did y'consider," asked the policeman, "that someone simply stole it?"

"Sure," McIntyre replied, over a spoonful of oatmeal. "But who? I think Lord Dunraven would be above burglary. Evans was twenty miles away, explaining things to the judge. Anyone else rushing to Nugent's cabin would have been announcing that they were implicated in the shooting. No, I think he mailed it off to Isabella."

The policeman had been doodling on a page of his pocket notebook and watching McIntyre. "I'm wondering," he said at length, tapping the doodle he had been making, "if ye've thought t'inquire at your police station for the bit of lead that killed him. Any one of our chief inspectors, now, would preserve the murder bullet."

"That would be interesting, I suppose," McIntyre replied, pushing his empty bowl away, "but a bullet wouldn't tell me anything I don't already know."

"It might." The policeman turned the notebook so that McIntyre could see his doodling. It was a set of stick figures—one stick figure stood on the ground pointing his stick gun at two other stick men, who were riding two stick horses. Behind them, there was a crude rectangle representing a wagon, with circles for wheels. He had drawn a dotted line to represent the bullet's trajectory, a line that angled steeply upward from the gun and past the head of the mounted man.

"As y'see," he said with the patient tone of an expert explaining the obvious to a layman, "for your ricochet theory t'be any good at all, either Mister Evans or that wagon wheel would hae t'be a couple of feet taller than the man on the horse. No, Mister McIntyre, I think y'll find that your Mountain Jim had his back t'the shooter. If your police station or your coroner kept those pellets, a ballistics expert could tell you if they had struck iron before striking the victim's head."

McIntyre was silent, letting the significance sink in.

"I'd be willing to bet money on one thing," the constable said.

"What's that?" McIntyre asked.

"That bullet didna come from a ricochet."

"But it's the only possible explanation," McIntyre said. "Three or four of the eyewitness accounts agree on that point."

"All I know," the constable said, "is that, if that's the only explanation you've got, you'd better be searching around for another one. But now tell me more about this valuable manuscript, and why y'think it's in Tobermory, and whether anyone is likely t'bash your head in to get it."

McIntyre's eyes snapped up from his coffee at that, and it cost him another round of neck pain. "What?"

"Just professional interest. If they do for ye, it's me that has to fill out the paperwork."

Chapter Seventeen

". . . and that's all I know at this point," McIntyre finished. "I don't believe anyone in Tobermory would know about Nugent's manuscript, let alone want it. Or beat me up to get it, if I had it. I'd settle for a photocopy. It doesn't really have much to do with Isabella Bird. More to do with Nugent's murder, I think."

"It's a topic of considerable interest," the policeman said. "But y'said the murderer had turned himsel' in?"

"Yes. I'm sure he thought he was guilty, but I think he was just a tool. I'd like to find out who gave Evans the nudge. Even Isabella didn't believe that Evans would shoot Jim Nugent on his own initiative."

The policeman exchanged a glance with McCulloch. "Then," he said, "was Lord Dunraven at fault? Y'say the family doesn't want y'getting too close to Ireland. What did this fellow call himsel', the one who gave ye the writing about spirits and such?"

"Holstrand. Major Holstrand. Didn't catch his first name. His wife referred to him as the major."

McCulloch was grinning and putting the breakfast dishes in the sink. The policeman also wore a grin.

"You two find this pretty funny?" McIntyre asked.

"In a way," the policeman said. "In a way." But his face went serious when he leaned on his elbows to look McIntyre in the eye. "Look," he went on, "while y'do your poking about in Tobermory, be more careful t'tell folks what y'd be up to. I'm fairly satisfied . . . and so's McCulloch . . . that those burleys last night were told t'rough ye up a bit. And while it's true enough that they don't like foreigners lookin' over the galleon wreck, someone put 'em up t'pounding you. And that person is no friend of yours. Just tak' care what y'do while ye're here."

"Well who's my mysterious enemy? Couldn't I just watch out for him?"

"It'd be better if y'just let me get the word around about what you're up to. Once folk know what y'want here, things should go right. They've made a mistake, that's all."

"Fill me in," McIntyre suggested.

"Can't do it. Too much risk o' spoilin' an on-going investigation. Take it on faith . . . it's bigger than a galleon or manuscript gone missing. I can tell ye one thing . . . over in Ireland there's more factions than football players, and they keep a close eye on each other. Major Holstrand, for instance, seldom goes anywhere without bein' followed by the I.R.A."

McIntyre remembered the other man at Fort William, the one the bartender said had taken an interest in him. McIntyre had assumed he was part of Holstrand's team. "So," he said, "you mean Holstrand is with British Intelligence or M5 or the S.A.S. or something? He's a cop?"

"No," the police constable said, "he's not wi' the law at all. But he is high up in an organization dedicated to riddin' Ireland of th' bleedin' Republicans. Evidently . . . and mind ye, I'm only speculatin' . . . Holstrand was seen t'give ye that envelope. And him pretendin' t'be on a bus tour and ye pretendin' t'be a tourist. Anyone watching, y'see, would take the pair o' ye for spies."

"That's the dumbest thing I've heard yet!" McIntyre exploded. The other two men laughed with him.

"Of course, it is," the policeman said. "But ye have t'know that we're not that far from Ireland here. Even a rowboat can make that crossing. And the law dogs of England and Scotland don't have much call t'come visiting in the Hebrides very often, of course. It's an attractive hidin' place, if ye tak' my meaning."

"A Scottish Hole-in-the-Wall." McIntyre grinned.

"Hole-in-the-wall?" The policeman frowned.

"Never mind. It was a hide-out for outlaws back in the Old West."

"I wouldna call us a hide-out. An Irish travel destination, ye might say."

"It goes back a ways," McIntyre said. "Even Columba came here to get out of Ireland."

"Aye. And even Columba was nae the first t'leave there and end up here."

"OK. So," McIntyre said, "you're saying that somebody, maybe an I.R.A. terrorist, a fugitive from Her Majesty's cops as well as the FBI, could be hiding out on Mull, near Tobermory. The major, involved in Irish politics but for a different faction, was seen giving me something. Maybe information about this Irish outlaw's whereabouts. I take the packet and make a beeline for Tobermory. The local sympathizer wants me to go home, so he rounds up some village primates to beat me up. That about it?"

"Aye. That's about it," the policeman said.

"And you can't tell me who this character is, at all?"

"Y'see," McCulloch said, "until we find where our refugee is hiding, we don't want tae tip our hand. We know who the local agent is, but not the hiding place. It might be on another island, for all we know. All we have is that one person to follow, and y'could easily spoil that. If you knew anything, that is."

"Which I don't. Better yet, I don't want to. What's this *we* stuff? You're with the police, too?"

"Just a friend, as far as ye're concerned," replied McCulloch. "Doing what I can."

The policeman stood up to leave. "I'll do what I can to set people straight about ye," he said. "I'm sure they'd be happy to look for your manuscript, wherever it is. And y'can count yoursel' lucky that searching for it didna get ye killed."

Back in his room, McIntyre gingerly brushed his teeth and tenderly combed his hair and experimented to see if he could smile his ingratiating smile without wincing or whimpering, which would ruin the whole effect. His thoughts were on Fiona Owen. He thought his first order of business, this fine sunny morning now that breakfast was out of the way, should be to pay her a visit and lay all his cards on the table. He would also tell her that he hoped he had not caused any friction between herself and . . . what, a local suitor? He was lying to himself, of course. What he wanted was just to gaze at her again. He wanted her to touch his bruises and kiss his wounds and coo soothing words of sympathy. He wanted her to be interested in him.

Facts did not matter to him, not in his state of mind. Not the fact that he needed to get off Mull within the next twenty-four hours, if he was going to catch his flight out of Glasgow. Not the fact that there was a Mrs. attached to her name. Not the fact that three heavyweights had strongly suggested he forget her altogether. McIntyre, grown young again that morning, added a brown tie to his checked shirt, knotted it in a natty Windsor knot, and sallied forth.

At the museum, he found a sign in the door saying **Closed Today**. Perhaps it was left there from the day before. It was early; maybe she would be coming along in a few minutes.

McIntyre went a-touristing down the street, stopping in at The Gallery, an upscale shop for Scottish items. No tourist junk here—the tightly woven blankets and rugs, the finely made sweaters, the jewelry and the china were, as they say in the States, the real McCoy. And McIntyre found one item that he had to have. He should have thought of it before. A blackthorn, the heavy walking stick of the isles. First cousin to the Irish social accessories named for the town of Shillelagh. South African colonists called it the knobkerrie. The wood of the blackthorn weighs like iron and is stronger than oak; the thick end was carved into a persuasive knob. Blackthorn sticks were sometimes used for walking, but were always considered essential items of dress for any gent who anticipated getting into any serious knuckle discussions. Best of all for McIntyre, when a tourist carried a blackthorn club, it looked like a souvenir. That was deceptive. McIntyre's odd assortment of skills—some more odd than others—included a passing familiarity with the use of a stick as a weapon.

Having no idea where Fiona Owen might live, McIntyre passed his time walking the street, swinging his new stick to feel its weight and balance. He examined each building's architecture, and checked his watch against the clock in the stone tower. Then, while he stood on the sea wall, watching some men clean a fishing boat, Hamish came hurrying out of a narrow street and straight up to him.

"Good morning!" McIntyre said to Hamish, saluting with the blackthorn. "And what are you up to today?"

"You said you didna need a house," Hamish began. "If you find those pages, y'll leave?"

"That's right," McIntyre said. "I find my pages, and I'm outta here."

"She told me. Ah could show you a cave," Hamish said. "She told me. Someone told me . . ."—he paused to recall the name she had given him—"maybe Mister Duweyer. They used to hide things inside. The sea can't get at things, not 'way inside. Too high. She told me Ah could show you, but today."

"Your mother? Somebody thinks the papers . . . the manuscript is in a cave somewhere?"

"Not Mother. My mother has too much tae do tae be mucking about with the likes of us. That money doesna grow on the trees, you know. Some folk has tae work, you know. 'Twas Missus Owen. She told me. You should come tae the cave."

"Where is this cave? Is she going to be there, is that what she said?"

"Ah think so," Hamish replied.

McIntyre's heart gave him a nice kick. Fiona Owen, that lovely-limbed beauty in the little kilt. She was a rascal! She had closed up the museum and told Hamish to watch for him. She wanted to meet him at this cave. This was turning out to be a beautiful day.

"Where is the cave?" he repeated.

"Sea cave. You know. Like Fingal had."

"Like Fingal? Oh, like Fingal's Cave!" The Hebrides had dozens of tidal caves, carved into the cliffs by eons of pounding sea. High-roofed and sometimes hundreds of yards deep, some were legendary for harboring smugglers and political dissidents. Some were said to be haunted. Fingal's Cave was famous, although MacKinnon's Cave on Mull attracted its share of daring explorers. McIntyre thought of old Grandpa McCulloch's nonsense rhyme about a tin box hidden in rocks too high for the sea.

"We need your car," Hamish said. "Ah have to show ye."

From the McCulloch house, they drove past fenced fields and open flats on a road that seemed to keep getting farther from the coastal cliffs. After several minutes, Hamish said—"Stop."—and got out. He walked ahead a few yards, searching, then pulled aside the underbrush and motioned for McIntyre to bring the car. It was a very dim track in the sandy soil, its junction with the main road almost impossible to see. It led through bracken and heather to the edge of the cliff.

McIntyre did not want to leave his blackthorn in the car, but it looked like he would need both hands free to scramble down the cliff to the beach. Again Hamish went searching ahead, like a bird dog on the scent, until he found the path.

"We go down here?" McIntyre asked. The path angled steeply down the precipice into a dark crevice behind a mono-lithic chunk of the cliff that had pulled away. There the path became a set of eroded steps leading down into the shadows.

"Down here," Hamish replied.

McIntyre saw the fresh prints of a hiking boot. There were also some animal tracks. He pointed these out to Hamish.

"Goats," the hulky boy said. "Wild, Ah guess, now."

They emerged from the ominous crevice onto a rock ledge scarcely wide enough to stand upon. The goat tracks had van-ished. It was a long drop to the beach. Overhead, gulls cried to each other in the blue sky. The sea swells made a far-off rumbling.

Fiona Owen had certainly picked a remote and private place for this rendezvous, McIntyre thought. It would be a little awkward with Hamish along, but they could probably send him back to wait at the car. He could even walk back to town. *Whoa, boy!* McIntyre said to himself. *I'm getting ahead of things here. What about Fiona's car? Where is it?*

Hamish studied the skinny fragment of ledge until he found the place to go down, a set of handhold niches that looked ancient. Following, McIntyre took his time, memo-rizing the way. The tide was out, but, when it came back in, they would need these steps. The beach was clean, meaning that the sea tide came up high here, so high that it swept away the kelp and driftwood, all the way up the cliff.

Hamish led McIntyre scrambling over a jut of boulders and sharp stones where tiny tidal pools held miniature crabs and urchins. They went along a narrow strip between the sea and the rock cliff where McIntyre looked up apprehensively at the way the sheer cliff straight above them seemed to lean outward, looming over the little strip of sand. They saw the goat tracks again, in single file. They finally came around the corner of the cliff and saw the mouth of the sea cave.

"Urd's Cave," Hamish announced.

"Urd?" McIntyre wondered. What did Urd stand for, unless it meant something like lonely?

"My mother says Urd was No One." Hamish was watching the goats. By some unseen trail, they had scrambled onto a lip of shattered rock overhanging the cave, fifty yards above the sand. They were grazing on rough grass.

No One. Urd. McIntyre suddenly realized what Hamish was saying. He had just been reading about it in the guidebook. "Oh, you mean Urdhr, one of the Scandinavian Norns. One of the goddesses of fate. Sure. This would be Urdhr's Cave."

"Ah have my torch," Hamish said, producing from his pocket a small plastic flashlight.

McIntyre had not seen any more boot tracks since the stone outcrop, saw no evidence that anyone had been here since the last tide. He followed Hamish. The cave's mouth was thirty feet high and a hundred feet wide, so daylight penetrated a good distance. But back deep inside the cavern, where the air began to smell like old sea-salted vegetation rotting in darkness, there was a close, cold feel. McIntyre paused to let his eyes adjust.

The sand floor angled upward. The cavern turned to the right. This might indicate that they were out of reach of the rising tide. If they were trapped back here by the tide, however, the concussion of waves slamming against the opening would leave them bleeding from the ears and mouth. If they lived through it—which was doubtful if the pounding lasted for more than an hour—they would emerge with their eardrums burst. And maybe driven insane. If sane men would be in here in the first place. McIntyre had read about MacKinnon's Cave on Mull, where, according to legend, some cave dwelling evil fairy-folk set upon a group of explorers and killed them all. All except for a piper, and they let him live so long as he could keep piping his music. When he stopped, exhausted, they killed him in the cave. Happy thought.

McIntyre and Hamish were now looking at a large square block of basalt set back in the darkness. Hamish's flashlight showed that it was like a table, or altar. Suddenly Hamish twisted around to look back.

"Heard someone," he said. "Somebody's coming."

They returned to the mouth of the cave, but there was no one there. No tracks, no sign of life except for a rattle of gravel and soft bleats from above.

"You must have heard the goats up there," McIntyre said. "I'm going to find some soft sand inside the cave and sit down to wait." He headed toward a spot where the sun reached in to warm one wall of the cave.

Hamish followed him, then turned again, and hurried outside. "Somebody whistled!" he said over his shoulder.

McIntyre just grinned and shut his eyes and leaned back with his fingers laced behind his head. It was warm and sunny and lovely right here. He could even take a nap while waiting for Fiona to show up. He wondered if she would bring a picnic basket.

The shout and the crash brought him to his feet instantly.

He found Hamish sprawled face down just outside the cave. His head was gashed and bleeding. A jagged rock the size of a cannonball lay next to him. McIntyre looked around, but all was still. Possibly a goat up on the ledge had knocked this stone loose, and Hamish's shout had then frightened it away. Or . . . ?

McIntyre dampened his handkerchief in the surf and cleaned the blood away. It wasn't a deep wound, but it was a big one. The falling rock must have caught the poor kid full force, right over the ear. Hamish was out cold.

"Better get you out of here, just in case," McIntyre muttered. If someone above had deliberately dropped that rock, both he and Hamish were now in a good spot for it to happen again. So he hoisted the large fellow under the arms and pulled and lunged backward along the sand until they were under the protection of the brow of the cave.

With Hamish unconscious, the whole place grew quiet and lonely. McIntyre heard his own breathing over the hissing and roiling of the sea as it came up the beach and retreated, a few inches nearer each time. When a larger wave came, it boomed and echoed into the cavern as it slammed into the sand. McIntyre tried to revive Hamish.

Two things were becoming clear to him. First, Fiona was not going to meet him for a picnic or to give him a manuscript or anything else. Second, if he couldn't arouse Hamish and get him to move, the both of them could drown. He considered dragging Hamish far back into the cave, where the water couldn't reach, but dismissed the idea, thinking of the dank air, the darkness, and the possibility of the sea rising to cover the cavern entrance. A wave larger than the rest broke on the sand and hissed at Hamish's shoe. McIntyre shook him by the shoulders. "Hamish!" he shouted. "Come on, boy! Time to get going!"

The boy stirred a little, then suddenly sat up. A wave covered his feet, which he pulled back with a scowl. "Tide is rising," he said.

"You're right," McIntyre agreed. "Time for us to get out of here."

Hamish stood up, swaying, looking vaguely disoriented. McIntyre maneuvered his shoulders under Hamish's arm and urged him along the sand as the water continued to rise, alternately burying them ankle-deep in swirls of foam and sucking sand. Halfway to the rocky outcropping, the salt water was knee-deep. They slogged along with wide steps like men trying to herringbone up a snow slope, the water grabbing at them, swelling up to float them, momentarily, off their feet. Just as a deep swell caught at him, McIntyre made the rocks. He scrambled up, got a handhold, reached back to haul Hamish up after him.

Now they stood on a bit of eroded basalt the size of a doormat with the higher waves breaking against their ankles. Ahead of them, where there had been a slim crescent of trail at the foot of the curving cliff, there was now only seething, churning water. The water slammed and growled at the sheer rock.

"Can you swim?" McIntyre asked Hamish, wondering if even a strong swimmer could make it across that heaving caldron without the foaming waves knocking him unconscious against the cliff. And, even if he could made it across, how would he get to the handholds and footholds before he would be dragged off the cliff face by the tidal surge?

"It's higher than this," Hamish said, pointing to the water line on the cliff above and then looking at their pitiful perch.

We'll both shout for help, McIntyre thought. Maybe someone had been up there on top of the cave, and the rock had been accidentally pushed, and . . . or had it been the goats? Goats. Something about the goats was mushing around in his brain. The trail down through the crevice, the narrow slot that opened onto a ledge—there had been goat tracks and boot tracks. But none on the ledge and none on the beach. There must be a way from the crevice to the brow over the cave. And it had to be almost directly above them.

"Hamish," he said, "can you stand on my shoulders, do you think? See, up there on the cliff? If you could get to that big rock, I think you could pull me up. I think that's where the goats went."

Hamish studied the cliff, then suggested that McIntyre stand on his shoulders, since he was the larger one. But McIntyre shook his head. "I think I can hold you, if you climb on my shoulders," he said, "but I'd never be able to pull you up after me. Quick, give me your belt." Hamish complied.

McIntyre looped his own belt and Hamish's together, then he squatted down so Hamish could stand on his shoulders, steadying himself against the cliff. McIntyre rose, keeping his back as straight as he could, letting his leg muscles do the lifting. His body, bruised and battered from the roughing up the night before, shrieked in protest. If he got out of this . . . he would have a strong word or two with Fiona Owen.

Hamish gave a grunt and lunged at a handhold, ending up hanging awkwardly. McIntyre twisted around to get a hand cupped under one of Hamish's feet and then pushed up with all his strength. Hamish's other foot sought a foothold in a sea-eroded cavity, but it broke off. He found another. This one held. Next he got an arm around the stub of rock and finally heaved himself up to lie full length on the ledge.

McIntyre looked up as the cold sea water clutched at his chest, half floating him, moving him off the rocks. It was a pulling surge. Hamish's face, looking down at him, was crimson. And, for a face that did not show much emotion, it was registering fear. For coming into the crescent curve of cliff was a wave as high as a house, a wave that would surely slam McIntyre into the stone wall. McIntyre frantically whipped the looped belts up toward Hamish's clutching hand, but Hamish wasn't quick enough to snatch it as it went by. He tried again. Another miss. The wave rolled closer with a huge indifferent rumbling as if plowing the sea bed as it came.

Once more he attempted to flip the looped belts into Hamish's hand. A projection of rock caught it, snagged it for an instant, and Hamish, reaching down with one blunt hand to slap at the belts, caught the loop and pulled for dear life. The leading swell lifted McIntyre. The leather loop pulled him toward the stub of rock where Hamish lay. His feet flailed at the cliff, caught on something, helped him up. Hamish caught his arm at last, nearly wrenching it from the socket, and McIntyre was landed like a flopping sea salmon. Flat out on the ledge, he felt the full weight of the wave hit, the rock shuddering with the blow.

Afterward, Hamish sat quietly staring out at the foaming sea. McIntyre explored the goat tracks, his soggy clothes like lead and his body hurting all over. It turned out that he had been right about somebody being above them. He saw how the goat tracks came from the crevice and led along this wide ledge to the top of the cave. The goats would make a leap up to it; a man could do it by scrambling. And there were boot prints in the sand and gravel on the brow over the cave. There was also a freshly uncovered indentation in the earth, the size and shape of the rock that had come plummeting down. Someone had lifted it and thrown it over the cliff. Who had it been? Unless Hamish had some serious enemies on the island, which McIntyre doubted, the falling rock had not been meant for him. One of the men from the attack on the jetty? The man in the woods who had been watching the two of them with binoculars? Maybe he and Hamish had both stumbled onto something they shouldn't have. Then McIntyre thought of Fiona. What if the rock-thrower had caught her as she had headed toward the cave? She could be in even more trouble than he and Hamish were.

Enough was enough, McIntyre thought. I.R.A. terrorist or jealous boyfriend, whoever had dropped the rock had the mentality of a fanatic. That person had not known whether the rock would kill its target, whether it would be Hamish or himself, or if the tide would finish off the intended victim. Neither had this person seemed to give a damn. If it was the fugitive the constable had spoken of, he was a very dangerous man. And so were his friends on the island.

For now, McIntyre's first job was to get Hamish to a doctor, then to try to find Fiona, and finally to contact the police constable. As soon as he had verified that Fiona was OK, he was going to head for Glasgow and catch his flight home. He didn't want to miss the plane, he didn't want to endanger anyone else, and he did not want to die searching for a manuscript. McIntyre smiled his wry smile. If he did die here, Dean Rolman would have a field day with it. He'd probably create a memorial scholarship and use it to raise funds for the college.

McIntyre went to help Hamish to his feet. "Think you can make it back to the car?" he asked. "We're going to get you to a doctor for that scalp wound."

"Ah know the doctor," Hamish said.

"I know you do," replied McIntyre. "I know you do."

"Where is Missus Owen?" Hamish asked, holding his aching head.

"I don't know," McIntyre replied. "She didn't come. We

didn't see any car, or car tracks, except our own. Would she have walked?"

"No," Hamish said. "Bicycle, maybe. It would make tracks."

Possibly. But McIntyre's gut was telling him that she had never come. As he and Hamish went back along the trail, moving slowly, McIntyre lined up all the details he could remember. During that first meeting in the museum, Fiona had seemed very friendly, as if she had known who he was. And despite his feigned interest in the galleon, her taking him to see it, and suggesting lunch in a place that would require them to take a long walk together, she hadn't really bought the story. Now that he thought about it, she had gone along with his whole line much too readily. Did she, too, think he was working for Major Holstrand? Was she the Tobermory citizen hiding an Irish terrorist somewhere among the cliffs and forests of Mull? Instinct told him she had never come to the cliff. Paranoid instinct told him she had been there, above the mouth of the sea cave, when the stone was dropped.

By the time they reached the car, McIntyre had made a revision to his scenario. In the revised version, he would get a doctor for Hamish and then get the hell off the Isle of Mull.

Chapter Eighteen

The bland routine of my vacation days seemed even more anemic whenever I found myself thinking about Scotland and the good times Lachlan must be having. At those moments I would become lost in thought, picturing the cozy pubs, the cool evenings with fine Scotch, and strolls across heather-covered hills. Some days it was all I could think of.

At least, I had the annual convention of the Cultural History Association to look forward to. There would be old acquaintances to renew and research developments to catch up on. And this year the CHA was to meet in Salt Lake City, a venue far more interesting than many.

All academic conferences go the same—you wake up in a sterile hotel room, breathing the same air that was there the day before, then you indulge yourself in a long hot shower, dress, then join your conference chums at breakfast and listen to invigorating reviews of the previous day's presentations. The rest of the morning is spent sitting on folding metal chairs, going numb on both ends as the speakers drone on. During the coffee breaks, the fast-paced conversations resume. But too soon the posterior and cerebellum are again subjected to the deadening effects of metal seats and monologues. By four o'clock it is time for the cocktail critiques. Or to escape.

Having faithfully completed two days of professional improvement, my friend Lynne and I decided to skip some sessions and visit the venue. After all, one should not leave Salt Lake City without seeing Temple Square and the Tabernacle.

216

Lynne persuaded me that we also had a professional obligation to investigate the LDS archives. The genealogical archives, arguably the most complete in the entire world, were now accessible on the church's computers.

"And maybe," Lynne said, "maybe they'll let us look up our families! Wouldn't that be fun?"

Fun may not be the term for it, but fascinating might be, at least for an historian. The heart raced and the mouth went dry just to be in control of so much information. My fingertips on the keyboard touched the complete accounts of anyone in the world who had ever had any relative, no matter how distant, associated with the Latter-Day Saints.

My natural impulse was to look up my own family name. The index indicated that the branches of the Palmers could keep me in the archives the rest of the night, perhaps for the remainder of the week. Besides that, I knew as much about the Palmer family history as I cared to, thank you very much. There had to be some other family name I could use to play with this amazing computer. What about Lachlan's principal suspects? What if I uncovered some scrap of information to add to the discoveries I already had waiting for him? What a wonderful way to make Lachlan squirm. When he got back, I'd exaggerate the hours I spent on his project while he had been stretched out beside some Scottish trout stream, some leggy highland lassie beside him, sipping the national export.

I decided to try it alphabetically. Entering the name William Brown nearly caused a power outage the width and length of Utah as computers whirred and labored to catalog all of the Browns—not a few of whom were in direct descent from Mormon founding families. Dunraven brought up several names, none apparently connected to the Irish lord. And for the life of me, I could not recall Lord Dunraven's birth name.

217

The next name I entered was Griffith Evans. Lachlan may have a knack for serendipity, but Palmer ingenuity had struck Mormon pay dirt. A descendant of Griffith Evans, Welshman, resident of Colorado and later Kansas, had joined the Saints.

What lovely tools, computers. Thirty minutes later, when Lynne reminded me that we had to dash to the convention's grand banquet—rubbery chicken and peas of dubious vintage—I had enough to make Lachlan not only squirm, but salivate. At the command *print* the computer poured forth dozens of pages of information. Lachlan would be in my debt for the remainder of his tenure.

I love computers.

Two weeks later I was seated on the embroidered cushion of a little Queen Anne chair in the parlor of a refurbished Victorian farmhouse, not far from the village of Niwot, sharing Saturday afternoon tea with Miss Jenny Sarah James, schoolteacher.

"When you first called and said you were interested in my great-grandmother's days in Estes Park, I couldn't imagine how you had found me!" she said, passing the tiny sandwiches. "But, of course, it would be through the Mormon records, because of my grandfather."

"My colleague would call it serendipity." I smiled. "Serendipity is his research method. I was thunderstruck to find you living within a half hour's drive of Boulder!"

"Well"—she smiled—"my grandmother, Nell, lived in Boulder. In fact, Great-Grandmother Jane died there in Nineteen Twenty-One. She and Great-Grandfather Evans . . . Griff . . . are buried up at Jamestown."

Our chat went on and on, and, as the sun slipped down behind the horizon of trees, I offered to take Miss James to supper at a local restaurant. We should have driven farther out of town—this was one of those places where the salad comes drenched in that peculiar viscous orange slime that Westerners term "French" dressing, and where dessert is pronounced "sher-burt" and has the flavor and texture of a carnival sno-cone.

Over coffee, I finished telling Lachlan's story.

"So you see, Professor McIntyre would be very interested in any family papers or records you happen to remember seeing. And family stories about Estes Park, that sort of thing."

"Tell me," she said, her large eyes quite frank behind the plain spectacles, "is he going to publish whatever he finds? And will it dredge up that horrible business of Griff Evans's shooting Mister Nugent? Rocky Mountain Jim?"

"I imagine so," I replied candidly.

"You see, that's my problem. For as long as I remember, my father and my grandmother have been very, very hesitant to discuss that murder. It's not very nice, having a murderer in the family, even if he did live in the wild and lawless West. Being from Missouri and named James, there is already a certain degree of embarrassment . . . Frank and Jesse James, you know . . . and when you add Griff Evans's crime to that, well. . . ."

"I understand," I told her. "I perfectly understand. And was it rather a burden, a sort of albatross to your great-grandmother?"

"Oh, my yes! Grandmother often spoke of it as the reason the family had to leave Estes Park. Had Griff Evans been able to stay there, he could have made a fortune in the tourist business. Just think," she laughed, "I might have been the heir to a mountain resort hotel, if Great-Great-Grandfather Griff had not been ostracized as a murderer."

Miss James demurred at my suggestion of a drink in the adjacent cocktail lounge. "Local schoolteacher, you know," she said, "really shouldn't be seen drinking in a lounge." But she invited me back to the farmhouse for a glass of sherry.

"I will tell you something," she finally said. "And you may pass it on to Doctor McIntyre, if you wish. I wouldn't mind speaking to him, if he would care to come to Niwot. My great-grandmother, Jenny Evans, did keep a large leather-covered box full of papers from that Estes Park period in the family history. It was known as Griff's Tooled Box, not because it ever held tools but because he had tooled the leather on the lid of it. My grandfather inherited the box after Jenny's death, and inside there was a note attached to a bundle of papers. It was from Jenny, instructing the recipient to burn this particular parcel, unopened. Grandfather gave me the box when he was a very old man. He told me how he had once begun to burn the wrapped stack of pages on a grate. The paper wrapping had burned off quickly, but the tight stack only smoldered. When he went to stir it, he saw that the handwriting was unusual, very stylish and clear, and it was about the mountains and Estes Park and so forth. Seeing that, he hesitated because it might have some historical value. He pulled it from the grate. The edges are charred, and some of the last pages, the ones on the bottom, were destroyed. I don't know how many, of course. But I do have it."

She smiled politely at my astonishment. "Your Doctor McIntyre," she continued, "if he can be trusted, might be allowed to look through the pages. However, do realize that it's a rather large family embarrassment. Even if I am the only surviving direct descendant, I must respect the family name."

"Embarrassment," I repeated, setting aside my sherry glass. "You mean because Griff became a murderer, of course."

"Yes. That's a chapter of family history I'd rather not have opened. In addition to that, my great-grandmother's wishes were never carried out, and that seems disrespectful. Oh, I know that it's old past history, and that, if the manuscript has any historical value, we should by all means let it be made available. But there's the other thing."

"The other thing," I echoed. "What might that be?"

"Well, Jenny Evans stole it, you see."

"What?"

"She stole it. According to family legend, James Nugent was in love with her. He wrote letters and poems to her. And what frightened her, frightened her very much, was Mountain Jim's book. Jenny was certain that she was a central figure in at least one chapter . . . a time when she had gone riding with Mountain Jim without telling her parents. Knowing the man's vivid romantic imagination, she must have imagined all sorts of stories he had written about their relationship. She had not been indiscreet, you understand, but she had somewhat encouraged him. And had disobeyed her father's command that she have no contact with the desperado."

"So she saw a chance to steal the manuscript."

"Yes. A young man staying at the Evans place noised it about that he had seen the manuscript. Or some papers, at any rate, in Jim's cabin." Miss James paused, frowning at my sudden smile.

"A coincidence," I explained. "Just recently I read Isabella Bird's account of that nosy boy. She calls him obnoxious."

"Oh. Well, the family story doesn't really say who it was. At any rate, Jim was shot. He was taken to Fort Collins. Griff Evans rushed off to Longmont to surrender. This gave Jenny her opportunity, you see. Possibly the only opportunity she would have. So she rushed to Jim's cabin and seized every sheet of paper she could find. She took it all. There might have been a love poem to her, or a letter, or Jim's description of their rides together."

"And then she had to hide it," I said.

"That's right. She would have destroyed it, but Jim lingered and lingered. It was possible he could return and would want to know what had become of his property. Griff was acquitted, but lost his reputation. Up until then, he had been known as a friendly innkeeper. Now he was a killer. No one was afraid of him, but he had become a local curiosity. Finally, he sold his place to the Dunraven company and moved the family away. Jenny didn't have the nerve to do anything but hide the stolen papers. As time went on, it became a sentimental treasure to her. A reminder of those days."

"Perfectly natural," I said. "Jenny didn't want Jim's papers to survive her. Perfectly natural. Professor McIntyre will certainly be interested in this story, I must say. If you don't mind my telling him, that is."

She did not. And that night in my study, as I wrote in my journal the details of my meeting with Jenny Evans's great-granddaughter, I smiled. For once, David Lachlan McIntyre's serendipity had given me the edge. There he was, overloading his credit card in Scotland. And here I was, right at home, with the Nugent manuscript practically within my grasp.

Miss James had said that she would get Griff Evans's tooled box and the manuscript out of storage, if I would care to see it. It was like asking a pit bull if he'd like to see a pork chop.

A little before eleven in the morning, I returned to her

farmhouse. I was not surprised that she had coffee and tiny sweet cinnamon rolls ready. Also in the kitchen, laid out on the table, were the contents of the tooled box.

"These are the papers," she said. "That's the box over on the counter."

"How many pages are here?" I asked, gingerly touching the crisp edge of the top page. The largest stack was about an inch high; the two other piles were smaller.

"I've never counted them," Miss James replied, "but I'd guess that there are at least a hundred. I did try to read it, years ago, but I gave up. That old-fashioned handwriting is very tiring. Besides," she laughed, "Mister Nugent was not the most captivating author in the world!"

"What are these?" I asked, indicating the other two piles.

"Those seem to be various notes, some torn from a notebook. Random jottings. A few poems. The others are drafts of letters, just business dealings. One is a draft of a letter to the territorial governor, but the rest are everyday correspondence. I read through them while waiting for you this morning. There are inquiries about livestock and responses to people who had asked Nugent to be their guide to the mountains. You're welcome to look."

I put aside my coffee and peeled a few of the sheets from the stack of letters. They were, indeed, mundane. So were the notes. The note pages, of various sizes and thicknesses of paper, contained hand-sketched maps of Muggins's Gulch and MacGregor's homestead, a few crude portraits of a dog, notes from a trip into the Rockies, and dozens and dozens of random jottings such as any writer will make in a notebook. **Is population self-limiting?** one said. **Do essay from viewpoint of ancient crag standing sentinel over the valley**, another said, and still another: **Will statehood spoil the mountains?**

"Would these be of any interest to Professor McIntyre, do you think?" she asked.

"It's hard to say," I replied. "Frankly, Lachlan is rather a romantic. He's hoping to find a complete book manuscript. And he wants it to show, once and for all, that Griff Evans was exploited in order to get rid of Rocky Mountain Jim."

"I see," she said. "I don't understand how he hopes Nugent's book would do that. But I would like to see Great-Grandfather's reputation improved."

"We'll see," I said. "It's up to Lachlan, of course. It's his project."

"May I ask you something?" Miss James said, rising to bring the coffee carafe to the table.

"Certainly. What is it?"

"It might be rather personal. I'm curious about something regarding your relationship with Professor McIntyre."

"Go ahead," I said bravely.

"I've noticed that you sometimes refer to him as Lachlan, and other times you call him Professor McIntyre or Doctor McIntyre."

"I do, don't I?" I replied. "To make matters more confusing, many of his colleagues call him David or even Dave. But I have always seen him as a Lachlan. I suppose I say Professor or Doctor McIntyre when I'm speaking to someone who doesn't know him. Formality, you know. A psychiatrist could write a rather weighty monograph about my images of that man."

"I know what you mean," Miss James said. "I have a friend named Edward, and I never know which name I want to use for him, when I'm with him. Edward, or Ed? Either one somehow sounds too intimate, as though I'm flirting. To his friends he's Ed, but he doesn't seem like an Ed to me. I suppose there are just certain men like that, men who keep a woman off balance."

"Amusing, isn't it?" I said, winking. Miss James's large eyes blinked in surprise behind the plain spectacles. Her hand flew to her mouth to cover a giggling laugh.

I would be curious to learn more about Edward.

She left me alone to read through the manuscript. In the main, it was a description of Mountain Jim's life in the Estes Park valley. A few poems were scattered in the texts, along with lists of dates and names and details concerning the settling of the valley. At best, it was an ordinary chronicle by a rather biased amateur historian. And it was clearly an early version. There were notes in the margins, long passages crossed out, blank places left to be filled in later with facts, all manner of indications of a rough draft.

After perhaps fifty pages of how Rocky Mountain Jim had single-handedly built his cabin at Muggins's Gulch and had explored all the high peaks, alone and in the worst kinds of weather, I came to a set of pages written in a different shade of ink. No, I decided after closer inspection, it was a different pen; the strokes were much cleaner and more legible, the lines broader. This was what we had been looking for. Part of it, at any rate. And my time was running short, much to my dismay. Having spent too much time on the trivia, I now had to hurry. I hated skimming and skipping, but at least I could be certain of one thing—it was complete.

"Miss James," I said, carrying the pages to the living room where she was reading the Sunday newspaper, "do you know what this is?"

"Oh, please call me Sarah," she smiled.

"Of course. Sarah. This is most exciting. It appears to be Mountain Jim's own account of climbing Long's Peak with Isabella Bird. Have you read her book, A LADY'S LIFE IN THE ROCKY MOUNTAINS?"

"Yes, several times. And now that you mention it, I do remember reading part of that portion of the manuscript. A long time ago. I didn't make the connection, though. Perhaps I hadn't read Bird at that time."

I read a few passages to her. Neither of us had any doubts but that it was Jim's version of that well-known climb. How frustrated and disappointed I felt that I couldn't stay long enough to study it.

"What if I had a copy made, and sent it to you?" Sarah asked.

"That would be wonderful. I'd be only too glad to pay for the copying and postage," I said. *Lachlan will be elated*, I thought.

In the end, that is what Sarah did. I arrived back in Boulder Sunday evening, and on Thursday the package arrived, containing Mountain Jim's narrative of the Long's Peak climb with Isabella Bird, a major piece of the puzzle. I actually hugged it, envisioning months of lovely expensive dinners paid for by the grateful Professor David Lachlan McIntyre, Ph.D.

Feeling rather full of myself, that evening I prepared a quiet celebration. Next to my armchair I set a fancy plate of three kinds of cheese, two types of crackers, and translucent slices of apple. I popped the cork from a split of Cordon Negro and got out one of my Waterford champagne flutes. I turned off the ringer on the phone, lowered the lights, and sighed down into my chair to read my James Nugent manuscript.

It was like opening a door into the past, reading the actual words of Isabella's "dear desperado" in his own handwriting.

In places, his account of their ascent of Long's Peak agreed with hers. In other places, however, the mountain man's male ego took over and described how he and he alone was responsible for the group's safety, how he had brought the beauty of the place to Isabella's attention, how he had gotten them safely down again. Nugent ended his narrative with this:

Turning in our saddles we took a long and lingering look backward at the now cloud-shrouded summit where we late had stood and marveled at the thought that we had actually been there where the Rockies seem to uphold the heavens, had forded those glacial torrents, leapt the boulders guarding the great head of the peak . . . and had seen the western slopes of these ranges with our own eyes . . . as snow began to glaze that impressive pinnacle, Miss Bird pronounced it "sublime" and "rapturous."

All in all, the seventeen-page version written by James Nugent was more verbose and certainly more melodramatic than that written by Isabella. As with the other fragments, this one contained internal references that proved the existence of other chapters. Lachlan was going to be very, very pleased with it. Only one thing could spoil my triumph, and that would be that he had found the full manuscript at Tobermory.

Chapter Nineteen

Dr. David Lachlan McIntyre's trip to Scotland could have ended with a romantic evening. Or he could have taken a few days for a tour of whisky distilleries on the Isle of Islay. But it ended instead in the Glasgow airport security office. The other persons in the office included two uniform policemen, a plainclothes inspector from Scotland Yard, and her sergeant. McIntyre sat on a metal folding chair, his luggage on the floor. The inspector sat at the desk; her sergeant and the other two policemen stood. One of them studied McIntyre's blackthorn walking stick and said: "So, sir, you say you were not aware that this sort of a thing is not allowed on commercial aircraft."

McIntyre forced a little laugh to show that the joke was on himself. "Heh. I should have guessed, I suppose. I tried to put it in my bag, but it was just too long. Even diagonally. Bought the thing as a souvenir. But I know I shouldn't have tried to board the plane with it."

"Security was right in stopping you, sir."

"Oh, sure! No argument there. I wouldn't want anyone coming on my plane carrying a club. Not even a ski pole."

"There are places in the airport that will ship it for you. Or you might purchase a case for it so it could go as luggage. The sort of heavy tube they send fishing rods in."

"Could do that, I guess."

The inspector stood and strolled over to look through the steel bars of the window. The policeman who had spoken said nothing more. McIntyre became even more uncomfortable. He saw no reason to be nervous, however; his flight was already gone, and the police did not seem interested in prosecuting him for trying to board an airplane with a lethal weapon.

Finally, the inspector turned to him. "Actually, Doctor McIntyre," she said, "the flight attendant could store your walking stick with the hanging luggage, as they would were it a cane or pair of crutches. The stick is not the reason we asked security to detain you."

"Ah, I wondered about that. And I wondered why security called in four of you. It's a lot of law enforcement for one man with one walking stick."

"We have information that you could be carrying documents out of the islands. Documents of historical value. There is a National Antiquities and Treasures Act prohibiting the export of such items without explicit and formal government sanction. May we search your luggage?"

The question was merely rhetorical. A policemen had already placed McIntyre's smaller bag on the table and was looking at the lock. He held out his hand for the key.

"I feel," continued the inspector, "that I must warn you. You have been seen in company with certain suspicious persons, one of whom is under serious surveillance. One was seen giving you what are believed to be the documents."

"I didn't realize England and Scotland are under such tight security."

"Ordinarily not, sir. There do happen to be those few whom we monitor, in the interest of public safety."

McIntyre pointed to his other bag. "The envelope is in the pocket of that one," he said.

The policeman went on examining the contents of the smaller bag. "I'll just have a look through it all, if you don't mind, sir."

McIntyre got up and stretched while he dug his luggage

keys out of his trousers pocket. The institutional chair had made him numb. "Can I ask something?" he said. The inspector nodded for him to go ahead. "At Fort William, I saw someone . . . couldn't get a good look at him . . . watching either me or Major Holstrand. Was that one of your people?"

"I think we can answer that," she said, looking at the sergeant. "Yes. We had word that morning that Holstrand had inexplicably joined a tour group headed for Fort William. One of our detectives was able to get there ahead of him."

"So . . . if someone from certain parts of Ireland joins a tourist tour suddenly, he comes under surveillance?"

"You have no idea, Doctor McIntyre, the lengths to which some of the political extremists might go. Tours are particularly good cover for a certain kind of objective, as they allow the operative to enter public buildings and travel in anonymity. Tour people tend to carry large shopping bags, large camera cases, backpacks, all manner of bulky items. Without suspicion."

The policeman brought the large flat envelope to the inspector. "Here you are, ma'am. Nothing more to be found in the luggage."

She resumed her seat at the desk and withdrew the papers, which she proceeded to examine as carefully as if she expected to discover a page from the Magna Carta. At last, she looked up. "These appear to be photocopies of some kind of narrative," she said. "The writing has an old-fashioned tone to it. Can you tell me why you have these?"

"I've been over half of Scotland looking for more of it, believe it or not. But I need it for a project. I'm investigating a Colorado manuscript written in the Eighteen Seventies that turned up missing. If you want to hear the whole story. . . ."

"No," the inspector interrupted him. "I should have asked

you why you have only photocopies. You weren't interested in the originals?"

"Oh, no. The originals are only artifacts. To reconstruct the book, all I need are good clear copies. I might eventually want to examine the originals, but only, if for some reason, I wanted to authenticate the date, look at the paper and ink used, that sort of thing. My main goal is just to prove it existed, and what was in it."

The inspector placed her finger on the Dunraven letter accompanying the photocopy. "This certainly looks legitimate," she said. "This letter from the family gives you permission to reprint the document. Curious, though . . . they do not want you to credit them as the owners of it. They expressly prohibit it, in fact. Can you explain that?"

"All I know is what Major Holstrand told me. The family values its privacy. He says they're worried that publicity would bring hordes of would-be researchers to their door, looking for more old documents."

"Some of the old families are like that," one of the policemen said. "Or they might have a skeleton in the closet. Some family shame or other. Very touchy about those things, too, some of 'em."

The inspector consulted her wrist watch. "I'm afraid you have missed your flight," she said.

"I suppose there'll be another one," McIntyre replied. "If I may, could I ask a purely hypothetical question? What would prevent someone from sending historical documents by mail? Surely there are dozens of ways to ship contraband."

"It's not so much the matter of materials," the Scotland Yard inspector said, "as it is the transfer of monies. The various Irish political factions are continually in need of finances. Like any complex organization, they have on-going inflow and outflow matters which must be attended to. With the government monitoring the banks, they resort to various ways of laundering money. Had you, for example, been in sympathy with Major Holstrand's group, you might pose as a scholar bringing him American dollars for some ostensibly authentic scholarly artifacts . . . when in reality you were carrying contributions from American supporters of the cause."

"But now you've decided that I'm just a plain ol' professor looking for material?"

"Yes. And don't flatter yourself that it's your charm that's won us over. You would be surprised to learn how much we know of your background." She smiled to show him all was well. "Tell me," she continued, "did you observe anyone else with Major Holstrand, anyone else with an Irish accent, for instance, who may have approached you?"

McIntyre did not have to think very long about that.

"Sure there was," he said. "The man at Ben Nevis."

"Ben Nevis?" said one of the policemen.

"Beautiful place," McIntyre said. "I had hoped to make the walk up to the top, but it was raining, and the trail was so slick that I turned back almost as soon as I had started out."

"A very wise decision," the policeman said. "I've done the climb myself, many times. Hobby of mine, mountaineering. You were right to turn back. Very dangerous place in bad weather, very dangerous, indeed. I'm reminded of a time when it was only a drizzle. . . ."

"Sergeant?" interrupted the inspector. "I would like to get on with this."

"Sorry, ma'am."

"Now, Doctor McIntyre, under what circumstances did you encounter this person?"

"I found him breaking into my car in the parking lot there at Ben Nevis. I . . . um, can I be arrested for assault for this? . . . I slipped up behind him and got a stick across his throat."

"This stick, sir?" asked the sergeant.

"No. I bought that stick later. No, it was just a good tough piece of tree limb I found. Years ago, when I was a shooting instructor, I learned some of the finer points of using sticks in hand-to-hand encounters. Anyway, this character was trying to pick the lock of the car. He said he was looking for something else, but he was the one who told me about the Dunraven manuscript."

"Can you describe him?"

"Not really. My height, slender. I had probably twenty pounds on him. Sort of sandy hair. No beard or mustache, cloth jacket . . . tweed, like a sports jacket. One of those tweed hats, or cap, like half the men over here wear."

"Would you know him, sir, should you see him again?"

"No, I don't . . . well, come to think of it, I believe I would. Yes, I'm sure I would."

"Anyone else, then? Anyone you didn't know who seemed to be following you?"

"Only Corrigan. He seemed to follow me all over the damn' place."

"Ah, our friend Corrigan," said the other policeman. "And did he ask you to take anything through customs for him? Nearly everyone we see him speak with has to be double-checked through security."

"But you're more interested in Holstrand."

"Yes, sir," the police sergeant replied. "Any other incidents you recall?"

"Just that fugitive or whatever he was, on Mull. I only had a glimpse of him."

"What fugitive would that be, sir?"

"According to the Tobermory constable, there was a man hiding out somewhere in the area, a fugitive from Ireland. I stumbled across a place one day that could have been his hide-out. The next morning, somebody tried to drop a rock on me, or drown me, or both, and it could have been him. Or somebody who was helping him. If they wanted to scare me out of town, it worked. I had to catch my plane, anyway."

"Does that explain the bruise along the side of your chin, then?" the inspector asked.

"That was a day earlier. A little territorial dispute with a few local lads. They either thought I was going to single-handedly raise a Spanish galleon that they had staked out as their own, or they were annoyed because I'd been holding hands and having lunch with one of the local ladies. Anyway, that was where I got the incentive to buy myself a walking stick."

"It has been several weeks since we were in communication with the police at Tobermory," she said. The sergeant made a memo in his notebook. "Tell me something, Professor McIntyre. These men who assaulted you at Tobermory, did they seem in any way connected with a woman named Owen?"

"How did you know that? She was the one I had lunch with." The matter-of-fact question had taken McIntyre by surprise. "She's the reason I went to the sea cave where somebody tried to drop a rock on my head. I was told she wanted to meet me there. Don't tell me she's on your list of suspects."

The inspector took her time in answering.

"Let me just say you appear to have been the victim of co-incidence. Not terribly difficult to understand, but coincidence, nonetheless. The I.R.A. people watching Holstrand saw him give you an envelope, and then learned of your plans to go to Tobermory where one of their leaders has been in hiding. I can't say more, except that Missus Owen probably knew your every move and the whereabouts of the fugitive."

"But she was visiting a sick relative on Skye when I arrived on Mull."

"Sick relative?" the inspector repeated, her eyebrow cocked inquiringly. "And as a professor, Doctor McIntyre, how often have you heard that?"

McIntyre laughed. "Everytime a paper is due or an exam is scheduled," he said.

There were more questions for him, but eventually the inspector brought proceedings to a close by noting that the afternoon was growing late. One of the policemen made three telephone calls. With the first, McIntyre was cleared through customs and security; with the second, he was assured a seat on a morning flight; and with the third he was booked into a hotel room in the Forte Crest Hotel just across the street from the airport terminal building. At the expense of the British government.

The inspector hoped that McIntyre had not been too much inconvenienced, wished him a safe flight home, and left. The two policemen thanked him for his trouble, returned his stick, and wished him a safe flight. The inspector's sergeant offered McIntyre supper.

"It's off duty for me," the sergeant said, "and my car's just outside. What say we drive into Paisley for a bite at one of the pubs? I'd like to hear more about this hundred-year-old murder of yours. By the way. . . . the name's Alden. Jim Alden."

"Not John?"

"That's my father." Alden smiled. "And a cross it's been for him to bear these years. Shall we?"

Driving toward Paisley, Sergeant Alden of Scotland Yard described his hobby of collecting accounts of Nineteenth-Century murders. "Like Jack the Ripper," McIntyre suggested. "Done to death," Sergeant Alden said, laughing at his own pun. There were, however, thousands of equally grue-some homicides that few people knew about.

Over a plate of fish and chips and a brace of good ales, McIntyre told Alden the story of Mountain Jim being shot in 1874 by Griff Evans.

"And so the motive was that this Lord Dunraven and company wanted Nugent's land? Why not just buy him out?"

"Good question," McIntyre said between bites. "Dunraven certainly could have. The shooting could have been arranged by someone else, someone who for some reason couldn't buy Nugent's place. Or didn't want to. There could be another motive. This Lord Haigh character seemed to have been genuinely afraid of Nugent, for example."

"But you're sure it was Evans who pulled the trigger . . . or triggers, I should say?"

"He admitted it," McIntyre replied. "His motive might have been his daughter's honor, although he never mentioned it in any of the depositions. My guess is that someone got him drunk and told him he had to shoot Nugent to defend Haigh. But like I said, that business of the shots hitting the wagon wheel and bouncing back, that sounds to me like Evans didn't shoot to kill. Maybe he tried to miss. After all, he and Nugent had known each other a long time."

"Was the bullet recovered?" Sergeant Alden asked.

"A surgeon dug it out, yes. Doctor Kingsley described it as a bullet that had split in half. Another account called it a small fragment and a much larger fragment."

"Too bad you're in America," the sergeant went on. "Over here, police departments like to keep homicide souvenirs. Daggers, bullets, poison vials, hangman's nooses, that sort of thing. They knew nothing about ballistics back then, of course. But that split bullet might tell you something. For example, whether it was a blue whistler or not, whatever that is."

"Why wouldn't it be? Two sources say the shotgun was loaded with blue whistlers."

"I'm thinking," Sergeant Alden said, "just for speculation, mind you . . . that Evans could have missed his target, as you said, and someone else tried to finish Nugent off with another gun."

McIntyre ordered a fresh round of ale. This was a new tangent. Haigh may have fired the lethal shot, after Nugent was down. "You've given me an idea," he said. "As soon as I get back, I'm going down to the sheriff's office and see if they do have a record of it. Maybe that bullet is there, in some forgotten drawer somewhere."

"Could well be, sir," Sergeant Alden said. After that, the conversation turned to law enforcement in general, following which the sergeant entertained McIntyre with an account of an 1870 murder in Scotland. At the conclusion, he tilted his glass to let the last drop of ale run down his throat. "Getting late, I'm afraid," he said. "I'll be needing to drop you at your hotel and get on home to my missus."

McIntyre thanked him for the ideas and the round of drinks. "I noticed a second-hand bookstore across the street, near where you parked the car. I think I'll browse around there, then grab a bus back to the hotel. Who knows? I might find an old book on firearms that would tell me what blue whistlers are."

"If that's what you want to do, that'll be fine," the sergeant said. "When you're ready, just ask where to catch the bus to the airport hotel. Enjoyed the chat. Have a smooth flight, then."

It was one of those very old book stores with dusty air pungent from centuries of leather bindings and yellowing paper. McIntyre could imagine the odors of pipe tobacco and damp tweed jackets.

Of the several volumes dealing with firearms, none contained any reference to blue whistlers. This did not surprise McIntyre, of course. Thinking it through, he decided that it did not have to be an English term at all. Most likely it was the brand name of a particular kind of shot, a name used by locals and written down by Kingsley as a quaint bit of color. Mountain men in the 1830s and 1840s used DuPont and Galena as generic terms for gunpowder and lead—why not call shotgun pellets blue whistlers?

Still, Sergeant Alden had planted the seed of an idea. Had anyone checked to see if the fatal bullet matched the load in Evans's shotgun? Jim Nugent, in his letter to the Fort Collins *Standard*, said that Haigh "finally wanted to empty the contents of his brave English pistols into me when I was pronounced dead." McIntyre imagined the scene, with Nugent lying face down on the ground from the blast of Evans's shotgun. There must have been confusion. There was the blast of the gun, the horses snorting and rearing, Evans and Haigh and Brown and who knows who else shouting—and, in the confusion, Haigh could have fired his English pistol at the back of Nugent's head, hitting him in the thick part of the skull just behind the ear.

That version was at least as logical as a ricochet from the wagon wheel.

McIntyre did a more or less methodical search of the bookstore's section on weapons, and then curiosity led him to the travel section. The words **TRAVEL LITERATURE** were hand-printed on a strip of cardboard tacked to a shelf. The cardboard had turned crisp and yellow, and the tack heads had oxidized. The assortment of used travel books had long since overflowed into the surrounding shelves. Some shelves were alphabetically arranged by author, others by country, and still others appeared to be organized either by the date, or not organized at all.

He found the usual titles by Isabella Bird. Nothing new there. But nearby, whether by accident or by geographical placement, there stood not one but two complete copies of Dunraven's two-volume PAST TIMES AND PASTIMES published in 1922 by Hodder and Stoughton, Limited, London.

There was the frontispiece photo of "The Earl of Dunraven, K.P." himself, a man in his seventies. The carefully brushed and trimmed mustache, the thrusting chin, the clear eyes with their steady gaze all indicated a man of great dignity and poise and aristocratic bearing. Born in 1841, he had waited until 1920 to "spend the autumn evenings in jotting down reminiscences" of his life and travels, forty years after the Estes Park episode. But this aristocrat in double-breasted uniform jacket and yachting cap was not the thirty-year-old young lord who had coveted a hunting preserve in Colorado. This was a man of family and position and the dignity of age. His account of the murder was at best anecdotal.

McIntyre wanted this book. At twenty pounds it was more than he wanted to spend, but the only copy he had found in Colorado was in the university library special collections, which meant that he could not check it out. It would be nice to have his own copy. He would spend the evening browsing through it, then put it into his carry-on bag to read on the long flight across the Atlantic.

Back in his hotel room, McIntyre phoned to confirm his flight reservation, asked the switchboard for an early wake-up call, and then indulged in that great pleasure of pleasures, a long hot shower. The Forte Crest, an accommodation priced beyond McIntyre's ordinary means, provided not only endless quantities of delightfully hot shower water and large bars of soft rich soap but gigantic towels as well, warmed upon an electrically heated towel rack. He wrapped himself in one of the hotel's thick terry robes and slid his feet into the complimentary slippers. He stacked three of the four over-size pillows against the headboard, made sure the remote control for the large-screen television was within easy reach, and stretched out luxuriously on the wide bed to relax. All this comfort, and all this quiet, and the airport terminal just across the street. Thoughts of his fruitless search, the frights and the discomforts, began to turn into nothing but warm memories.

What with the drone of the BBC-TV and his attention to Lord Dunraven's book, McIntyre did not hear the soft knock on his door. The second rapping, being somewhat more firm, made him switch the television to mute and listen. A third knocking came.

He had not ordered room service. Who else could be rapping on his door at this hour? For that matter, the Forte Crest did not as a rule allow people to go wandering through the hallways disturbing the guests. Any legitimate visitor—even room service—would have phoned up to the room first.

McIntyre cast an eye at the heavy cardboard tube in which he had packed his blackthorn so that it could ride home in the luggage compartment. He should probably get it out before opening the door. Instead, he put his eye to the peephole and saw, in the dim light of the hallway, a familiar figure. A cloth hat, a smallish frame, a rounded knob of a nose made to look even more so by the optic effect of the peephole lens. Corrigan.

McIntyre unlocked and opened the door. "Nice of you to drop by to see me off," he said.

"Think nothing of it," Corrigan replied, "nothing at all." As the small man walked through the room toward the armchairs, it seemed to McIntyre that his bright little eyes darted everywhere, as if taking complete inventory of the place. Occupational habit, no doubt. He dropped his worn raincoat across the bed. He did not remove his cap.

"Drink?" McIntyre offered, gesturing toward the small refrigerator.

"Don't mind at all. Would there be a bottle of stout in there, by chance?"

McIntyre handed him the darkest bottle he could find and helped himself to a bottle of Tennent's ale.

"You're a long way from home," McIntyre suggested.

"Would you believe it," said Corrigan, "if I told ye that I've come to Glasgow on business? Me, eh, business associate mentioned t'me that he'd seen the police escorting a man of your description into the airport security."

"And this associate works in the departure area of the airport somewhere, I'd assume. Well, it took you long enough to find my hotel room. You must be slipping."

"None of it," said Corrigan. "Not at all. I needed to wait until your shadow from Scotland Yard had given up and left the lobby. He was no doubt expecting ye to go out again, or to have visitors."

"Who do you mean? Sergeant Alden? Medium-size man, no hat, light trousers, nice tweed sport coat?"

"The same."

"I'll be damned. And here I thought he had left me in Paisley. The son-of-a-gun must have waited outside the bookstore and followed me clear back here again." It didn't matter. There was no reason for McIntyre to worry about the law, that was sure. "So what brings you here, Mister Corrigan?"

"Oh, the very luckiest thing. I laid me hands on an old portrait that a fellow in Canada is keen to have for his wall. An ancestor, he thinks. And just by luck, a pal of mine is off to

Canada tomorrow to do a bit of fishing, so he agreed to deliver it for me."

"Ah," McIntyre said, gesturing with his drink in the direction of his large suitcase and the cardboard tube containing his walking stick. "He's carrying his fishing rods in a tube such as that one, I'd imagine. Wrapped in paper or canvas to protect them, right?"

"It could be," Corrigan laughed, "it well could be. Nothing illegal about it, of course."

"Of course."

"Let me bring us to why I'm delighted to find you here, though, Doctor McIntyre," said Corrigan. "Y'remember me saying I had a friend who had the ways and means of doing research in the old London post office vaults, I believe?"

"Yes. And?"

"And after our conversation there in London, I asked if he wouldn't just keep an eye out, in case there would be a misdirected parcel or letter pertaining t'the name Bird or Bishop."

McIntyre's heart gave a leap. Had Corrigan unearthed the manuscript, after all? Was this the last minute happy ending to his trip? He drew his breath deeply and tightened his lips, fighting down a wave of trembles that rose from his chest to his face.

"Just by chance, of course, since he wouldn't be the kind of man t'go scavenger hunting on government time. . . ."

"Of course," McIntyre interjected.

"He just happened on an envelope someone had tossed into the dead letter pigeonholes. In Nineteen Oh-Four, I believe it 'twas."

1904. The year Isabella Bird had died.

"What brought it to my friend's attention," Corrigan continued, "was the return address being that of Missus Isabella Lucy Bird of Edinburgh."

"Not Bishop? She was married . . . and widowed . . . by then."

"No, Bird. That, and she had written down Albermarle Street."

"That's wrong," McIntyre said. "Understandable, though. She confused Murray's street with her own. She had probably written to her publisher on Albermarle Street hundreds of times. Of course, she hadn't lived at Walker Street for some years, either."

"I don't know about all that," said Corrigan, "but it came back to London Central as sender unknown."

"Who was it sent to, then? Who was the original addressee?"

"Missus Virginia Evans, I believe he said. In Colorado somewhere. It was also marked addressee unknown."

"OK." McIntyre leaned back to process all this. A letter. For some reason, Isabella Bird-Bishop had written to Griff Evans's wife thirty years after leaving Estes Park. She hadn't bothered to answer Enos Mills's inquiry, and then had written to Mrs. Evans. No. Wait a minute. McIntyre squeezed his eyes shut, trying to recall the name of Griff's wife. The letter was to *Jenny* Evans, the daughter. No one at the Estes Park post office would know where she had gone, after all those years, and so had sent the envelope back to Edinburgh with addressee unknown written on it. The Edinburgh post office had not recognized the return address or name.

"But why London?" he said.

"No doubt," said Corrigan, "some postal employee of superior intelligence remembered Albermarle Street was in London and sent the envelope there. But as there isn't such a thing as Twelve Albermarle, I'm thinking it went dead."

"And so what is in this letter? I assume you'd like to sell it to me?"

"That is the issue, yes." Corrigan took one of the Forte Crest postcards from the table and wrote his address on it. Next to it he wrote a figure, then pushed the card over to McIntyre.

McIntyre looked at the figure and whistled. "That's a lot of money," he said. "Especially for a pig in a poke like this."

"Shipping and handling costs," said Corrigan. "However, if it's not the original y're interested in, which would entail some additional acquisition expense, y'understand, me friend could manage a photocopy of the document. For half that amount, shall we say?"

"Shall we say a third? I don't think anything written after Nineteen Hundred is going to be related to my project."

"Done for a third!" Corrigan exclaimed, finishing his stout and setting down the bottle. "I'll have it posted to ye directly I get back to London. The check y'can mail upon receipt."

"Fair enough," McIntyre said.

"And now," said Corrigan, "at the risk of seeming rude, I'll take me leave of ye." He picked up his coat on his way to the door. "But when y're in the grand old kingdom again, do let me know."

McIntyre grinned as he held the door to usher Corrigan out. "I have a feeling," he said, "that you'd know without me having to tell you."

Chapter Twenty

I didn't need to be reminded that D. Lachlan McIntyre, Ph.D., owed me several expensive dinners. Why, then, one could ask, had I offered him supper at my house? Well, when he phoned to say he had arrived home and had much to tell me, I knew I didn't want to hear it in a noisy restaurant. Besides that, I had a few choice bits of news myself. And finally, Gordon had left a bottle of wine—this Merlot everyone was so keen on—and I thought that it would be just lovely with some filet mignon.

"And so," Lachlan was saying, after supper, as we moved into the living room for coffee, "I wrote you that long letter from Fort William, and the next day this Major Holstrand showed up with another chapter from Nugent's manuscript. Wait until you see it! Pretty weird stuff. Nugent must have given it to Dunraven as an attempt to establish common ground. People haven't been giving Nugent enough credit for being civilized and educated, you know. I think Isabella Bird had him pegged right, better than anyone since. Dunraven wasn't such a bad guy, either . . . he soon tired of the land scheme and went home to the wife and kids. It was Theodore Whyte and his buddy, that cousin of Dunraven's, who kept the land scheme going. They built The English Hotel."

"That situation was borne out by my research as well," I said. Correcting in mid-sentence for the passive voice, I added: "In fact, I think I've uncovered quite a few interesting details about it. But . . . are you up to hearing all this? You look as though your flight is catching up to you."

"I'm OK. The strange thing, see, is that the Dunraven descendants tried to use the manuscript to get rid of me. Just like that bunch of loonies at Tobermory was supposed to distract me . . . I thought from the manuscript search, but it didn't have anything to do with that. But it would have, except for this book." The book in question was one he had brought with him to the couch.

"Wait," I interrupted. "What loonies? What happened at Tobermory? One of us isn't being as lucid as usual, and I think it's the one who just had the long airplane trip."

He opened to the title page and held it up for me. PAST TIMES AND PASTIMES by the Earl of Dunraven, K.P., C.M.G. The facing page was a photograph of a handsome older man in yachting uniform. The earl himself. Looking at the aristocracy in that visage, I felt like making a curtsy.

"Now listen to this," Lachlan went on. His page marker was a reply coupon torn from an in-flight magazine. "*This* is what the family hoped I wouldn't find. They hoped I would take their gratuitous piece of the manuscript puzzle, ecstatic that I could reassemble the whole document, and forget about Nugent's murder. Nugent's murder is the skeleton in the Adare closet."

"You're kidding!" I said. "You can't seriously think that the Earl of Dunraven himself killed Mountain Jim."

"I'm not kidding. Listen to what the good earl writes on page one hundred and forty. I quote . . . 'Evans lived in quite a decent, comfortable log-house, and Jim in a shanty some fifteen miles away. Evans and Jim had a feud, as per usual about a woman—Evans's daughter. One fine day I was sitting by the fire, and Evans asleep on a sort of sofa, when some one rushed in shouting "Get up . . . here's Mountain Jim in the coral, and he is looking very ugly." Up jumped Evans, grabbed a shot gun, and went out. A sort of duel eventuated, which ended in Jim getting all shot up with slugs: no casual-

ties on our side. . . . After a while we got him back to his
shanty. Dr. Kingsley went with him and reported that he
could not possibly live, for he had one bullet in his skull and
his brains were oozing out, and he did not know how many
more slugs were embedded in various parts of his person.'
There's more," Lachlan concluded, "but that's the kernel of
it."

"I'm afraid I don't see your point," I said.

" '*I* was sitting by the fire!' Evans asleep on the sofa!
Dunraven was the man in the cabin with Evans! In his
memoir, years and years later, Lord Dunraven said that he
was the mysterious motivation behind Evans's act of murder.
He was awake, he heard someone yell that Jim was coming,
he saw Evans wake up and seize the shotgun. And if
Dunraven didn't outright encourage Evans to fire, at the very
least he didn't lift a finger to stop it. Remember the other version, too, in which an *English voice* begged Evans to protect
him by killing Jim. That's what the Dunraven descendants
didn't want me to stumble across. Those other reports agree
on one thing . . . somebody with Evans urged him to take the
loaded shotgun and go out to shoot Nugent. Nugent said it
was Haigh who was in the cabin, but neither Dunraven nor
Kingsley . . . and make a note of that . . . mentioned Haigh
being there at all."

"What about Kingsley? Was he there?"

"No, and that's a crucial point. He was off hunting somewhere. But in Kingsley's version . . ."—Lachlan went rum-
maging through his attaché case, looking for the file marked
Kingsley—"in Kingsley's version, and I quote . . . 'Griff, the
Welshman, dozing in his bed by the open door, and a wandering Englishman, who was dawdling about in those parts
under the pretense of hunting, seated on the doorstep . . .
when Jim evidently tried to draw a bead on the seated

Englishman . . .' and so on."

"Proving what, if anything?" I asked.

"Look at the language. Kingsley called him an *Englishman*. He made a light-hearted jibe about him *dawdling* and pretending to hunt. And he made absolutely no mention of Dunraven being anywhere near. Or anywhere. That's because he had already told the reader where Dunraven was. . . . or where he thought he was. Later on, Kingsley wrote that Dunraven 'behaved very kindly in the matter' by insisting on Jim being taken down to a hospital. But if you know Dunraven's version, you would tend to interpret Kingsley's description as a direct reference to Dunraven. It would confirm the earl's presence. Or, at least, that's what the Dunraven family probably thinks."

"Beg your pardon? You spoke with the family?"

"No, no," Lachlan said. "But if the family has a copy of Dunraven's PAST TIMES AND PASTIMES, they are certain to own a copy of Kingsley's NOTES ON SPORT AND TRAVEL. The two men were lifelong friends. I think someone in the past hundred years put the two accounts together, noticed the discrepancies, and came to the conclusion that the illustrious ancestor had been the one in the cabin, and that he probably got Griff Evans drunk and sent him out with the shotgun to kill Nugent. Hardly a noble thing to do. The Dunraven family was already associated with land theft in Estes Park. . . . they don't need this added to the story."

"So," I said, "you are now going to publish the real story?"

"No, not this story," Lachlan said. "No need to. Besides, I don't believe it."

"You don't believe Dunraven's own account? I'd love to hear you explain that! It should be fascinating. But first let me tell you what I found out about Isabella Bird. . . ."

"OK, here's the situation," Lachlan said. The professor

was clearly too full of himself to listen to me. "It's very, very common with Victorian travel accounts. Mark Twain, for instance, made mistakes in ROUGHING IT because he relied on his brother's diary to augment faint recollections. Here was Lord Dunraven, the earl, seventy years old, writing his memoirs in the autumn of his life. It had been forty years since he was in Colorado. He tried to recollect the things that happened there. Now look at this." Lachlan showed me the first page of the Foreword to PAST TIMES AND PASTIMES. "Dunraven began by describing the collision of his yacht *Valkyrie II* with the *Satanita* at Hunter's Quay on the Clyde in Eighteen Ninety-Four. And he said that his personal belongings, including his diary, went to the bottom of the sea. He asked the reader to forgive him for gaps and errors because he had lost his diary in that accident. If his diary contained a first-hand account of Mountain Jim's murder, it lies in the master's cabin of a wrecked yacht in twenty fathoms of water."

"And you are going to go look for it?" I smiled, removing the coffee cups and setting out the cognac decanter and two snifters.

"You never know," Lachlan said. "But my point is that his memory needed help, and he said so in his Foreword. Did he use Kingsley's book, which had been published in Nineteen Hundred? Sure he did. In fact, Dunraven's chapter on Colorado was in a section called 'Travel and Sport,' a virtual copy of Kingsley's title. So, follow this. The killing was a long time ago. Dunraven found it hardly worth writing about . . . in one paragraph he wrote about the shotgun slugs and Jim's brains oozing out, and in the next paragraph he nonchalantly went on to describe how irrigation and cultivation affects the weather. He had been reading Kingsley's version. It was full of good memories of when they were young, bright lads of good family, larking about in Colorado. Both of them were witty and subtle. Kingsley at one point joked that the air was so pure in Estes that nothing can die of infection there, so Mountain Jim had to go elsewhere to perish.

"No doubt with a smile of reminiscence wrinkling the corners of his mouth, Dunraven began to examine the sentence about this 'wandering Englishman who was dawdling about in those parts under the pretense of hunting.' Who could Kingsley have been referring to? Dunraven himself, of course. It would have been just like Kingsley to kiddingly call him *English* as many Americans had before learning that his fine accent was upper-class Irish. How like Kingsley, that rascal, to have said he was *dawdling* and *pretending* to hunt. The good old earl might even have assumed that Kingsley was covering up for him. Calling him English and all that. Gradually, the Earl of Dunraven constructed a false memory of the event. Dunraven didn't remember Haigh. Or William Brown. He added the detail of the *coral*, as he called it, and called the shooting *a kind of a duel* even though witnesses had said that Griff was the only one to pull a trigger. No, Hank," Lachlan finished, toasting me with the Courvosier, "the Dunraven family has been protecting an empty closet, for there ain't no skeleton in it. Just an old man who misread one whimsical sentence."

"I'd love to find that lost diary of his," I said.

"You would? You? Why, Hank! That's very encouraging! Maybe the Nugent project has given you the literary anthropology bug, after all. Really, it's a whole new you. Let's take off next summer and go diving in the Clyde."

"You just want to get me into one of those tight rubber suits, you lech."

"You're right," he confessed. "But that's enough of that. Tell me what you found while I was playing around in the land of kilts and honeys."

After extracting a promise of an elegant dinner, I brought out my box of papers. While Lachlan sorted through them, I told him about Isabella's reference to that obnoxious boy which proved, to me at least, that Isabella was aware of the manuscript's existence. My other news, the revelation that Nugent had sold his homestead claim months before his murder, puzzled Lachlan as much as it had puzzled me.

"You know," he said, "that's just one more loose end. Like Dunraven thinking he was the man behind Evans. It just doesn't solve anything. We are overlooking something, my dear Watson, and I have no idea what it is. We have different accounts of the shooting, and your latest revelation takes away the motive. If somebody set up this murder, but not to get rid of Nugent, then it doesn't add up."

"Dunraven wrote that the motive was Evans's daughter," I reminded him. "In that case, it wouldn't matter whether Jim had sold his claim or not."

"Baloney. Too convenient. *Everybody* would think that. Mills thought so . . . Bird seems to have thought so. It's the good old romantic cliché, isn't it? But tell me . . . how many actual murders have you heard of in which a father shoots his daughter's admirer? Outside of romance novels, I mean. Besides that, if Jim sold his place, it would mean he was going to leave Estes Park. Why murder him?"

I saw his point, of course.

Lachlan was thrilled that I had uncovered Mountain Jim's account of the Long's Peak ascent. As soon as he recognized what it was, he seized it in one hand and began pacing dramatically through my living room, waving his snifter for emphasis, reading it in a grandiloquent soliloquy.

Finally he flopped onto the couch, looking as exhausted as if he had been climbing the peak with them. After resting—

and sipping a bit of restorative cognac—he began laying out the manuscript chapters, each in its file jacket, on the floor beside my coffee table.

"No good," he said. "Too much missing, still. Nope, Professor Palmer, we just don't have a book here. And look how good the handwriting is. Neat margins, too. These are handwritten second copies. Somewhere, somehow, I've overlooked the first copy, the complete version of Mountain Jim's manuscript. He *had* a full, clean copy. Where is it?"

"Perhaps when your friend . . . what was his name? . . . Corrigan? . . . sends you Isabella's letter," I said, "it will be the clue you need. Perhaps she told Jenny Evans where the manuscript was, suspecting she had little time left to live. Perhaps the letter was to tell Jenny that the manuscript was coming."

"Perhaps you should just dream on," the professor said, looking at his watch. "Guess what time it is? If we go on talking for another half hour, it'll *perhaps* be time for me to buy you breakfast. Or would you rather go to bed?"

I looked for the leer behind that last question, but Lachlan's face showed an innocent blankness. His features were as travel-rumpled as his sports jacket. Even though he was wrinkled around the eyes, he was still quite handsome. But he lacked his lecherous sparkle. *Jet lag*, I thought. Nasty stuff!

"Bed, I think. Good night, David."

" 'Night, Hank," he said, picking up his jacket from the chair. "I can just leave all these files and stuff here tonight, can't I? Suddenly very tired, don't feel like wrestling with it."

Too tired to wrestle? Either the jet lag had been particularly hard on Lachlan, or my charms were slipping. I hoped it was jet lag. I gently closed the front door behind him and turned to survey the wreckage. Loose sheets of paper had floated to the carpet, notes on torn notebook pages and

252

stickum tags in three different sizes littered the couch. The coffee table centerpiece I had carefully arranged was surrounded by yawning file folders weighted with empty snifters.

The place was an academic war zone, and we still had nothing. Correction. *Lachlan* had nothing. Who had told Evans to pull the trigger? Where was James Nugent's manuscript? We were no closer to finding out than we had been three months ago.

It was a more neatly pressed and rested Professor McIntyre who was shown through the Larimer County Sheriff's Department offices to the cubicle of Deputy Sheriff Wayne Bissell. The partitioned enclosure was crammed with boxes of files, stacks of books, and baskets full of correspondence. Deputy Bissell's Army surplus desk was shoehorned into one corner, where the partition met the radiator, and another desk acted as a clutter repository in the corner opposite.

The deputy was busy at a computer keyboard, but waved in the direction of an empty chair. The chair, like its companion at the other desk, looked like a courtroom cast-off.

"I read in the *Post* that Larimer County is asking voters for a new office building," McIntyre said. "Now I see why."

"No kidding," the deputy replied, his fingers flying across the keys and his eyes darting from a paper on his desk to the monitor. "Just give me a minute to finish this."

McIntyre found a copy of *Guns and Ammo* under his chair and flipped through it while he waited. Bissell finished typing, punched in the print command, then the save command, then swiveled around to face McIntyre.

"OK. That's done. Now, what can I do for you?"

It did not take a genius to know that the deputy's work schedule was as overburdened as his office cubicle, so McIntyre tried to make the facts as succinct as possible.

"While looking for this manuscript, I've uncovered some inconsistencies in accounts of Jim Nugent's murder in Eighteen Seventy-Four. The court records are gone, that much is certain. A Scotland Yard inspector wondered if the sheriff's office kept a collection of murder artifacts. Maybe the shotgun pellet that killed Nugent would still be around, somewhere."

Deputy Bissell looked about the cluttered little office space. "You can pretty much see how much room we have. Anyway, they wouldn't have kept anything like that. The coroner, or whoever dug the lead out of the victim's brain, would probably have tossed it out. There wouldn't be any way to match it to a weapon, not in Eighteen Seventy-Four. Especially not a shotgun. You say it entered the back of the victim's head?"

"That's right," McIntyre explained. "Doctor Kingsley, who was the first doctor to see Nugent after the shooting, found minor wounds on the face and on one arm. His written version accounted for all six balls from the shotgun load."

"Six?"

"Yes. Four hit Nugent around the face, one went through his biceps . . . he was probably shielding himself with his arm up, like this"—he demonstrated—"and the sixth one hit the steel rim of a wagon wheel behind Nugent and bounced back. The ricochet entered his skull just behind the ear. That's the one that killed him."

The deputy leaned forward, interested. "I'd like to see that piece of lead myself," he said. "Tell me about this Doctor Kingsley. Why did he expect to find six balls?"

"I don't know. That's just what he said . . . an unaccounted-for sixth bullet . . . were his words. Called them blue whistlers and heavy shot, but I haven't been able to find out what blue whistlers are."

Deputy Bissell picked up his letter opener, the handle of which was a brass cartridge case, and played with it, deep in thought. "You know the size of the gun?" he asked. "The gauge?"

"No. It was possibly English."

"Probably a Ten or Twelve Gauge. Hand me that big book on the shelf there, would you? The thick, brown one."

He searched the index, did not find blue whistlers listed, then turned to a page of tables comparing shotgun loads and bore sizes. He showed it to McIntyre.

"Let's assume it was a Ten Gauge, which would have been the most popular size in Eighteen Seventy-Four. Depending on the size of balls they loaded into it, it could have been used for rabbits, ducks, coyotes, skunks, deer, even men."

"Evans had trouble with skunks. And porcupines. They got under his cabins. Somebody mentioned that a young brown bear had been a nuisance, too."

"Large shot, then. And Kingsley said there should have been six pellets. Did he know his weapons?"

"I imagine he did," McIntyre said. "He and Dunraven hunted all the time, all over the world."

"Well, he was wrong this time," the deputy said, pointing his letter opener at the ballistics table. "There it is. A Ten Gauge load of Number Zero buckshot weighs between seven-eighths and one and three-eighths ounces . . . that's the maximum a reasonable powder charge could push any kind of distance. Let's look at the maximum load, one and three-eighths ounces of black powder. And let's assume it was Number Zero buckshot. This table says there would be twelve pellets to the load. When they're as big as Number Zero we call them bullets or balls."

"Oh?" McIntyre said. "How big would a Number Zero ball be?"

Deputy Bissell consulted a chart on the next page. "Thirty-Two caliber," he said. "Thirty-Two one-hundredths of an inch across."

McIntyre whistled in amazement. "I was imagining something the size of a B-B, not the size of a Thirty-Two! No wonder that single ball killed him. It would have lost power, bouncing off the wagon wheel, but still have been able to penetrate the brain. But why would Kingsley say that he expected to find six?"

"Don't know," the deputy said. "But if I was investigating this murder, I would find that a very interesting question. How did he know what the gun was loaded with? First, it's because he was the one who had loaded it. Probably a muzzle-loader, so the loader knows what he put in. Maybe he just put in six balls for some particular reason. Second, somebody else who loaded it told him, probably after the shooting, that there were six balls. Did Evans load it, maybe? Or Dunraven?"

"Now I have another puzzle on my hands." McIntyre laughed, starting to get up. "Well, I appreciate your time. . . ."

"The real puzzle is in the ricochet," the deputy said.

McIntyre sat down again.

"Know what those are?" Bissell asked, pointing the letter opener at a photograph tacked to the partition. It showed Bissell and two other deputies standing beside three human-size target silhouettes.

"Targets," McIntyre answered. "Probably the police shooting range."

"Steel plate targets," Bissell said.

McIntyre looked closely. The targets did seem to be made of steel. The paint was chipped by bullets. "OK," he said, "you got me. What am I supposed to see here?"

"When we go out for target practice, we shoot at steel targets. The reason it's safe to do that is because the bullets don't ricochet straight back. An occasional bullet will splatter, which is why we wear goggles. But a slug doesn't bounce straight back. It would have to hit the steel at an angle. If it didn't splatter, it would fly off and keep going. Remember physics? It's impossible for a ricochet to come straight back."

"So you're saying that a shotgun ball couldn't have bounced off a wagon wheel and hit Nugent in the back of the head," McIntyre said.

"Not if it went past him to begin with." Deputy Bissell took a sheet of graph paper and began to make a sketch. As he drew, he went on with his explanation. "Your ricochet could possibly happen, but only if the wagon wheel was located somewhere between the shooter and the victim. And if the victim had his back to the wheel. But if four balls hit the face, how could the other one hit him in back? And you said that the ball they found in his skull was split in half?"

"Well, in two pieces."

"OK, think of the odds of that happening. If the ball hit the wheel, and, if by some quirk of physics it bounced back *and* penetrated farther than any of the direct hits had, what are the odds that both pieces of it would still hit in the same place?" Deputy Bissell turned his diagram for McIntyre to look at. Like the Tobermory constable's sketch, it showed a man on the ground, holding a gun with a long barrel, and a man on a horse. There was a line from the muzzle of the barrel to the man's head. "This is the shooter," he continued, pointing at the first figure. "Let's assume the muzzle of the shotgun was about five feet from the ground. Then let's say that the head of the man on the horse was about eight feet from the ground. Make the distance about thirty feet, and look what happens to the trajectory angle. He's shooting way too high to hit a wagon wheel behind the victim, unless that wheel was about twenty feet tall."

McIntyre studied the stick figures. The logic was inescapable. "Well," he said, "that blows the ricochet theory all to hell. What about this . . . Kingsley wrote that Nugent was sheltering himself behind the wagon, drawing a bead on the man sitting outside the cabin. Kingsley was the only one to tell it that way. But would that account for the ricochet?"

Deputy Bissell thought a moment. "If I was the officer looking into this homicide, I wouldn't believe anybody. One witness said Nugent was on a horse, and another one said he was hiding by a wagon. One guy said he was riding by with his gun across his saddle. And then there are one or more people who know how the gun was loaded. And wounds in both the front and back of Nugent's head. There's something missing here."

"That's been the story of my life this month," McIntyre said, rising to go. "Any suggestions?"

"Beats me," the deputy said. "Whoever loaded that gun would be my first suspect. For some reason, he told the doctor to look for six shotgun balls. But something else happened there. Something the witnesses didn't see happen. Even Nugent didn't see it happen. All these different eyewitness accounts seem to be trying to account for something they can't quite account for. You know, we had a case here in Larimer County once. Family dispute. Woman took a shotgun and fired at her husband, but missed. He died anyway. The autopsy couldn't find a single pellet in him . . . turned out he had died of a heart attack. Maybe Nugent had a stroke when he heard the gun go off!"

"Maybe," McIntyre said, "helped by that bullet in his brain. Well, I have to go. Thanks for all your help."

"Keep me posted," Deputy Bissell said. "Take my card. It has my e-mail address on it. I'd like to hear what you come up with."

McIntyre made his way out of the maze of cubicles, hoping the county would get its new facility. Crossing the lawn to get to his truck, he aimed an imaginary shotgun at an imaginary man on horseback.

"Boom," he whispered. Shotgun pellets flew skyward. Thick white smoke filled the air, enveloping Evans. Brilliant sunlight hitting the smoke dazzled Evans. He was drunk. He had just emerged from a dark cabin into the bright day. Between the glare and the smoke and the whisky, McIntyre reflected, Evans hadn't seen where the shot went. He probably hadn't seen Nugent fall. There's the roar of the blast, finally the smoke clears, and Evans was standing there, clutching the gun, and somebody told him he'd killed Mountain Jim.

McIntyre stopped. OK, imagine that Jim wasn't on horseback. He was hiding behind some wagon wheel, drawing a bead with his rifle. Now Evans, drunk and blinking from the morning glare, faced a real sharpshooting challenge. All six balls, if there were six, needed to miss the spokes and the rim and the rifle stock that Jim had against his cheek. As five of them get through the obstacle course to strike Jim in the face, a sixth bullet needed to circle around and hit him behind the ear. Could be.

Afterward, Jim had fallen behind the wagon, which no one mentioned, not even Kingsley. Again, the sun was glaring, Evans was drunk, and the gun blast made his ears ring. The thick white gunsmoke obscured everything for a minute. Evans stood there with the gun, waiting to see what he had hit. Or maybe waiting for Jim to shoot back. Evans couldn't have seen what happened, not right away. Neither could Kingsley, who wrote the version in which Jim was behind the wagon. Kingsley, by his own account, was far up the valley, tracking a bear.

The man most likely to know what had happened was Nugent himself. He wrote that he had been on his horse. He had seen Evans raise the gun, and the next thing he knew he was on the ground with head wounds. He had heard an English voice say—"Give him the other barrel."—and then he had passed out.

McIntyre drove away thinking about his friend Jon Iron Snake Manley, a modern-day buckskinner who was an expert in black powder guns and owned a riding mule. Maybe he'd be willing to help reënact the shooting of Mountain James Nugent.

Chapter Twenty-One

If nothing else, McIntyre's Scotland expedition had provided a needed respite from academe. He had returned to Boulder with fresh zeal and vigor, eager to tie up the loose ends of the Mountain Jim murder case and bring some kind of resolution to the manuscript mystery. He outlined an article about the shooting, hoping some regional publication would pick it up. The dean frowned upon *popular* publication by faculty, but that made things even—McIntyre frowned upon the dean.

The manuscript chapters he had uncovered would go into a monograph to be printed at his own expense, unless he could get a grant. For that he would wait until Corrigan sent the Isabella Bird letter—if Corrigan ever sent it, and if it ever arrived, and if it seemed legitimate. Lots of ifs. Meanwhile, he would work at getting all the different versions of the shooting to make sense.

If serendipity guided McIntyre's field research, method was the muse of his writing. He made photocopies of all material, turning odd-size scraps and over-size documents into uniform size for filing. He labeled and stored the originals in document boxes. He typed out his notes, identifying each page with a key term in the upper right corner. On a yellow legal pad he wrote down all questions, large and small, that an account of the murder should answer. He struck lines through questions that were irrelevant, redundant, or frivolous, then copied the remainder onto another sheet and categorized them.

There were questions of geography. In what Fort Collins

house did James Nugent die? Where was he buried? There were questions of motive. What would Evans gain? What would Dunraven gain? Who else stood to gain anything? Then there were questions of minor technicalities. How was Nugent armed? Was Brown armed, and why wasn't he wounded? How did the news reach Isabella Bird? Finally came the miscellaneous loose ends. Who impersonated Dunraven in Denver? Was Jenny Evans jealous of Isabella Bird?

After a week of organizing his material, McIntyre was ready for more field research. In this case, field research referred to a visit with that Grand Lake woman, but with Trail Ridge Road closed by winter snow, it was impossible. He settled for an investigative trip to Estes Park.

McIntyre sipped gingerly. The problem with a stainless steel vacuum bottle was that the coffee came out scalding, and the little metal cup got hot enough to blister the lips. The truck's heater kept the November chill at bay as he sat in the cab looking down into the valley. Cold radiated from the window glass and crept in around the edge of the doors. He was parked where Highway 66 affords the first vista of Estes Park, on the east end of a causeway across Lake Estes. This was as near the site of the Evans cabin as he could drive; somewhere under that icy black water, somewhere within his field of vision, was the submerged foundation of the cabin where the fatal shot had been fired.

With Trail Ridge Road closed and the Front Range lying frozen under its tree-deep smother of snow, the Estes Park valley was a dead-end, a cul-de-sac barricaded by granite peaks. There must have been times when James Nugent had seen the park as a symbol of a life wasted. Literate, intelligent, energetic, and ambitious, he had ended up here in an evil-smelling shanty, eking out a dirty existence by killing animals and guiding overbearing aristocrats.

Isabella Bird's visit must have been a kind of epiphany for Nugent, a gust of fresh air. Here was a woman traveling across the world—a woman!—with limited means and a modest education, but writing books, her mind and her pen as fearless as her journeys. In Bird's presence, Nugent must have been ashamed of the way he existed. Like a man asking penance, he might have told her how much he abhorred his past and raged at the circumstances that had brought him to his present state. He had education and he had civilized tastes, but he had been forced to live like a rogue boar in a smelly cabin, hiding from his outlaw past. And in her example he had seen his own escape from the dead-end into which his existence had blundered.

McIntyre sipped from the steel cup. He closed his eyes and imagined the broad meadow as it had looked in 1874. He imagined the morning of Friday, June 19, 1874 and the events that had happened.

James Nugent and William Brown were riding across the valley, toward Evans's cabin. Nugent wrote that he was "riding peacefully along a highway in company with one William Brown," the only highway or public road running east and west through Evans's land. They had probably set out from Muggins's Gulch after breakfast, taking an hour to ride over Park Hill to the Evans place.

The cabin was on an open meadow near where a small stream converged with the Thompson River. The vantage was excellent; anyone at the cabin could have seen riders at a considerable distance. The cabin faced south or southeast, since the prevailing winds of winter made deep drifts on the north and west sides. Kingsley had written that the Englishman was sitting outside the door, enjoying the sun—evidence that the door faced south.

Riding west, Nugent and Brown had the cabin on the right-hand side of the road. Nugent had to be riding on the side nearest the cabin, since he was hit with the first blast of the shotgun while Brown went unscathed.

McIntyre confirmed this with a detail from Kingsley's narrative: "Amongst other injuries the grizzly bear had scratched across the right eye, causing an adhesion between the lid and the eye itself . . . in consequence of the state of his right eye he could only shoot from his left shoulder." McIntyre put his hand over his right eye. Brown would have ridden on Nugent's left so the mountain man could look at him, as they talked, without twisting his head clear around.

The two horsemen rode past the timber machine or set of wheels or old wagon or whatever it was, the assumed cause of the improbable and fatal ricochet, leaving it slightly behind them and on their left.

The Englishman jumped to his feet and rushed into the cabin, yelling: "Jim's on the shoot!" Brown shouted a warning to Nugent; Nugent twisted around to see the cabin door with his good eye, his horse turning at the same time. Brown ended up immediately behind Nugent, and Nugent ended up facing the cabin.

That explained why Brown wasn't hit, McIntyre reflected. He drew his own pencil sketch of two men on horses, one to the left and slightly behind the other, a cabin to their right, and a man standing by the cabin with a gun. Then he started his note recorder and described the scene again, recorder in one hand and hot coffee in the other.

"And so," he stated, "Evans burst from the cabin with this shotgun. He was groggy, dazed in the sunlight, somewhat drunk, alarmed . . . his thumbs worked at the hammers, putting the shotgun on full cock. He swung the muzzle up.

Nugent was between Evans and Brown, fully exposed to the blast, all because of his blinded eye. Another reason Brown escaped was the angle of fire in Deputy Bissell's sketch. It's common for someone to shoot too high when they're aiming upward . . . ask any hunter who has tried to shoot a deer upslope. Any of Evans's bullets that missed Nugent would have gone three or four feet over Brown's head. . . . Damn!"

The hot coffee hit McIntyre's lap, and he slopped more as he slammed the cup down on the dashboard. With coffee soaking into his jeans and the recorder still running, he could only stare straight ahead. He had just realized what had really happened to James Nugent. The steam from the coffee was fogging the windshield, making things look hazy, but to McIntyre it was as though he could see right through the mist and fog, through the years and the confusion. He knew what happened as clearly as if he had just seen it take place.

"Well," he finally said, talking to nobody but himself, and grinning at his revelation, "that settles the questions about Mister Brown."

McIntyre leafed through the box of file folders on the seat beside him, drawing out the one marked **Dunraven**.

"OK, Lord Dunraven. Let's see what kind of motives you might have had . . . or might *not* have had. Were you a greedy man, an angry one? Vengeful, spiteful, threatened by rivalry?" McIntyre pulled out a list of books pertaining to the Irish earl, replaced the file, put the Dodge in gear, and drove into Estes Park. The defroster quickly cleared the fog from the windshield.

At the Estes Park Library, McIntyre searched through pamphlet files, newspaper files, document boxes, and rare volumes. But he came up with nothing new, nothing that he had not seen before. Then, on a bookshelf in plain view, he found a pamphlet. It was called "Estes Park from the Beginning" by Dave Hicks. McIntyre took it to one of the armchairs and began to read.

Mr. Hicks was a researcher to be reckoned with. His thin volume was not the usual re-telling of the old Enos Mills version, sprinkled with the usual quotations from Kingsley. This work contained details, facts, dates. It included a William Henry Jackson photo of Estes Park, made in 1873, showing the river and the park and the cabins. It included records of deed transfers, including the names of some thirty-seven men who transferred land deeds to Theodore Whyte and The English Company between May 6, 1874 and May 27, 1879.

McIntyre's investigation had not told him much about Theodore Whyte. Dunraven and Kingsley had found the man useful and amusing, and Dunraven had left Whyte to run the estate while he took his friends out shooting and fishing. Hicks described Whyte as a dandy who carried all the paraphernalia of an English gentleman when he arrived in the park. Whyte was one of The English Company—the chief executive of it, in fact. Later on, he supervised the building of The English Hotel on the site of Dunraven's cabins.

Whyte enjoyed dressing for the hunt. In his red jacket and tight white trousers he led the English guests on chases after the park's coyotes and wolves. First-hand accounts described him dressed in English riding habit, jumping a fence, and then turning back to open the gate for his guests. One visitor wrote that Whyte followed Lord Dunraven around the park like an apprentice in aristocracy, imitating Dunraven's manners, his taste in food and drink, his speech, and even his choice of horses.

Through Hicks, McIntyre began to see Dunraven, Lord of Adare, in a new light. It was not really logical to see him as a land-grabbing megalomaniac. He had an active, vigorous life that kept him busy at other things, things such as steeple-chase riding, yachting, and hunting. He was in search of sport and adventure by his own admission, and not some fiefdom in America to manage. He had a feudal empire of his own in Ireland.

Lord Dunraven's own PAST TIMES AND PASTIMES showed him to be a man of good humor with an almost self-deprecating sense of reality. When he realized what was happening in Estes Park, he did not hire armed thugs to guard the perimeter for him. Dunraven wrote:

Folks were drifting in prospecting, fossicking, pre-empting, making claims; so we prepared for civilisation. Made a better road, bought a sawmill at San Francisco, hauled the machinery in, set it up, felled trees, and built a wooden hotel. . . . Neither I nor my chum stayed there long. People came in disputing claims, kicking up rows; exorbitant land taxes got into arrears; we were in constant litigation. . . . So we sold for what we could get and cleared out, and I have never been there since. But I would like to see the place again. Estes Park has long ago become civilised, highly civilised, indeed fashionable.

These were hardly the words of a man bent upon building himself an empire, not a man to condone murder, even by proxy. Another time Dunraven came across as an easy-going, jolly sort of gent. A man was circulating around Denver one week, telling people he was Lord Dunraven. This scoundrel threw drunken parties with local prostitutes, engaged in loud arguments in Denver taverns, and ran up hotel bills in Dunraven's name. If Dunraven had been as ruthless as some have claimed, he would have hired roughnecks to find this impersonator and shoot him—or, at least, beat him and dump him on the prairie. But Dunraven took it with a grain of salt:

I got into trouble in Denver through a scoundrel impersonating me during my absence. Vicariously I committed many atrocities. I acquired an evil reputation, and, of course, knew nothing at all about it, till accident brought the facts to light and the mess was cleared up. Impersonation was not infrequent—I suppose because, in those days, lords were scarce. . . . I remember the monotony of one voyage home being relieved by the society of a charming young lady. When we went our several ways at Liverpool she said, "Well, good-bye, I have had a nice time, but it is funny. Of course you know that I know you are not Lord Adare?" Well, "I did not know it," I replied. "What makes you think that?" "I don't think at all, I know it," she said. "I danced with him at a Patriarch's ball the night before we sailed, and you are a very bad likeness of him." I wonder who my understudy was in New York!

Accident brought the facts to light and the mess was cleared up. The easy-going subtlety of that sentence was deceptive, McIntyre thought. It contained a strong implication that Dunraven knew, and forgave, the impersonator. All in all, this was not the language nor the attitude of an offended snob. Nor did it indicate any vindictiveness.

However, while Lord Dunraven enjoyed his vast private hunting preserve and shrugged off offensive impersonations, his administrator and foreman, Theodore Whyte of the Estes Park Company, Limited was being serious and shrewd about acquiring land in Estes Park. Besides building the hotel and monopolizing lumber and agriculture—the English dairy was a sole source of milk—the corporation kept acquiring land by unscrupulous means until it owned over eight thousand two hundred acres outright and controlled at least seven thousand more.

McIntyre let the booklet fall into his lap and leaned back. All this beautiful valley, full of game, blessed with pure air and water, carpeted with thick grass. On the hillside above Fish Creek sat a fine hotel surrounded by outbuildings, stables, a dairy; elegant English gentlemen and ladies came and went, posing for Jackson's camera or watching Albert Bierstadt make paintings of the park. Whyte and Haigh dressed in red riding coats and rode English jumpers, leaping gates while ladies looked on from beneath French parasols. In the evenings chefs, imported from Europe, prepared continental cuisine; servants brought crystal glasses of the best French brandy to complement fresh cigars.

Away down the hill, near the river where mosquitoes and gnats made meals of human blood, common Welshman Griff Evans sat outside his low log cabin next to the major highway into the park, smoking a pipe of foul-smelling tobacco, drinking brew of his own making. His children, dressed in homespun hand-me-downs, brought in the few cows or horses from the pasture and then played wild games in the fields or hopscotch in the dusty road.

Evans had loved rubbing elbows with the gentry, as Abner Sprague had put it in his "An Historical Reminiscence." "Haigh soon learned that Evans was flattered by being made a friend of by him, and that things would be winked at that could not be done in a civilized or settled community."

Eight miles away, where the road to Estes Park passed Muggins's Gulch, Mountain Jim Nugent stretched his animal skins on crude frames and hung them from the eaves of his shanty. His clothing consisted of soiled, ragged waistcoats over homespun shirts, buckskin pants stained with blood and grime and grease and sweat, a floppy hat pulled down over his horridly scarred face. When folks came along the road, looking toward the end of their long ride up from Longmont, eager for their first glimpse of the fine hotel and their gracious continental hosts, it was Mountain Jim who greeted them. Often, if reports were true, at gunpoint.

The shanty Irishman named Nugent and the seldom-sober Welshman named Evans were an embarrassment to The English Company, a blight on the social landscape, and serious obstructions to development and profit. And in Colorado history, one rule always prevailed toward anyone who stood or squatted in the way of development and profit, be they Indians, Mexicans, or European commoners.

They had to go.

"So," I said, after the hovering waiter had gone away with the wine list and menus under his arm, "how difficult was it, shoveling your way across the pass to Grand Lake Village?"

"Very droll, Palmer," Lachlan replied. "Quite droll, indeed. And has Gordon discovered that you and I drank his bottle of Merlot?"

"Checkmate. Well played, Professor! I believe that gives us a point apiece. Now, before we're interrupted by the escargot, I want to hear all about your eye-opening discovery. When you said eye-opening earlier, I naturally assumed you to be in reference to Grand Lake Gwendolyn."

"Glenda," he corrected. "And it's not about her. Tell me . . . what does it take to make a murder in all those television dramas you watch? Motive, means, and opportunity, right?"

"Correct."

"But we need one thing more . . . a precipitant."

"A what?"

"Something to precipitate the act itself. If the motive has been building up slowly, it takes something to trigger it, to cause the killer to go from wishing someone dead to actually dropping the hammer on them."

I had gone to Lachlan's place that morning with a few notes about early Estes Park hotels, including The English Hotel, and he had given me copies of what he had discovered in the Hicks book. His anxiousness to tell me all about it, together with my very, very discreet reminder that he was in my debt, was what had *precipitated* the dinner invitation. David Lachlan McIntyre has excellent taste in restaurants, I'll say that for him. I always appreciated him asking me to dine. Nevertheless, I did choose to wear my high-neck, sleeveless black dress rather than the low-cut one—I do hate to show him *too* much appreciation.

"As I see it," he said, his smile crinkling the corners of his eyes as if amused by my choice of dresses, "it was Whyte who was the ambitious, grasping, cold-blooded villain of our little Estes Park soap opera. When he and Haigh weren't on horseback, pretending to be English peers, they must have been scheming how to get hold of more land and turn the park into an exclusive country club for gentry. Now, three men were in their way, spoiling things, two of whom were giving a shabby look to the blue-blood hunting reserve. One was an odorous trapper and self-appointed mountain guide who had one eye and glared at strangers with it, and the other was an overly friendly little alcoholic Welshman with delusions of innkeeping. For The English Hotel owners, it was like spending thousands to landscape your house, then having the neighbor pile junk cars in his front yard. Ever read Frederick Jackson Turner?"

Ever hear the term non sequitur? I thought. I nodded with what I hoped was dignified disdain for the question. To ask a history professor if she had read Turner. I mean, *really*, Lachlan.

"Jim Nugent and Griff Evans were members of what Turner had called the intermediate wave of frontiersmen, men who built crude cabins and lived by hunting or primitive agriculture and soon moved on, making room for settlements with glass windows and brick chimneys, settlements with bridges and roads and civic improvements. Jim and Griff should have picked up, packed up, and followed the frontier farther west. But they stayed put, instead."

"You mean John Mason Peck, not Turner," I said. "Turner quoted Peck's theory of frontier waves."

"Whatever. Evans and Nugent were eyesores to the English. They were working-class slobs, and that's putting it mildly. All the fancy guests coming into Estes in their expensive coaches or riding their purebred horses had to go right past Nugent and Evans. Their shanties were the first thing visitors saw. And," Lachlan added, tasting the Bordeaux and nodding to the waiter, "Nugent's drying animal hides and Evans's whisky still, not to mention their latrines and manure piles, were the first thing the visitors smelled."

The waiter left the wine and hurried away. Obviously, he wasn't accustomed to professorial chit-chat. I'm afraid I giggled. I dipped a slippery bit of escargot in melted butter sauce and sucked it slowly through my sensually parted lips, but Lachlan wasn't watching. At least, the wine was complimentary. "Who else was in the way?" I asked. "You said there were three men. Is the other man your faceless Mister Brown?"

"No. Brown had no more land to sell to the company, didn't seem to work for anyone, had no reason to stay. After the shooting he vanished. No, it was Lord Dunraven."

"*Dunraven?*"

"You bet. Whyte and Haigh were enterprising men out to

make money and improve their position. Dunraven and his chum had more gold than God and more titles than a library, and they were getting bored with the whole deal. Can you see young Lord Dunraven actually getting interested in setting up a sawmill and welcoming tourists? Just for the heck of it, Hank, let's pretend you're Theodore Whyte."

Picture me as a man? I raised an eyebrow over my wine glass—but Lachlan's mind was not among those present at our table. I sipped my wine.

"You're Whyte, and you want this English Company land scheme to work, in the worst way. You aspire to peerage, you're ambitious, you're in a hurry to get on with it. Dunraven's a nice guy and spends money lavishly, but he's a drag when it comes to active development of the hunting preserve. Worse yet, he brings other lords and earls to Estes Park as guests . . . they cost the company thousands of pounds in food and lodging. You'd like to see Dunraven resume his travels. Then you'd be free to use his name and his resources. Besides, Dunraven was an ethical man, and ethics weren't something found within a hundred miles of Colorado land development. To this very day."

"Lachlan," I said, "I'm missing something here. You are saying, or you are about to say, that Whyte framed Dunraven for Evans's shooting of Nugent?"

"In a way, yes. In a way. I think he . . . Whyte . . . had already tried it. On a smaller scale. Remember that paragraph about the men who impersonated Dunraven?"

"Oh. That was Whyte?"

"Why not? Try this scenario and see how you like it. Whyte went with Dunraven to New York to see him off on his visit to Ireland . . . one of his jobs, since he was Lord Dunraven's right-hand man. The evening before the boat sailed, Whyte went out for the evening. He ended up at the

Patriarch Ball, where he conned the young lady that Dunraven later encountered aboard ship. Think about it . . . who else in New York City knew Dunraven well enough to get away with it? How many people in New York would have called him Lord Adare, instead of Lord Dunraven?

"So, months later, Whyte was looking for a way to once again get Dunraven out of Colorado and out of the way. He went to Denver and played a more elaborate charade, running up hotel and bar bills, spending time with prostitutes, getting into drunken fights, all the time posing as Dunraven. The idea was that Dunraven's reputation would be ruined. He would be so irritated that he'd go home to Ireland for good, and guess who would volunteer to stay behind to manage the Estes Park investments?"

I interrupted Lachlan's hypothesis. "Where's your evidence for all this?" I asked. "That he learned it was Whyte, I mean. Who would have told him?"

"Haven't got any idea, but I've got a guess. Evans owed Isabella Bird more than a hundred dollars, and Isabella had to go all the way to Denver to find him to collect it. She found Evans living there, but he didn't have the money. Evans evidently had used it for drinking, and, as small as Denver was, I'd be surprised if he hadn't run into Whyte, alias Dunraven, at one of the whisky mills on Larimer Street. That could have been the *accident* that Dunraven's book referred to. Around the same time . . . according to a story I found in Sprague's reminiscence . . . Haigh gave Jim Nugent a hundred dollars. Nugent was to go to Denver and give it to a certain lady to induce her to spend the winter with Haigh. Jim came back with no woman and no money. Horny and enraged, Haigh swore to shoot Jim. Jim poked a cocked rifle against Haigh's neck and invited him to try."

"So?"

"So there were few places in Denver where a man could drink and consort with low women. Again, there's an excellent chance that Nugent had run into the imitation Lord Dunraven and had recognized Mister Whyte. Why didn't Dunraven name the impostor in his book? Why did he take it as a prank? Because he valued Whyte's services. And he didn't suspect Whyte's real motive. It would *also* go a long way toward explaining why Whyte would want to trick Evans into shooting Jim Nugent."

I slid a thin morsel of filet between my lips, then sipped my Bordeaux. "Now, Professor," I said, "let me summarize the lesson. Whyte, or Haigh, or both, conspired to get Griff to shoot Nugent and to put the final blame on Dunraven, is that it? I detest admitting it, but you are making sense. If their scheme worked, Mountain Jim would be dead and out of the way. Griff Evans would either be jailed or so shunned that he would leave Estes. And Lord Dunraven's reputation as an aristocratic bastard would have made him want to go home to Ireland. Very slick, I must admit. The company obtains the Nugent place, the Evans place, and a free hand every place. Very slick. But what was the precipitant you spoke of?"

"Slick?" Lachlan grinned over his forkful of *bourginon*. "You *are* mastering the Western idiom, Hank. There's several things that could have lit the fuse. Evans, or Nugent, might have spilled the beans to Dunraven about who was imitating him. Or, Whyte might have finally heard that Nugent had sold his claim. Or it could have been the shouting match between Haigh and Nugent. Whyte would have wanted to exploit the argument before it was forgotten."

I corrected him for saying "there's several," of course, and then we ate in silence except for yet another solicitous interruption by the waiter, who kept refilling our water glasses so often that we began referring to him as Gunga Din. Fortunately, he also kept the wine glasses topped up.

Eventually Lachlan spoke again. "I think," he said, very deliberately and seriously, "I think you can write to Jenny James and tell her that it was not her great-grandfather who killed Rocky Mountain Jim. William Brown did it." Lachlan sat back and grinned.

My napkin stopped dead in the air on its way to my lips, and my mouth dropped open for an instant. He kept grinning. In retaliation, I leaned toward him, resting my elbows on the tablecloth, wishing now that I had worn the low-cut, black dress and could have made *his* jaw drop. I whispered when I spoke. "Explain yourself."

He did. Beginning with the fact that, while sitting in his truck looking down at Estes, he had seen it all fall into place. The number of pellets in the shotgun, Brown's convenient disappearance, the ricochet that could not have happened, the size of the blue whistlers, Evans's behavior afterward, all of it.

"First, there was the set-up," Lachlan began. "When Griff Evans went to Denver with Isabella's money and spent it all, it gave Whyte and Haigh an idea. Haigh asked Mountain Jim to go to Denver with a similar amount that he could use to persuade a certain lady to return with him to Estes Park. The Englishman had met this woman in Denver and was eager to bring her to the park to be his companion. If the Ansel Watrous version of the story is credible, Haigh had been beaming his masculine charms on the maiden Jenny Evans, making Nugent jealous . . . so, one can easily infer that Jim would have been more than eager to bring Haigh a fancy Denver woman. The lady refused to go to Estes Park, however, and Jim spent all the expense money.

"Was this part of the plot? It would have been no trick at

all for Haigh to have paid the woman so that she would detain
Jim and make him spend the money. And while Jim was gone
on his errand, which took a week or ten days, according to
Sprague, Haigh had plenty of time to ingratiate himself with
Evans and put himself under Evans's protection should the
unpredictable Mountain Jim go into one of his murderous
moods."

Lachlan paused to pour me the remainder of the wine.

"The story of the Denver woman in Abner Sprague's
reminiscence came from Brown. Supposedly Haigh and Jim
had a public argument about the woman and the money . . .
an argument that ended when Jim pushed the muzzle of his
rifle into Haigh's neck and *forced him to take back what he had
said.*

"Griff Evans, acquainted with Jim Nugent's violent
temper and reputation as a desperado, was by now convinced
that Haigh was in mortal danger. Evans, who missed no opportunity to be of service to the lords of The English Company, would protect his house guest with deadly force.

"The next step was to arrange the stage for the drama.
Dunraven, his own memory of events notwithstanding, was
not on the scene. Neither was his friend and physician,
Doctor George Kingsley. The conspirators had a clear field.
Whyte, you will remember, once offered to give Isabella Bird
a little Thirty-Two caliber revolver. It was a black powder
percussion cap weapon, and it shot a round ball. A round ball
the exact size of a blue whistler pellet.

"It was probably while loading a shotgun for a day of sport
that Whyte realized the similarity between a Number Zero
buckshot and a Thirty-Two ball. If witnesses saw a man shot
with a shotgun, and subsequently found a Thirty-Two caliber
ball in his brain, they would swear on a stack of Bibles that the
ball had come from the shotgun.

"At the cabin that morning, Haigh got Evans drunk. Brown put the Thirty-Two revolver in his pocket and went to fetch Mountain Jim, probably telling him that Haigh was ready to apologize for the previous day's fracas.

"Brown and Nugent rode down from Park Hill, across the valley, and up the slight hill toward the Evans cabin. Brown suggested that they stop at Evans's cabin to water their horses.

"Meanwhile, with Griff snoring away, either Haigh or Whyte took the scatter-gun from its usual place by the door and modified its load by pouring out some of the powder. They reloaded it with *five* balls, not six . . . later, they could tell Kingsley that it was a half load, to scare skunks with, and he should find six wounds. The sixth would be the one from the pistol. The light load of powder and the reduced number of balls greatly decreased the odds that Brown would get hit. The shotgun blast didn't have to be lethal . . . Evans only had to *think* that it had been lethal.

"Now enter the victim. Brown let his horse lag behind so Jim's body would shield him. He slipped his right hand into his pocket and cocked the revolver. Haigh, who had been sitting outside the cabin, yelled . . . 'Jim's on the shoot!' Whyte, inside the cabin, pulled Griff Evans to his feet and thrust the scatter-gun into his hands. Haigh hid behind the Welshman, crying . . . 'Evans, Rocky Mountain Jim is coming, you will not see me shot down like a dog, will you?'

"With a push from one of the Englishmen, Griff Evans stumbled out into the sunshine, cocked the gun, took aim, and fired. At the same moment, Brown extended his arm, put the pistol inches from Jim's skull . . . just behind the right ear, since Jim had his head twisted around to see Evans out of his one good eye . . . and fired the fatal shot. The pistol ball hit the thickest part of the skull . . . a fragment of lead flew off and lodged in the fracture. The rest of the ball penetrated far into the cerebellum at an upward angle, coming to rest deep in the brain.

"Evans's scatter-gun held only half a powder charge and only five balls that left the muzzle and dispersed in a random pattern. Some hit Jim in the face and in the upper arm but did not penetrate far. One went through the bridge of his nose, or left a wound indicating that it had.

"If the horse was killed, as one account says, what happened to its corpse? When Jim's estate was settled, both of his horses were included in it. Another question is whether Evans shot again? Perhaps he fired the second barrel after Jim dropped to the ground, but odds are that it would have been another ineffective shot. The conspirators would have changed the loads in both barrels, not knowing which one Evans would trigger first. And Evans was drunk and not too likely to be accurate. The roar of the shotgun rang in Evans's head, people shouted at him, and the air was full of gunsmoke. In all likelihood, he did not see exactly where Jim fell, and there is a possibility that Evan's second shot killed the horse, perhaps because Jim fell off the far side, and Evans tried to aim past the horse to hit him again. No one saw Evans aim a shot to hit Nugent in the back of the head.

"In the aftermath, Evans, who was still confused and somewhat drunk, was urged to go immediately to Longmont and turn himself in. Somewhere along the road to Longmont, as he sobered up, Evans decided that it would be a better idea if he swore out a complaint against Jim for assault and attempted murder. A good offense is the best defense, after all. But in his heart, Evans knew what Colorado Territory was going to hear from the eyewitnesses and the press . . . that he had shot Mountain Jim Nugent.

"William Brown told his version of the shooting to Abner

Sprague, and then vanished. Significantly, out of all the people in the park at the time of the shooting, only Whyte, Haigh, and Brown failed to record their versions. Others described it, but those three wrote nothing down. Brown was never heard of again, and never came forward to tell his version as one might expect . . . after all, it was a popular topic. Twenty years later, people still remembered the event and described it to Enos Mills. In Nineteen Hundred, Doctor Kingsley wrote his memory of it. Dunraven wrote his in Nineteen Twenty-Two. But no one, except Abner Sprague, mentioned hearing or reading a single word from Brown.

"Dunraven left Estes Park before the grand opening of The English Hotel. Kingsley and the other Dunraven chums went with him. Evans and his family left the valley, too, selling their holdings to The English Company. James Nugent died in Fort Collins and was probably buried there.

"One of the great ironies was that Nugent had sold his Muggins's Gulch claim and had been preparing to leave. This had little bearing on Whyte's motives . . . he didn't want Nugent's homestead so much as he wanted to be rid of Evans and Dunraven. Nugent's decision to sell simply meant that the whole scheme had to be put into operation before the key victim escaped."

"Jenny will be very, very pleased to hear your version," I said. We adjourned to a small candlelit table in a hushed corner of the lounge, where Lachlan enjoyed an after dinner cognac. My head felt a little light, so I had coffee.

"You are a hero, you know," I said. "After all, in one brilliant stroke you have exonerated Lord Dunraven, solved the riddle of the ricochet, and cleared the name of Griffith Evans, Esquire."

"Yeah," Lachlan growled, "but I didn't find the damn' manuscript."

"Never mind," I said, leaning closer. "You deserve a reward."

"What did you have in mind?" he asked.

"I thought a kiss would do," I whispered. And I did not give him a peck on the cheek, either. I rewarded Professor McIntyre with a long, long kiss, one that left the taste of his cognac on my lips and tongue.

Chapter Twenty-Two

It was odd that, in the days that followed, it began to appear as if my spontaneous kiss had dampened the ardor of D. Lachlan McIntyre, rather than the other way around. To me, it was no more than the wine and the stimulation of a fine dinner, together with an impulse prompted by David's enthusiasm. To him, however, it represented a step beyond friendship. One would expect a man to pursue the opportunity, but Lachlan's response was four days of silence. When he did finally ring up, it was to ask if he might drop over to see me that evening.

"Yes, of course," I said carefully. "Any time, really. I'm usually through with supper by six or six-thirty."

"OK. About seven, then," he said. "I got that letter from Corrigan. And I got back my pictures of Scotland, if you'd like to see them."

I told him I was free for the whole afternoon. It was a nice day . . . perhaps a walk in the park, or down along the river? But he had an appointment to see his doctor.

"Oh?" I said. "Aren't you feeling well?"

"I'm fine. I left him some questions about the Nugent shooting, and he called to say he had some answers. That's all."

"See you at seven, then."

Dr. Carlos Zavala's interest in crime and forensics was quite keen for a family practitioner. One question McIntyre had asked him was: if it was a murder plot, and the conspirators were alone with Nugent after Evans rode off in hot haste for Longmont, before Dr. Kingsley and others arrived, why hadn't one of them finished him off with a second shot in the head?

Dr. Zavala answered that they had seen no need. Nugent was bleeding from numerous head wounds and would in all probability die. "Your average person, seeing someone who has been shot and who is bleeding, automatically assumes that the bullet is in the wound. Even after they clean off the blood, it still looks like an entrance hole. In Nugent's case, they had seen bloody wounds on his face and had assumed that several bullets had gone into his head, or through it. But according to the autopsy, only one of them really had gone in . . . the rest must have hit him and fallen off. If he did not die there, then that bumpy forty-mile trip down through the mountains to Fort Collins would certainly kill him. Or so they would have thought."

Next McIntyre and Dr. Zavala discussed the two pieces of lead found in the mortal wound, the wound beneath the ear on the right side of the skull.

"Could bone split a lead bullet?" McIntyre asked.

"Oh, sure," Dr. Zavala answered. "The report made it appear that the projectile cracked his skull, leaving a small chunk of lead in the fracture. That part of the skull is extraordinarily thick. Besides that, you have to think about the lead. Might have been faulty."

"Faulty?"

"Sure. These guys made their own bullets in molds, right? They used old bullets over and over again, digging them out of deer, or out of trees. It's easy to imagine a contaminated batch of lead making flawed bullets."

"And," McIntyre suddenly realized, "that would be more likely in a pistol ball than in a shotgun load! Lead shot was usually bought ready-made. That's more evidence the bullet came from a pistol and not a shotgun."

About the post-mortem report, Dr. Kingsley's description had said that the only bullet found, in spite of five or six wounds, was the one in the skull. The report had said that the other bullets *passed through*, such as the one that supposedly went right through Nugent's arm and the one described as having *passed through* the bridge of his nose.

Dr. Zavala's answer was gruesome. A typical exit wound in human flesh is more than twice the size of an entrance wound, often much more than that, and is ragged. He laughed because one witness had theorized that the bullet which entered the base of Nugent's skull exited through his nose. "Not without taking most of his forehead with it," Dr. Zavala chuckled.

They agreed on the logic of assuming that Evans's gun had contained only a partial load of powder and shot. The wounds to Jim's face, between his eyes, on his cheek, and biceps were no doubt bleeding bruises, the bullets having hit him and dropped to the ground. Dr. Kingsley had marveled at how quickly the wound in the biceps had healed over.

"Why not just have put a blank charge in Evans's gun to begin with?" McIntyre wondered out loud.

"They probably wanted to have wounds on Jim, and on the horse, to prove that Evans had done it. Besides that, an experienced hunter like Evans would have felt the difference between a blank and a full load. The kick would have been significantly less."

McIntyre agreed. But there remained one puzzling weak spot in his theory. It was William Brown. Even if he had been shielded by Nugent's body, there still would have been a chance that a stray shot would hit him. Would he have taken that big of a chance? It was doubtful. Maybe he wasn't part of the plot, after all.

"Sure he was!" Dr. Zavala said, caught up in the zeal of the murder puzzle. "Sure he was. Try this theory . . . Haigh, or Whyte, recruited Brown to bring Jim to the cabin and shoot him from behind. They told Brown that they would fix it so that Evans would be shooting blanks. But they lied."

"So then why give Evans a loaded gun?" McIntyre asked.

"Hey, David, be a detective here! It's a double-cross. The Englishmen didn't care whether Brown got hit or not. If he didn't get hit, and managed to shoot into the back of Jim's skull, fine . . . by the way, did you notice the nice parallel? That Brown would have put his gun right in the same spot that Jim had put *his* gun to Haigh's neck in the argument earlier? Probably not an accident. I'll bet Haigh had told Brown he wanted Jim shot right in that very spot. Anyway, if Brown didn't get hit, it was still OK. They would pay him off, and he would vanish."

"Right. Which he did."

"And if he got killed, it was better for them. Then it would be said that Evans had killed *two* men. He wouldn't be back to Estes Park, either. Plus it got rid of a witness."

"OK, but what if Brown was only wounded? Then he would have known it was a set-up."

"Yes," Dr. Zavala said, "and he would also have known that he was dealing with two dangerous and treacherous individuals. Same result . . . if he was smart, he'd leave town and keep his mouth shut. For all we know," he added, "your conspirators later killed him and made the body disappear."

They finished their conversation with speculations about Kingsley's medical background and reliability, and more about the six balls, and how Kingsley had expected six wounds.

"Well," McIntyre said, "Whyte could possibly have told

Kingsley to look for six wounds. Or Haigh could have said it. Whoever had loaded the gun."

"It would make sense," Dr. Zavala added. "If you're keeping a loaded shotgun around to scare prowling animals, why waste lead with full loads? I mean, that could have been Haigh's explanation. Evans, he would say, had just had six balls in each barrel, for the skunks don't you know. So Doctor Kingsley looked for six wounds."

"Ah!" McIntyre said. "And he assumed all six hit, because Evans had been so close to Nugent when he had pulled the trigger! Later on, maybe at the hospital, Kingsley or another surgeon found an entrance wound in the back of Nugent's head. So somebody . . . Brown, maybe . . . came up with the ricochet story to explain to Kingsley where that bullet came from."

"There you go. A hundred years ago, forensics wasn't much of a science. You know us doctors. We believe whatever we're told. Well," the doctor concluded, "I've got to be going. Hospital rounds. I'll send you my consulting bill, David."

"Oh, yes, you do that," McIntyre replied. "And I'll send you a check. Believe it."

It was obvious, that evening, that Professor McIntyre was pretending the kiss never happened. He was in a blue mood as well. So I just made cheerful small talk from the kitchen while I brewed fresh coffee to go with the pie.

"Tell me," I shouted, "seriously, and because I'm terribly nosy and curious. Do you think you'll be seeing Glenda again, the woman at Grand Lake? It sounded promising when you first told me about it."

"Not really," came his answer from the other room. "I don't see anything serious there. We might get together for some hiking. She knows the trails on that side of the National Park. But, no, there's not that chemistry, that electricity, whatever."

We had our pie and coffee at the coffee table. McIntyre took some sheets of paper from a large envelope and sank back against the cushions. I was wishing his voice had more of its usual zest.

"Want to read Isabella's letter, or do you want me to read it to you?"

"You read it." I relaxed on the couch with my coffee.

"OK. First, this explains the mixed-up address mystery, since Corrigan sent us a photocopy of the envelope along with the copy of the letter."

At least, he was still using the plural pronoun.

"Mind if I ask you what Corrigan charged you for all this?"

"Yes, I do," he said, and went on. "Isabella had the inside address wrong . . . you see? She gave it as Albermarle Street, Edinburgh. Poor lady. Then someone else apparently copied it onto the envelope for her. Look . . . different handwriting. It's Nineteen Oh Three, and she was in an Edinburgh nursing home, so I think someone there, some nurse or assistant, was helping her with her correspondence. She'd been writing to John Murray about another trip to China, not knowing she'd be dead in a few months. Being ill and seventy-two years old, it's no wonder she was a bit disoriented when it came to addresses and such. Seventy-two years old. Anyway, it was addressed to Jenny Evans:

Edinburgh, 17 September 1903
My Dear Miss Evans,
You cannot imagine my delight at receiving your letter. To see the postmark Colorado USA brought back delighted memories of the fine clear air and high

mountains, the rich scents of the pines and meadow. Apparently much has befallen both of us since those carefree days in the Rockies when I was young & in good health (for the most part) and you of course were a "mere slip of a girl" with all life before you. Now it seems we two are left alone much as two survivors of shipwreck would be to recount the story—"Mountain Jim's" last two loves, if I'm not mistaken and may presume to call you so. Pray you grant an old lady patience and my narrative shall make clear why I presume to call you one of James Nugent's last loves. Never fear, the story is safe between us, although do take care against yourself, for some brash investigator *has* written me recently, probing and prying, trying to dig up old skeletons, etc.

Our old friend of the mountain parks would be pleased—as I think we both know well!—of your desire to see his book published at last—and you do very well in corresponding with me concerning that. What a shame the papers in your possession are fragmentary, I am sorry for your sake since they are most fascinating reading, and applaud your dear bravery, (and you not much more than a girl at the time!) in rescuing Mr. Nugent's "written remains" from pillagers and enemies. More of that in a moment, or anon as the poet says.

You say, dear Miss Evans, that you do this literary labour partially out of memory of a friend and partially as a way of expiating the unfortunate involvement of your father in Mr. Nugent's untimely death, God rest your father's cheery and generous soul.

Let me rush to clarify what must by this point seem a wildly rambling letter written by an old woman whose mind must seem as palsy-twitched as her handwriting (this partly due to hurry and excitement, I am so pleased to hear from you after all these long years since that season in Estes Park, and I rush to record my account to you).

Not a dozen days, perhaps as much as a fortnight following receipt of the *sad*, *sad* doleful news of Mr. Nugent's passing, the postman one afternoon delivered a thin envelope to me that seemed a correspondence from the grave, for it was a missive penned by Mr. Nugent and addressed to me as he lay in a Fort Collins home expecting to recover from his wounds and once more ride his beloved mountain trails. He confided to me that he had shipped a parcel—had exchanged his deed to the Muggins's Gulch property for ship passage money—would *follow* as soon as able to—are you prepared, my dear—to London! Imagine our mountain man in London. What a picture it conjures.

He had sent ahead his book in hope that I might read it and further it to my friend, the publisher, M. John Murray. In those days of riding and evening chats in the mountains I had said I could do him such a service with M. Murray, but thought "such stuff" to be casual conversation as I have had with other aspiring writers in my travel—the bloom of our camaraderie passing and both of us knowing such an exchange of draft and influence shall not take place.

We underestimate Mr. Nugent, however, and in the course of time his book did arrive. More of that matter later—please indulge and forgive my straying.

Mr. Nugent, I must caution you, my dear Miss Evans, came away from the shooting with a dim and garbled idea of what had actually transpired. Set it down to his confusion or wounds or perhaps to his genteel disposition to protect a lady from some unkind thoughts re: a man whose personality and hospitality I found to be without serious flaw. His letter to me would seem to exonerate your father. The letter now after these many years, alas, is not to be got at *from where I am* but the wording I remember plainly: "my first act as a whole man again is to find Evans and apologize for my impulsive tirade against him and then to set out to search the West, the continent if need be, for the man who really shot Mountain Jim. The vile assassin's very name speaks darkness and stain against him."

Mr. Nugent and his word puzzles. His "next act"— did I say?—was to be a journey to London to market his account of his life in the Rockies with which to begin a new life, a life as a travelling writer as I have been. His letter, though, did most clearly evince a willingness to forgive your father, which must raise a weight from the hearts of any who knew him, those near and dear to the memory of Mr. Evans.

My pen grows weary, dear Miss Evans, so I must rush to answer the gist of your inquiry. I do indeed, as you rightly suspicioned, have knowledge of his book and in fact as you are now apprised do have a fair copy of all of it in clean revision ready for the publisher to see. Whether it *should* be "published to the world" is more problematic as in nearly every chapter our dear desperado has managed to calumniate and vilify his en-emies and to aggrandize and awfully romanticize his friends. You are numbered among the latter, an entire chapter being devoted to the "Nymph of Lily Lake, the naiad of Silk Lake and the Columbine Meadows" and detailing some excursions the two of you enjoyed which, if only half as romantic as his account, must

have been thrilling indeed.

Please know that I am open to receive your thoughts and wishes in the matter of this book's ultimate disposition. You should know my intentions in the matter, thus I will confide to you that I have arranged it in my Will and Testament that the manuscript will be "entombed upon my death" where it will rest in a secure place along with the memory of my dear sister. Should you wish to retrieve it at some date following my own departure from this world, at your request I shall ask my solicitor to forward to you the necessary permission to have Mr. Nugent's written remains "disinterred."

No more—I tire quickly these days. Do write again soon and think of me whenever you contemplate those mountains "from whence cometh my strength."

Your Friend,
I.B.B.

McIntyre and I looked at each other in disappointment. Isabella's meaning was unmistakable—her copy, the *only* complete copy of the manuscript, had been buried. Probably with her sister. Henrietta died in 1880 and was buried in the family plot at Dean's Cemetery, Edinburgh. Isabella must have decided to lay to rest the last remains of her only sister and her only romantic love, together, and free herself to go on with her own life.

We reviewed the Bird letter with scholarly care. The date, 1903, explained Isabella's remark that "we two are left alone." Jenny's father, Griff Evans, had died in 1900. The 1903 date is corroborated by her passing reference to an "investigator" writing to her; McIntyre was sure that the writer was Enos Mills. His history of Estes Park appeared in 1905, so it's reasonable to assume that he wrote to her in 1902 or 1903.

"Lachlan," I asked, "how do you like this romantic image of Jenny, racing to Muggins's Gulch to *rescue his written remains from pillagers and enemies?* You could write a novel about Jenny and James. The excursion to Lily Lake and Silk Lake sounds like juicy material."

"Except that I don't do novels," Lachlan said flatly. "The important thing, I guess, is that I have proof that a complete manuscript did exist. And some chronology."

I read the paragraph in which Isabella had written that Jim did not blame Evans. Evans was someone's pawn, that seemed indisputable. It was interesting that Isabella recalled the riddle from the "letter which cannot be got at from where I am"—probably the nursing home in Edinburgh. Jim's riddle was that the assassin's name "speaks darkness and stain." Brown? Isabella, in all probability, had never heard of William Brown.

"I'm sorry. What were you saying about chronology?" I asked.

"Just that we have one. Isabella and Jim climbed Long's Peak in October of Eighteen Seventy-Three. In November, the Boulder *News* said that Mountain Jim was writing a book. He was in town to sell some fur and meat. Raising money to go to London? During the long winter months between December of Eighteen Seventy-Three and May of Eighteen Seventy-Four, he stopped sending random chapters to people, found someone to buy his land, and sent Isabella a clean copy of the manuscript. By spring, he was ready to go. When Haigh offered him some money to go to Denver and bring back that woman, he must have jumped at the chance to add to his travel funds.

"Now that I think of it, he might have mailed the manuscript from Denver while he was there! It would have been his last trip. After getting shot, in June, he wrote to Isabella that she could expect the parcel and then himself."

"What a picture," I inserted "Mountain Jim getting off the boat in London and looking about him for Isabella! I wonder what he would have been wearing?"

"He wouldn't have gone to London," Lachlan continued. "He expected to find Isabella in Edinburgh. Or even Tobermory. Her sister died in Eighteen Eighty, and Isabella was still using the Tobermory cottage, off and on. I think Jim would have landed at the Port of Leith, in Edinburgh. Probably looking quite ordinary in a decent suit of new clothes. A nice haircut, his beard shaved off. And that awful scar running over his eye and down his face."

I read Isabella's offer again. She said she would have the manuscript dug up if Jenny wrote and requested it. What if Jenny *had* received the letter? What if she had requested the manuscript from Isabella's solicitors? Any chance, do you think, of locating Isabella's last will and testament?" I asked. "Surely she had a solicitor in Edinburgh."

"Sure," Lachlan said, "and, while we're at it, we could look for Lord Dunraven's diary in his yacht at the bottom of the Clyde. Still, it would be a good excuse to go back to Scotland. She had no heirs that I know of, but she left some money . . . two hundred pounds, I think it was . . . for Tobermory to build a clock tower in memory of Henrietta. She included instructions, too. It was supposed to be designed after another clock tower she'd seen in Southhampton or some place."

"Did she see it finished, the one at Tobermory?"

"No," Lachlan answered. "Let me think a minute. I think it was finished in Nineteen Oh Five. Yes, I'm sure of it. Anyway," he continued, setting aside the letter and his notes and reaching for a packet of photos, "speaking of Tobermory's main architectural attraction, how'd you like to see my pictures?"

I moved over next to him. One by one, he handed me his photographs, explaining each one as he went. "You'll recognize this one," he said.

"Harrod's of London," I replied. "I can spend fortunes in there."

"Murray Publishing Company isn't far from there. Here's a couple of shots of the front of their building. These two show you what the inside looks like. Isabella Bird and John Murray probably sat in those very chairs there," he said, pointing at the picture.

He skipped through other shots quickly, mostly tourist-type scenes of downtown London. And then we got to Scotland.

"Ben Nevis. Clouds, rain, drizzle. Heather in bloom, up around Inverness. This is the ferry I took to get over to the Isle of Mull. Short ride, but I really enjoyed it." He shuffled through the photos. "Here we are at Tobermory. See, that's the house Isabella shared with Henrietta. Stone walls. Very plain." Lachlan sighed at the mention of the walls of stone. His face looked as though someone had dented his Dodge. "That's the wharf where I got beat up. When I took the picture I didn't know I was going to get beat up there."

"No pictures of the sea cave?" I asked.

"No. Luckily, I left the camera in my room that day. Otherwise, we wouldn't have these pictures, either."

"And no pictures of your Fiona Owen."

"Nope. If I had some, do you think I'd show them to you? You give me a hard enough time about women the way it is, without bringing you photographic evidence to work with! But here . . . here's a great shot of yours truly, the travelling professor, leaning against the famous clock tower. Mister McCulloch took it. Here's the village of Tobermory, kind of a panoramic shot from across the little harbor."

"Colorful."

"No kidding. If the word picturesque didn't exist, we'd have to make it up just to describe Tobermory."

"And how about words such as frustration and disappointment?" I tried to express sympathy. I mean, he had to face Dean Rolman with a report on what he had done with his leave, and had to pay off his credit card, and the most he could hope for was to publish some scraps of manuscript and an account of his fruitless search for it. All that travel, and getting beaten up—not to mention being disappointed by the fair Fiona—and almost drowned. Poor Lachlan. I shall have to take him out for a nice dinner, I thought, and see if I can't cheer him up.

"This is another shot of the harbor," he continued, handing me another picture. "You can just barely see Isabella's house on the hill there, next to the hotel I couldn't afford. Clock tower and quay in the picture there. That's a ferry boat coming in. I could have taken it direct from Oban, but I enjoyed driving across the island."

I looked closely at the photo. "What is the name on that ferry?" I squinted. "The *Caledonian Mac* something?"

"It's *MacBrane* or *MacByrne* or something. Doesn't matter."

It was then that I saw. I seized the stack of photos from him. I flipped back past the picture of the harbor and the panoramic view of the village.

"Lachlan!" I said, trying to control my voice, "do you remember that little rhyme McCulloch's grandsire would recite when they walked past Isabella's house? You know, the stone mason?"

"I walked all over that village reciting it to myself. It goes . . .

In a wall of rocks,
In a snug tin box,
Papers inside,
Too high for the tide.

"Well, Sherlock," I said, "we won't find the manuscript buried with Henrietta in Edinburgh."

"Oh?" he said. "Why not?"

Without a word, but with my eyebrow arched—you know the look—I turned the photograph to him. And I pointed. At the clock tower.

The End

Author's Note

Those interested in more detailed accounts of the events in my story are invited to consult the following source materials.

Louisa Ward Arps and Elinor Eppich Kingery: HIGH COUNTRY NAMES: ROCKY MOUNTAIN NATIONAL PARK (Denver: The Colorado Mountain Club, 1966).

Pat Barr: A CURIOUS LIFE FOR A LADY: THE STORY OF ISABELLA BIRD, A REMARKABLE VICTORIAN TRAVELER (Doubleday, 1970).

Isabella Bird: A LADY'S LIFE IN THE ROCKY MOUNTAINS (London: John Murray, 1879).

Mary Lyons Cairns: GRAND LAKE: THE PIONEERS (Frederick, Colorado: Renaissance House Publishers, 1991)

Harold Marion Dunning: THE LIFE OF ROCKY MOUNTAIN JIM (JAMES NUGENT) (Boulder: Johnson Publishing Company, 1967).

The Earl of Dunraven, K.P., C.M.G.: PAST TIMES AND PASTIMES, two volumes (London: Hodder and Stoughton Ltd., 1922).

David Hicks: ESTES PARK FROM THE BEGINNING (Denver: Egan Printing Co. and A-T-P Publishing Co, no date).

Evelyn Kaye: AMAZING TRAVELER: ISABELLA BIRD, THE BIOGRAPHY OF A VICTORIAN ADVENTURER (Boulder: Blue Penguin Publications, 1994).

George Henry Kingsley: NOTES ON SPORT AND TRAVEL, WITH A MEMOIR BY HIS DAUGHTER MARY H. KINGSLEY (London: Macmillan, 1900).

Enos Mills: THE ROCKY MOUNTAIN NATIONAL PARK (Houghton Mifflin, 1932)

Anna M. Stoddart: THE LIFE OF ISABELLA BIRD (MRS. BISHOP) (London: John Murray, 1906).

About the Author

James C. Work was born in Colorado where his family has lived for four generations. His mother's grandparents were in Leadville and Cripple Creek during the gold rush days, while his father's grandparents were pioneer farmers on Colorado's eastern plains. He grew up in Estes Park and attended Colorado State University and the University of New Mexico, and holds degrees from both. He now teaches literature and creative writing at Colorado State University. Western American literature first heard of Work in 1984 when he took on the job of restoring Jack Schaefer's novel SHANE for the University of Nebraska Press. Since then he has published PROSE AND POETRY OF THE AMERICAN WEST, an anthology that won the Colorado Seminars in Literature Annual Book Award. Of the one hundred or so essays he has written, a sampling can be found in FOLLOWING WHERE THE RIVER BEGINS. This work won the Charles Redd Award in Western Studies. He was also the editor of a collection of short stories entitled GUNFIGHT! which includes many stories by Western favorites. His first **Five Star Western** was RIDE SOUTH TO PURGATORY. His next **Five Star Western** is RIDE WEST TO DAWN.